Alfred Edersheim

The Bible History. Israel Under Samuel, Saul, and David, to the Birth of Solomon

Vol. IV

Alfred Edersheim

The Bible History. Israel Under Samuel, Saul, and David, to the Birth of Solomon

Vol. IV

Reprint of the original, first published in 1875.

1st Edition 2024 | ISBN: 978-3-38538-623-5

Verlag (Publisher): Outlook Verlag GmbH, Zeilweg 44, 60439 Frankfurt, Deutschland
Vertretungsberechtigt (Authorized to represent): E. Roepke, Zeilweg 44, 60439 Frankfurt, Deutschland
Druck (Print): Books on Demand GmbH, In de Tarpen 42, 22848 Norderstedt, Deutschland

BIBLE HISTORY.

VOL. IV.

From the Close of the Era of the Judges to
the Birth of Solomon.

THE BIBLE HISTORY.

By the Rev. Dr. EDERSHEIM, Author of "The Temple, its
Ministry and Services," etc.

VOL. I.—*The World before the Flood and the History of
the Patriarchs.* Crown 8vo. 2s. 6d. cloth boards.

VOL. II.—*The Exodus and the Wanderings in the Wilderness.* Crown 8vo. 2s. 6d. cloth boards.

VOL. III.—*Israel in Canaan, under Joshua and the
Judges.* Crown 8vo. 2s. 6d. cloth boards.

VOL. IV.—*Israel under Samuel, Saul, and David, to
the Birth of Solomon.* Crown 8vo. 2s. 6d. cloth boards.

In Preparation.

VOL. V.—*From the Birth of Solomon to the Fall of the
Separate Israelite Monarchy.* Crown 8vo. 2s. 6d. cloth boards.

LONDON: THE RELIGIOUS TRACT SOCIETY.

ISRAEL

UNDER

SAMUEL, SAUL, AND DAVID,

TO THE BIRTH OF SOLOMON.

BY

ALFRED EDERSHEIM, D.D., Ph.D.

AUTHOR OF

THE WORLD BEFORE THE FLOOD, AND THE HISTORY OF THE PATRIARCHS;"
"THE TEMPLE: ITS MINISTRY AND SERVICES," ETC.

PREFACE.

THE history of Israel, viewed as the Theocracy, or Kingdom of God, consists of three periods : *First*, that *under the guidance of Prophets* (from Moses to Samuel) ; *secondly*, that *under the rule of Kings* (from Saul to the Babylonish Captivity) ; and, *thirdly*, that *under the reign of High-priests* (from Ezra to the birth of Jesus Christ). Thus the Theocracy had passed through its full typical development in all its stages, when He came, to Whom they all pointed : Jesus Christ, the Prophet, King, and High-priest of the Kingdom of God. The period described in the present volume closes one of these stages, and commences another. The connecting link between them was Samuel — who alone fully realised the mission of the Judges, and who was also Divinely appointed to inaugurate the new institution of royalty in Israel. That royalty next appeared in its twofold possibility—or, as we might express it, in its negative and positive aspects. Saul embodied the royal ideal of the people, while David represented the Scriptural ideal of royalty in its conscious subjection to the will of the Heavenly King. Saul was, so to speak, the king after Israel's, David after God's own heart. But with the actual introduction of monarchy the first period had come to an end, and a new era begun, which was intended to continue till the third and last preliminary stage was reached, which prepared the way for the Advent of Him, Who was the fulfilment of the typical meaning of all.

From what has been said it will be inferred that the period about to be described must have witnessed the birth of new ideas, and the manifestation of new spiritual facts ; otherwise spiritual advancement would not have kept pace with outward progress. But it is in the rhythm of these two that the real meaning of Scripture history lies, marking, as it does, the *pari passu* inner and outer development of the kingdom of God. On the other hand, the appearance of new ideas and spiritual facts would necessarily bring out in sharper contrast the old that was passing away, and even lead to occasional antagonism. Of course, these new ideas and facts would not at first be fully understood or realised. They rather pointed towards a goal which was to be reached in the course of history. For nothing could be more fatal to the proper understanding of Holy Scripture, or of the purposes of God in His dealings with His ancient people, than to transport into olden times the full spiritual privileges, the knowledge of Divine truth, or even that of right and duty, which we now enjoy. It is not to do honour, but dishonour, to the Spirit of God to overlook the educational process of gradual development, which is not only a necessity of our nature, but explains our history. A miracle of might could, indeed, have placed the age of Samuel on the same spiritual level with that of the New Testament, at least so far as regards the communication of the same measure of truth. But such an exhibition of power would have eliminated the *moral element* in the *educational* progress of Israel, with the discipline of wisdom, mercy, and truth which it implied, and, indeed, have rendered the whole Old Testament history needless.

What has been stated will lead the student to expect certain special difficulties in this part of the history. These concern, in our opinion, the substance more than the form or letter of the text, and raise doctrinal and philosophical rather than critical and exegetical questions. The calling and later rejection of Saul; his qualification for the work by the influence of the Spirit of God, and afterwards the sending of a spirit of evil from the Lord; in general, the agency of the Spirit of God in Old Testament times, as distinguished from the abiding Presence of the Comforter under the Christian dispensation, and, in connection with it, the origin and the character of the Schools of the Prophets and of prophetic inspiration—these will readily occur to the reader as instances of what we mean. As examples of another class of difficulties, he will recall such questions as those connected with the ban upon Amalek, the consultation of the witch of Endor, and in general with the lower moral standpoint evidently occupied by those of that time, even by David himself. Such questions could not be passed over. They are inseparably connected with the Scriptural narratives, and they touch the very foundations of our faith. In accordance with the plan of progressive advance which I set before myself in the successive volumes of this *Bible History*, I have endeavoured to discuss them as fully as the character of this work allowed. Whether or not I may always succeed in securing the conviction of my readers, I can at least say, that, while I have never written what was not in accordance with my own conscientious conviction, nor sought to invent an explanation merely in order to get rid of a difficulty, my own reverent belief in the authority of the Word of God has not in any one case been the least shaken. It sounds almost presumptuous to write down such a confession. Yet it seems called for in days when the enumeration of difficulties. easily raised, owing to the distance of these events, the great difference of circumstances, and the necessary scantiness of our materials of knowledge—whether critical, historical, or theological,—so often takes the place of sober inquiry ; and high-sounding phrases which, logically tested, yield no real meaning, are substituted for solid reasoning.

As in the course of this volume I have strictly kept by the Biblical narratives to be illustrated, I may perhaps be allowed here to add a bare statement of three facts impressed on me by the study of early Old Testament history. *First*, I would mark the difference between the subjective and objective aspects of its theology. However low, comparatively speaking, may have been the stage occupied by Israel in their conceptions of, and dealings with God, yet the manifestations of the Divine Being are always so sublime that we could not conceive them higher at any later period. As we read their account we are still as much overawed and solemnised as they who had witnessed them. In illustration, we refer to the Divine manifestations to Elijah and Elisha. In fact, their sublimeness increases in proportion as the human element, and consequently the Divine accommodation to it, recedes. *Secondly*, even as regards man's bearing towards the Lord, the Old Testament never presents what seems the fundamental character of all ancient heathen religions. The object of Israel's worship and services was never to *deprecate*, but to *pray*. There was no malignant deity or fate to be averted, but a Father Who claimed love and a King Who required allegiance. *Lastly*, there is never an exhibition of mere power on the part of the Deity, but always a moral purpose

conveyed by it, which in turn is intended to serve as germ of further
spiritual development to the people. We are too prone to miss this
moral purpose, because it is often conveyed in a form adapted to
the standpoint of the men of that time, and hence differs from that
suited to our own.

Of course, there are also many and serious critical and exegetical
questions connected with such portions of the Bible as the two
Books of Samuel and the first Book of Chronicles. To these I have
endeavoured to address myself to the best of my power, so far as
within the scope of a volume like this. Whether or not I may have
succeeded in this difficult task, I am at least entitled to address a
caution to the reader. Let him not take for granted that bold assertions of a negative character, made with the greatest confidence,
even by men of undoubted learning and ability, are necessarily
true. On the contrary, I venture to say, that their trustworthiness
is generally in inverse ratio to the confidence with which they are
made. This is not the place to furnish proof of this,—and yet it
seems unfair to make a charge without illustrating it at least by
one instance. It is chosen almost at random from one of the latest
works of the kind, written expressly for English readers, by one of
the ablest Continental scholars, and the present leader of that
special school of critics.[1] The learned writer labours to prove that
the promise in Gen. iii. 15 "must lose the name of ' Proto-Evan-
gelium,' which it owes to a positively incorrect view" of the passage. Accordingly he translates it : " I will put enmity between thee
(the serpent) and the woman, and between thy seed and her seed :
this (seed) shall lie in wait for thy head, and thou shalt lie in wait
for his heel"—or, as he explains it : "man aims his attack at the
head of the serpent, while it tries to strike man in the heel." It
may possibly occur to ordinary readers that it scarcely needed what
professes to be a record of Divine revelation to acquaint us with
such a fact. Very different are the views which the oldest Jewish
tradition expresses on this matter. But this is not the point to
which I am desirous of directing attention. Dr. Kuenen supports
his interpretation by two arguments. *First,* he maintains that the
verb commonly rendered "bruise," means "to lie in wait for,"
"according to the Septuagint and the Targum of Onkelos,"—and
that accordingly it cannot bear a Messianic reference. *Secondly,*

---

[1] *Prophets and Prophecy in Israel.* By Dr. A. Kuenen. London, 1877.

he, of course, implies that it is used in this sense by Onkelos in the passage in question. Now, the answer to all this is very simple, but quite conclusive. *First,* the Hebrew verb referred to is always used in the Targumim for " bruise," or " rub off," as will be seen by a reference to Levy's well-known *Dictionary of the Targumim,* Vol. II., pp. 462*b*, 463*a*.[1] *Secondly,* neither the word nor the rendering in question occurs in the Targum Onkelos, nor anything at all like it[2] (as implied in the language of Kuenen); while, *thirdly,* it *is* used, not indeed in the Targum Onkelos, but in the so-called Targum (Pseudo-) Jonathan and in the Jerusalem Targum (which in the whole of this history closely follow Jewish traditionalism), but in the sense of " bruise," with evident mystic reference—and what is more, *with express mention of its application to Messiah the King!*

I will not be so rash as to say, *Ex uno disce omnes,* but this instance may at least point the moral to our caution. In conclusion, I can only repeat the apostolic assurance, as in this sense also expressive of the feelings with which I close the present part of my investigations : " NEVERTHELESS THE FIRM FOUNDATION OF GOD STANDETH !"

ALFRED EDERSHEIM.

LODERS VICARAGE, BRIDPORT.

---

[1] Comp. also the full discussion in Roediger's *Gesenii Thes.,* Vol. III., p. 1380 *b*—the *positive* part of which it has not suited Dr. Kuenen to notice.

[2] Onkelos paraphrases : " He will remember what thou hast done to him at the beginning, and thou shalt keep in mind against him to the end."

Contents of the First Book of Chronicles (to beginning of Chap. XX.), and List of the Parallel Narratives in the two Books of Samuel.

CONTENTS.

ISRAEL:

UNDER SAMUEL, SAUL, AND DAVID.

CHAPTER I.

Purport and Lessons of the Books of Samuel—Eli—Hannah's Prayer and Vow—The Birth of Samuel—Dedication of the Child—Hannah's Song.

(1 SAM. I.—II. 11.)

ONCE more, after long and ominous silence, the interest of the sacred story turns towards the Tabernacle which God had pitched among men, and the Priesthood which He had instituted. The period of the Judges had run its full course, and wrought no deliverance in Israel. In this direction, evidently, help or hope was not to be looked for. More than that, in the case of Samson, it had appeared how even the most direct aid on the part of God might be frustrated by the self-indulgence of man. A new beginning had again to be made; but, as we have hitherto noticed in all analogous cases in sacred history, not wholly new, but one long foreshadowed and prepared.

Two great institutions were now to be prominently brought forward and established, both marking a distinct advance in the history of Israel, and showing forth more fully than before its typical character. These two institutions were: *the Prophetic Order* and *the Monarchy.* Both are connected with the history of Samuel. And this explains alike why the books which record this part of sacred history bear the name of *Samuel,* and why they close not with the death of David. as

B

might have been expected in a biography or in a history of his
reign, but with the final establishment of his kingdom (2 Sam.
xx.). At the close of 2 Sam. four chapters (xxi.–xxiv.) are
added as a sort of appendix, in which various events are
ranged, not chronologically, but in accordance with the general
plan and scope of the work, which is : to present Israel as the
kingdom of God, and as under the guidance of the spirit of
prophecy. This also explains two other peculiarities. In a
work compiled with such an object constantly in view, we do
not expect, nor do we find in it, a *strictly chronological arrangement* of events. Again, we notice large gaps in the history of
Samuel, Saul, and David, long periods and important facts
being omitted, with which the author *must* have been acquainted,—and to which, indeed, in some instances, he afterwards expressly refers,—while other periods and events are
detailed at great length. All these peculiarities are not
accidental, but designed, and in accordance with the general
plan of the work. For, we must bear in mind, that as in the
case of other parts of Holy Scripture, so in the Books of
Samuel, we must not look for biographies, as of Samuel, Saul,
and David, nor yet expect merely an account of their administration, but *a history of the kingdom of God* during a new period
in its development, and in a fresh stage of its onward movement towards the end. That end was the establishment of the
kingdom of God in Him to Whom alike the Aaronic priesthood, the prophetic order, and Israel's royalty were intended
to point. These three institutions were prominently brought
forward in the new period which opens in the books of Samuel.
First, we have in the history of Eli a revival of the interest
attaching to the priesthood. Next, we see in Samuel the real
commencement of the Old Testament prophetic order. Not
that the idea of it was new, or the people unprepared for it.
We can trace it so early as in Gen. xx. 7 (comp. Psa. cv. 15);
and we find not only Moses (Deut. xxxiv. 10), but even Miriam
(Ex. xv. 20; Numb. xii. 2) designated by the title of prophet;
while the character and functions of the office (if " office " and

not "mission" be the correct term) are clearly defined in Deut. xiii. 1-5; xviii. 9-22.[1] And although Joshua was not himself a prophet, yet the gift of prophecy had not ceased in his time. In proof we point not only to Deborah (Judg. iv. 4), but also to other instances (Judg. vi. 8). But on the other hand, the *order* of prophets as such evidently began with Samuel. The same remarks apply to the institution of royalty in Israel. It had been contemplated and prepared for from the first. Passing from the promise to Abraham (Gen. xvii. 6, 16), with its prophetic limitation to Judah (Gen. xlix. 10), we find the term kingdom applied to Israel, as marking its typical destiny (Ex. xix. 6), centering of course in *the* King (Num. xxiv. 17, 19). And as the character of the prophetic order, so that of this royalty also was clearly defined in Deut. xvii., while from Judg. viii. 23 we learn, that the remembrance and expectation of this destiny were kept alive in Israel. It was, however, during the period which we are about to describe, that royalty was first actually introduced in Israel. It appeared, if we may so express it, in Saul in its *negative*, and in David in its *positive* aspect; and to the latter all the promises and types applied which were connected with its establishment. Nor is it without the deepest significance in this respect that in the books of Samuel the designation "Jehovah of Hosts," occurs for the first time, and that Hannah, who was the first to use this title in her prayer (1 Sam. i. 11), prophesied of that King (ii. 10) in Whom all Israel's hopes were fulfilled, and Whose kingdom is the subject of grateful praise alike by the Virgin-mother, and by the father of the Baptist (Luke ii.).[2]

But to turn to the history itself. Once more the Sanctuary had been restored to its former and God-destined position, and Eli the high-priest judged in Israel.[3] Once more God

[1] This is well brought out in Ewald, *Gesch. d. V. Isr.*, vol. ii. (3rd ed.) p. 596.

[2] Comp. Auberlen, as quoted by Keil, *Bibl. Comm.*, vol. ii. s. 2, p. 17.

[3] Ewald suggests that Eli had attained the dignity of judge owing to some outward deliverance, like that of the other judges. But the Scriptural narrative of Eli, which is very brief, gives us no indication of any such event.

had visibly interposed to own the institution of Nazarites, which, more than any other, symbolised Israel's spiritual calling of voluntary self-surrender to God. Alone, and unaided by man, the Nazarite Samson had made war for God against the Philistines. In the miraculous strength supplied from on high, he had prevailed against them. But neither priest nor Nazarite of that time had realised the spirituality of their calling. Both had been raised up to show what potentiality for good there was in God's institutions ; and both were removed to prove that even God's institutions were powerless, except by a continuous and living connection with Him on Whose presence and blessing depended their efficacy. But already God was preparing other instrumentalities—a prophet, who should receive and speak His Word, and another Nazarite, voluntarily devoted to God by his mother, and who would prevail not in the strength of his own arm, but by the power of prayer, and by the influence of the message which he brought from God. That prophet, that Nazarite was Samuel. His birth, like that of Samson, was Divinely announced ; but, in accordance with the difference between the two histories, this time by prophecy, not as before, by angelic message. Samuel was God-granted, Samson God-sent ; Samuel was God-dedicated, Samson was God-demanded. Both were Nazarites ; but the one spiritually, the other outwardly; both prevailed : but the one spiritually, the other outwardly. The work of Samson ended in self-indulgence, failure, and death ; that of Samuel opened up into the royalty of David, Israel's great type-king.

Up in Mount Ephraim, due west from Shiloh,[1] lay *Ramah,* "the height," or by its full name, *Ramathaim Zophim,* "the twin heights of the Zophites." [2] From Josh. xxi. 20, we know

---

[1] Notwithstanding high authority, I cannot look for *Ramah,* as most modern writers do, anywhere within the ancient territory of Benjamin. The expression, "Mount Ephraim," might indeed be taken in a wider sense ; but then there is the addition "an Ephrathite," that is, an Ephraimite. Keil's suggestion that Elkanah was originally an Ephraimite, but had migrated into Benjamin, is wholly unsupported.

[2] Some of the Rabbis fancifully render it, "the watchers," or prophets.

that, amongst others, certain districts within the tribal possession of Ephraim were assigned to the Levitical families which descended from Kohath. One of these—that of Zophai or Zuph (1 Chron. vi. 25, 35)—had given its name to the whole district, as "the land of Zuph" (1 Sam. ix. 5). From this family sprang *Elkanah*, "the God-acquired," or "purchased," a name which characteristically occurs in the Old Testament only in Levitical families.[1] It was not in accordance with what "was from the first," that Elkanah had two wives,[2] *Hannah* ("favour," "grace") and *Peninnah* ("pearl," or "coral"). Perhaps the circumstance that Hannah was not blessed with children may have led to this double marriage. "Yearly"—as has been inferred from the use of the same peculiar expression in Ex. xiii. 10— "at the Feast of the Passover,"[3] the one above all others to which families as such were wont to "go up" (Luke ii. 41), Elkanah came to Shiloh with his household for the twofold purpose of "worshipping" and of "sacrificing" peace-offerings according to the law (Ex. xxiii. 15; xxxiv. 20; Deut. xvi. 16). Although, Eli being old, the chief direction of the services devolved upon his unworthy sons, Hophni and Phinehas, yet these were joyous occasions (Deut. xii. 12; xvi. 11; xxvii. 7), when the whole household would share in the feast upon the thank-offering. At that time Elkanah was wont to give to Peninnah and to her children their "portions;" but to Hannah he gave "a portion for two persons,"[4] as if to indicate that he loved her just as if she had borne him a son. Whether from jealousy or from malevolence, Peninnah made those joyous seasons times of pain and bitter emotion to Hannah, by grieving,

[1] With one exception—2 Chron. xxviii. 7—Levites seem in civic respects to have been reckoned with the tribes in whose territories they were located, as Judg. xvii. 7. This would be a further undesigned fulfilment of Gen. xlix. 7.

[2] The Mosaic Law tolerated and regulated, but nowhere approved it, and in practice polygamy was chiefly confined to the wealthy.

[3] If the inference be admitted, Judg. xi. 40; xxi. 19, must also refer to the Feast of the Passover. On the observance of this feast during the period of the Judges, comp. Hengstenberg, *Beitr.* iii. 79, etc.

[4] This in all probability is the correct rendering.

and trying to make her dissatisfied and rebellious against God. And so it happened each year : Hannah's sorrow, as time passed, seeming ever more hopeless. In vain Elkanah tried to comfort her by assurance of his own affection. The burden of her reproach, still unrolled from her, seemed almost too heavy to bear.

It was surely in the noble despair of faith—as if in her own way anticipating the New Testament question : "Lord, to whom shall we go?"—that Hannah rose from the untasted sacrificial feast, with the resolve to cast upon the Lord the burden she could not bear. It was early evening in spring time, and the aged high-priest Eli (a descendant not of Eleazar, but of Ithamar, to whom the high-priesthood seems to have been transferred from the elder branch of the Aaronic family, comp. Josephus' *Antiquities*, v. 11. 5)[1] sat at the entrance probably to the holy place, when a lonely woman came and knelt towards the sanctuary. Concealed by the folds of the curtain, she may not have noticed him, though he watched every movement of the strange visitor. Not a sound issued from her lips, and still they moved faster and faster, as, unburdening the long secret, she poured out her heart[2] in silent prayer. And now the gentle rain of tears fell, and then in spirit she believingly rose to the vow that the child she sought from the Lord should not be cherished for the selfish gratification of even a mother's sacred love. He would, of course, be a Levite, and as such bound from his twenty-fifth or thirtieth year to service when his turn for it came. But her child should wholly belong to God. From

[1] That Eli was a descendant of Ithamar, not of Eleazar, appears from 1 Chron. xxiv. 1, Abimelech being the great-great-grandson of Eli. Ewald suggests that Eli was the first high-priest of that branch of the family of Aaron, and that he was invested with the office of high-priest in consequence of his position as judge. Other writers have offered different explana- tions of the transference of the priesthood to the line of Ithamar (comp. Keil, *Bibl. Comm.* ii. 2, pp. 30, 31). But the Scriptural narrative affords no *data* on the subject. It gives not the personal history of Eli, nor even that of the house of Aaron, but of the kingdom of God.

[2] Ver. 13, literally rendered : "She was speaking to her heart."

earliest childhood, and permanently, should he be attached to the house of the Lord. Not only so—he should be a Nazarite, and that not of the ordinary class, but one whose vow should last for life (Num. vi. 2 ; comp. Judg. xiii. 5).

It leaves on us the twofold sad impression that such prayerful converse with God must have been rare in Shiloh, and that the sacrificial feasts were not unfrequently profaned by excesses, when such a man as Eli could suspect, and roughly interrupt Hannah's prayer on the supposition of her drunkenness. But Eli was a man of God ; and the modest, earnest words which Hannah spake soon changed his reproof into a blessing. And now Hannah comes back to those she had left at the sacrificial feast. The brief absence had transformed her, for she returns with a heart light of sorrow and joyous in faith. Her countenance [1] and bearing are changed. She eats of the erst untasted food, and is gladsome. She has already that for which to thank God, for she is strong in faith. Another morning of early worship, and the family return to their quiet home. But God is not unmindful of her. Ere another Passover has summoned the worshippers to Shiloh, Hannah has the child of her prayers, whom significantly she has named *Samuel*, the God-answered (literally : heard of God—*Exauditus a Deo*). This time Hannah accompanied not her husband, though he paid a vow which he seems to have made [2] if a son were granted ; no, nor next time. But the third year, when the child was fully weaned,[3] she presented herself once more before Eli. It must have sounded to the old priest almost like a voice from heaven when the gladsome mother pointed to her child as the embodiment of answered prayer : " For this boy have I prayed ; and Jehovah gave me my asking which I asked of Him. And now I (*on my part*) make him the asked

---

[1] Ver. 18, literally : " And her face was the same face no more to her."

[2] This we infer from the addition, "and his vow," in ver. 21.

[3] The period of suckling was supposed to last three years (2 Macc. vii. 27). A Hebrew child at that age would be fit for some ministry, even though the care of him might partially devolve on one of the women who served at the door of the tabernacle.

one unto Jehovah all the days that he lives : he is 'the asked one' unto Jehovah!"[1]   And as she so vowed and paid her vow, one of the three bullocks which they had brought was offered a burnt-offering, symbolic of the dedication of her child.[2]

Once more Hannah "prayed ;" this time not in the language of sorrow, but in that of thanksgiving and prophetic anticipation. For was not Samuel, so to speak, the John the Baptist of the Old Testament? and was it not fitting that on his formal dedication unto God, she should speak words reaching far beyond her own time, and even furnishing what could enter into the Virgin-mother's song?

"And Hannah prayed and said :

1   " My heart rejoiceth in Jehovah—
       Uplifted my horn in Jehovah,
       Wide opened my mouth upon my foes
       For I rejoice in Thy salvation ![3]
2   None holy as Jehovah—for none *is* beside Thee,
       Nor *is* there rock as our God !
3   Multiply not speech lofty, lofty—
       (Nor) insolence come out of your mouth,
       For God of all knowledge[4] is Jehovah,
       And with Him deeds are weighed.[5]
4   Bow-heroes are broken,[6]
       And the stumbling girded with strength.

[1] This literal rendering will sufficiently bring out the beautiful meaning of her words. It is difficult to understand how our Authorised Version came to translate "lent."

[2] They had brought with them *three* bullocks—two for the usual burnt and thank-offerings, and the third as a burnt sacrifice at the formal dedication of Samuel. The meat-offering for each would have been at least $\frac{3}{10}$ of an ephah of flour (Num. xv. 8).

[3] Possibly it would be more accurate here to translate, "deliverance."

[4] In the original, "knowledge" is in the plural ; I have rendered this by "all knowledge."

[5] Many interpreters understand this not of man's but of *God's* deeds, as meaning that God's doings were fixed and determined. But this seems very constrained. I would almost feel inclined to discard the Masoretic correction of our Hebrew text, and retaining the *Chethib* to translate interrogatively, " And are not deeds weighed?"

[6] The verb which agrees with *heroes* is used both in a literal and a metaphorical sense—in the latter for confounded, afraid.

5 "The full hire themselves out for bread
   And the hungry cease—
   Even till the barren bears seven,
   And the many-childed languisheth away!
6 Jehovah killeth and maketh alive,[1]
   He bringeth down to Sheol, and bringeth up.
7 Jehovah maketh poor and maketh rich,
   He layeth low and lifteth up.
8 He lifteth from the dust the weak,
   And from the dunghill raiseth the poor,
   To make them sit down with nobles.[2]
   And seats of honour will He assign them—
   For Jehovah's are the pillars of the earth,
   And He hath set on them the habitable world.
9 The feet of His saints will He keep,[3]
   And the wicked in darkness shall be put to silence,
   For not by strength shall man prevail![4]
10 Jehovah—broken they that strive with Him,
   Above him (over such) in the heavens shall He thunder;
   Jehovah shall judge the ends of the earth,
   And give strength to His King,
   And lift on high the horn of His Anointed!"

And so the child and his parents parted—where parting is ever best: leaving him "ministering unto the Lord." But yearly, as they came up to the twice-loved service in Shiloh, they saw again the child, still serving in the courts of the Lord's house, "girded with a linen ephod." And the gift they brought him each year from home was that with which Hannah's love best liked to connect her absent child—"a little Meïl,"[5] or priestly robe in which to do his service. She had made him "the God-asked," and present or absent he was ever such in her loving thoughts. But, as Eli had prayed, instead of the "asked one," who was "asked" for Jehovah, three sons and two daughters gladdened Hannah's heart. "But the boy Samuel grew up with Jehovah" (1 Sam. ii. 21).

[1] Cp. Deut. xxxii. 39; Psa. xxx. 3; lxxi. 20; lxxxvi. 13.
[2] Cp. Psa. cxiii. 7, 8.   [3] Psa. lvi. 13; cxvi. 8; cxxi. 3, and others.
[4] Psa. xxxiii. 16, 17.
[5] The *Meïl* was properly the high-priestly robe (Ex. xxviii. 31). Of course, Samuel's was of different material, and without border.

CHAPTER II.

The Sin of Eli's Sons—Eli's Weakness—A Prophet's Message—Samuel's First Vision—His Call to the Prophetic Office.

(1 Sam. 11. 12—111. 21.)

QUITE another scene now opens before us, and one which, as it shows the corruptness of the priestly family, also argues a very low religious state among the people.[1]   The high-priest Eli was "very old,"[2] and the administration of the sanctuary was left in the hands of his two sons, Hophni and Phinehas.   The energy, amounting almost to severity, which, even in his old age, Eli could display, as in his undeserved reproof of Hannah, was certainly not exercised towards his sons.   They were "sons of Belial," and "knew not Jehovah" in His character and claims.[3]   Their conduct was scandalous even in a decrepid age, and the unblushing frankness of their vices led "the people of the Lord to transgress," by "bringing into contempt"[4] the sacrificial services of the sanctuary. The main element of hope and the prospect of a possible revival lay in the close adherence of the people to these services.   But the sons of Eli seemed determined to prove that these ordinances were mainly designed for the advantage of the priesthood, and therefore not holy, of Divine significance, and unalterably fixed.   Contrary to the Divine insti-

---

[1] See the pertinent remarks of Ewald, *u.s.*, p. 10.

[2] The mention of this in Scripture is not intended to represent Eli as a man whose faculties were gone, but to account for the absolute rule of his sons, and for that indulgence which men in their old age are apt to show towards their children.

[3] *Belial* means literally *lowness*, that is, vileness.

[4] So literally.

tution, "the priest's right," as he claimed it,[1] was to take, if necessary by force, parts of the sacrifices before these had really been offered unto the Lord (Lev. iii. 3–5 ; comp. vii. 30–34).

Nor was this all. The open immorality of the high-priest's sons was as notorious as their profanity.[2] The only step which the aged high-priest took to put an end to such scandals was mild expostulation, the truisms of which had only so far value as they expressed it, that in offences between man and man, Elohim would, through the magistracy, restore the proper balance, but who was to do that when the sin was against Jehovah? Such remonstrances could, of course, produce no effect upon men so seared in conscience as to be already under sentence of judicial hardening (ver. 25).

But other and more terrible judgments were at hand. They were solemnly announced to Eli by a prophet (comp. Judg. xiii. 6), since by his culpable weakness he shared the guilt of his sons. As so often in His dealings with His own people, the Lord condescended to reason, not only to exhibit the rightness of His ways, but to lay down principles for all time for the guidance of His church. Had He not dealt in special grace with the house of Aaron? He had honoured it at the first by special revelation ; He had singled it out for the privilege of ministering unto Him at the altar ; for the still higher function of presenting in the incense the prayers of His people ; and for that highest office of "wearing the ephod" in the solemn mediatorial services of the Day of Atonement. Moreover, He had made ample provision for all their wants. All this had been granted in perpetuity to the house of Aaron (Ex. xxix. 9). It had been specially confirmed to Phinehas on account of his zeal for the honour of

[1] Notwithstanding high authority, I cannot accept the view which would connect the *first* clause of 1 Sam. ii. 13 (of course, without the words in *italics*) with the last clause of ver. 12.

[2] Ver. 22. "The women that assembled at the door of the tabernacle" were, no doubt, officially engaged in some service, although we know not wherein it consisted. Comp. Ex. xxxviii. 8.

God (Num. xxv. 13). But even the latter circumstance, as well as the nature of the case, indicated that the whole rested on a moral relationship, as, indeed, the general principle holds true : " Them that honour Me I will honour, and they that despise Me shall be lightly esteemed." In accordance with this, Eli and his house would become subjects of special judgment : none of his descendants, so long as they held office, should attain old age (1 Sam. ii. 31); in punishment of their own insolence of office they would experience constant humiliation (ver. 32);[1] another and more faithful line of priests should fill the highest office (ver. 35);[2] and the deposed family would have to seek at their hands the humblest places for the sake of the barest necessaries of life (ver. 36). Thus justice would overtake a family which, in their pride of office, had dared to treat the priesthood as if it were absolutely their own, and to degrade it for selfish purposes. As for the chief offenders, Hophni and Phinehas, swift destruction would overtake them in one day; and their death would be the sign of the commencement of those judgments, which were to culminate in the time of Solomon (1 Kings ii. 27; comp. Josephus' *Antiq.* v. 11, 5 ; viii. 1, 3).

But, uncorrupted by such influences around, "the child Samuel grew, and was in favour both with Jehovah and with men,"—in this respect also the type of the "faithful Priest," the great Prophet, the perfect Nazarite (Luke ii. 52). It was

---

[1] The Authorised Version renders, evidently incorrectly : " Thou shalt see an enemy in My habitation, in all the wealth which God shall give Israel." But the suggestions of modern critics are not more satisfactory. I would venture to propose the following rendering of these difficult expressions : " And thou shalt see adversity to the tabernacle in all that benefits Israel ;" *i.e.*, constant humiliation of the priesthood during the prosperity of Israel, a prediction amply fulfilled in the history of the priesthood under Samuel, Saul, and latterly under David, until the deposition of the line of Ithamar.

[2] I venture to think that this promise should be applied impersonally rather than personally. Thus it includes, indeed, Samuel and afterwards Zadok, but goes beyond them, and applies to the priesthood generally, and points for its final fulfilment to the Lord Jesus Christ.

in many respects as in the days of the Son of man. " The word of Jehovah" by prophetic revelation "was precious," it was rare, and prophetic "vision was not spread." [1] Meanwhile Samuel had grown into a youth, and was, as Levite, "ministering unto Jehovah before Eli." But as yet, beyond humble, faithful walk before God, heart-fellowship with Him, and outward ministrations in His sanctuary, Samuel had not other knowledge of Jehovah, in the sense of personal revelation or reception of His message (iii. 7). The sanctuary in Shiloh had become permanent, and we are warranted in inferring that "the dwelling," which formerly was adapted to Israel's wanderings, had lost somewhat of its temporary character. The "curtains" which in the wilderness had formed its enclosure, had no doubt been exchanged for buildings for the use of the priesthood in their ministry and for the many requirements of their services. Instead of the "veil" at the entrance to the outer court there would be doors, closed at even and opened to the worshippers in the morning. The charge of these doors seems to have devolved upon Samuel, who as "minister" and guardian lay by night within the sacred enclosure, in the court of the people—or, at least, close to it, as did the priests on duty in later times. The aged high-priest himself seems to have lain close by, probably in one of the rooms or halls opening out upon the sanctuary.

It was still night, though the dawn was near. [2] The holy oil in the seven-branched candlestick in the holy place was burning low, but its light had not yet gone out, when a voice calling Samuel by his name wakened him from sleep. As Eli's eyes had begun to "wax dim," so that he would require the aid of the young Levite on ministry, it was natural to infer that it was the voice of the aged high-priest that had called him. [3]

---

[1] So 1 Sam. iii. 1, literally rendered.

[2] The expression, "ere the lamp of God went out in the temple of the Lord," seems intended to mark the time, as indicated by us in the text.

[3] This seems to be the reason why the fact is mentioned, that Eli's eyes had begun to wax dim.

But it was not so, and Samuel again laid him down to rest. A second time the same voice called him, and a second time he repaired in vain to Eli for his commands. But when yet a third time the call was repeated, the high-priest understood that it was not some vivid dream which had startled the youth from his sleep, but that a voice from heaven commanded his attention. There is such simplicity and child-like faith, such utter absence of all intrusive curiosity, and such entire self-forgetfulness on the part of Eli, and on that of Samuel such complete want of all self-consciousness, as to render the sur-roundings worthy of the scene about to be enacted. Samuel no longer seeks sleep; but when next the call is heard, he answers, as directed by his fatherly teacher : "Speak,[1] for Thy servant heareth." Then it was that not, as before, merely a voice, but a vision was granted him,[2] when Jehovah repeated in express terms, this time not in warning prediction, but as the announcement of an almost immediate event, the terrible judgment impending upon Eli and his sons.

With the burden of this communication upon him, Samuel lay still till the grey morning light; nor, whatever thoughts might crowd upon him, did the aged high-priest seek to intrude into what might pass between that Levite youth and the Lord, before Whom he had stood for so many years in the highest function of the priestly office, and into Whose im-mediate Presence in the innermost sanctuary he had so often entered. Suffice it, the vision and the word of Jehovah had passed from himself—passed not to his sons and successors in the priesthood, but to one scarce grown to manhood, and whose whole history, associated as it was with that very

---

[1] It is remarkable, as indicative of Samuel's reverential fear, that his reply differs from that taught him by Eli in the omission of the word "Jehovah."

[2] This is implied in the words, "Jehovah came and stood " (1 Sam. iii. 10). The "voice" had come from out of the most holy place, where the Lord dwelt between the Cherubim; the "vision " or appearance, in whatever form it may have been, was close before Samuel. In the one case Samuel had been asleep, in the other he was fully awake.

tabernacle, stood out so vividly before him. This itself was judgment. But what further judgment had the voice of the Lord announced to His youthful servant?

And now it was morning, and Samuel's duty was to open the gates of the sanctuary. What was he to do with the burden which had been laid upon him? In his reverence for his teacher and guide, and in his modesty, he could not bring himself unbidden to speak of that vision ; he trembled to repeat to him whom most it concerned the words which he had heard. But the sound of the opening gates conveyed to Eli, that whatever might have been the commission to the young prophet, it had been given, and there could be no further hesitation in asking its import. Feeling that he and his family had been its subject, and that, however heavy the burden, it behoved him to know it, he successively asked, entreated, and even conjured Samuel to tell it in all its details. So challenged, Samuel dared not keep back anything. And the aged priest, however weak and unfaithful, yet in heart a servant of the Lord, received it with humiliation and resignation, though apparently without that resolve of change which alone could have constituted true repentance (1 Sam. iii. 17, 18).

By the faithful discharge of a commission so painful, and involving such self-denial and courage, Samuel had stood the first test of his fitness for the prophetic office. Henceforth "the word of the Lord" was permanently with him. Not merely by isolated commissions, but in the discharge of a regular office, Samuel acted as prophet in Israel. A new period in the history of the kingdom of God had commenced ; and all Israel, from Dan to Beer-sheba, knew that there was now a new link between them and their Heavenly King, a living centre of guidance and fellowship, and a bond of union for all who were truly the Israel of God.

CHAPTER III.

Expedition against the Philistines—The Two Battles of Eben-ezer—Death of Eli's Sons, and Taking of the Ark—Death of Eli—Judgment on the Philistine Cities—The Return of the Ark.

(1 SAM. IV.—VII. I.)

TIME had passed; but in Shiloh it was as before. Eli, who had reached the patriarchal age of ninety-seven, was now totally blind,[1] and his sons still held rule in the sanctuary. As for Samuel, his prophetic "word was to all Israel."[2] Some effect must have been produced by a ministry so generally acknowledged. True, it did not succeed in leading the people to repentance, nor in teaching them the spiritual character of the relationship between God and themselves, nor yet that of His ordinances in Israel. But whereas the conduct of Eli's sons had brought the sanctuary and its services into public contempt (1 Sam. ii. 17), Samuel's ministry restored and strengthened belief in the reality of God's presence in His temple, and in His help and power. In short, it would tend to keep alive and increase *historical*, although not *spiritual* belief in Israel. Such feelings, when uncombined with repentance, would lead to a revival of religiousness rather than of religion; to confidence in the possession of what, dissociated from their higher bearing,

[1] Literally, "his eyes stood" (1 Sam. iv. 15). Through a mistake, probably in reading the numeral letters (ע for נ), the Arabic and Syrian versions represent Eli as seventy-eight instead of ninety-eight years old.

[2] We regard the first clause of 1 Sam. iv. 1 as entirely unconnected with the account of Israel's expedition against the Philistines. Keil, following other interpreters, connects the two clauses, and assumes, as it appears to me, erroneously, that the war was undertaken in obedience to Samuel's word. But in that case he would have been the direct cause of Israel's disaster and defeat.

were merely externals; to a confusion of symbols with reality; and to such a reliance on their calling and privileges, as would have converted the wonder-working Presence of Jehovah in the midst of His believing people into a magic power attaching to certain symbols, the religion of Israel into mere externalism, essentially heathen in its character, and the calling of God's people into a warrant for carnal pride of nationality. In truth, however different in manifestation, the sin of Israel was essentially the same as that of Eli's sons. Accordingly it had to be shown in reference to both, that neither high office nor yet the possession of high privileges entitles to the promises attached to them, irrespective of a deeper relationship between God and His servants.

It may have been this renewed, though entirely carnal confidence in the Presence of God in His sanctuary, as evidenced by the prophetic office of Samuel, or else merely a fresh outbreak of that chronic state of warfare between Israel and the Philistines which existed since the days of Samson and even before, that led to the expedition which terminated in the defeat at Eben-ezer. At any rate, the sacred text implies that the Philistines held possession of part of the soil of Palestine; nor do we read of any recent incursion on their part which had given them this hold. It was, therefore, as against positions which the enemy had occupied for some time that "Israel went out to battle" in that open "field," which from the monument erected after the later deliverance under Samuel (1 Sam. vii. 12), obtained the name of *Eben-ezer*, or stone of help. The scene of action lay, as we know, in the territory of Benjamin, a short way beyond *Mizpeh*, "the look out," about two hours to the north-west of Jerusalem.[1] The Philistines had pitched a short way off at *Aphek*, "firmness," probably a fortified position. The battle ended in the entire defeat of Israel, with a loss of four thousand men, not fugitives, but in the "battle-

---

[1] For reasons too numerous here to detail, I still hold by the old identification of *Mizpeh*, notwithstanding the high authority of Dean Stanley, and Drs. Grove and H. Bonar.

array"[1] itself. They must have been at least equal in numbers to
the Philistines, and under favourable circumstances, since at
the council of war after their defeat, "the elders of Israel"
unhesitatingly ascribed the disaster not to secondary causes,
but to the direct agency of Jehovah. It was quite in accordance
with the prevailing religious state that, instead of inquiring into
the causes of God's controversy with them, they sought safety
in having among them "the ark of the covenant of the Lord,"
irrespective of the Lord Himself and of the terms of His covenant. As if to mark, in its own peculiarly significant manner,
the incongruity of the whole proceeding, Scripture simply puts
together these two things in their sharp contrast : that it was
"the ark of the covenant of Jehovah of Hosts, which dwelleth
between the cherubim," and that "Hophni and Phinehas were
there with the ark of the covenant of God" (1 Sam. iv. 4).

Such an event as the removal of the ark from the sanctuary,
and its presence in the camp, had never happened since the
settlement of Israel in Canaan.   Its arrival, betokening to their
minds the certain renewal of miraculous deliverances such as
their fathers had experienced, excited unbounded enthusiasm
in Israel, and caused equal depression among the Philistines.
But soon another mood prevailed.[2] Whether we regard ver.
9 as the language of the leaders of the Philistines, addressed
to their desponding followers, or as the desperate resolve of
men who felt that all was at stake, this time they waited not to
be attacked by the Israelites. In the battle which ensued, and
the flight of Israel which followed, no less than thirty thousand
dead strewed the ground. In the number of the slain were
Hophni and Phinehas, and among the booty the very ark of
God was taken ! Thus fearfully did judgment commence in
the house of Eli ; thus terribly did God teach the lesson that
even the most sacred symbol connected with His immediate

---

[1] So literally in 1 Sam. iv. 2 : "They slew in the battle-array in the field
about four thousand men."

[2] In vers. 7 and 8 the Philistines speak of God in the plural number,
regarding Him from their polytheistic point of view.

Presence was in itself but wood and gold, and so far from being capable of doing wonders, might even be taken and carried away.

Tidings of this crushing defeat were not long in reaching Shiloh. Just outside the gate of the sanctuary, by the way which a messenger from the battle-field must come, sat the aged high-priest. His eyes were "stiffened" by age, but his hearing was keen as he waited with anxious heart for the expected news. The judgment foretold, the presence of his two sons with the army in the field, the removal of the ark, without any Divine authority, at the bidding of a superstitious people, must have filled him with sad misgivings. Had he been right in being a consenting party to all this? Had he been a faithful father, a faithful priest, a faithful guardian of the sanctuary? And now a confused noise as of a tumult reached him. Up the slopes which led to Shiloh, "with clothes rent and earth upon his head," in token of deepest meaning, ran a Benjamite, a fugitive from the army. Past the high-priest he sped, without stopping to speak to him whose office had become empty, and whose family was destroyed. Now he has reached the market-place; and up and down those steep, narrow streets fly the tidings. They gather around him; they weep, they cry out in the wildness of their grief, and "the noise of the crying" is heard where the old man sits alone still waiting for tidings. The messenger is brought to him. Stroke upon stroke falls upon him the fourfold disaster: "Israel is fled!" "a great slaughter among the people!" "thy two sons are dead!" "the ark of God is taken!" It is this last most terrible blow, rather than anything else, which lays low the aged priest. As he hears of the ark of God, he falls backward unconscious, and is killed in the fall by "the side of the gate" of the sanctuary. Thus ends a judge-ship of forty years![1]

Yet another scene of terror. Within her house lies the wife

[1] The LXX. give it as twenty years, probably misreading the numeral letter מ for כ

of Phinehas, with the sorrows and the hopes of motherhood upon her. And now these tidings have come into that darkened chamber also. They gather around her as the shadows of death. In vain the women that are about try to comfort her with the announcement that a son has been born to her. She answers not, neither regards it. She cannot forget her one great sorrow even in this joy that a man is born into the world. She has but one word, even for her new-born child : " *I-chabod*," " no glory." To her he is Ichabod —for the glory is departed from Israel. And with that word on her lips she dies. The deepest pang which had wrought her death was, as in the case of her father-in-law, that the ark, the glory of Israel, was no more.[1] Two have died that day in Shiloh of grief for the ark of God—the aged high-priest and the young mother; two, whose death showed at least their own fidelity to their God and their heart-love for His cause and presence.

But although such heavy judgment had come upon Israel, it was not intended that Philistia should triumph. More than that, in the hour of their victory the heathen must learn that their gods were not only wholly powerless before Jehovah, but merely idols, the work of men's hands. The Philistines had, in the first place, brought the ark to Ashdod, and placed it in the temple of Dagon as a votive offering, in acknowledgment of the victory which they ascribed to the agency of their national god. Had not the ark of God been brought into the camp of Israel, and had not the God of Israel been defeated and led captive in His ark through the superior power of Dagon? But they were soon to feel that it was not so ; and when on the morn of its arrival at Ashdod, the priests opened the temple doors, they found the statue of their god thrown upon its face in front of the ark. It might have been some accident ; and

---

[1] As I understand the narrative, her only words, as quoted in the text, were Ichabod, as the name of the child, and the explanation which she gave of it in ver. 22. All the rest is added by the narrator of the sad tragedy.

the statue, with its head and bust of a bearded man, and body in the form of a fish,[1] was replaced in the *cella* at the entrance of the temple. But next morning the head and hands, which were in human form, were found cut off and lying on the threshold, as if each entrant should in contempt tread upon these caricatures of ideal humanity ; and nothing but the Dagon itself,[2] the fish-body, was left, which once more lay prostrate before the ark.

But this was not all. If the gods of Philistia were only vanity, the power and strength in which the people may have boasted, were likewise to appear as unavailing before the Lord. He "laid waste" the people of Ashdod—as we infer from 1 Sam. vi. 4, 11, 18—by that terrible plague of southern countries, field-mice, which sometimes in a single night destroy a harvest, and are known to have driven whole tribes from their dwelling-places.[3] While thus the towns and villages around Ashdod were desolated, the inhabitants of that city itself and of its neighbourhood, suffered from another plague, possibly occasioned by the want caused by famine, in the form of an epidemic—probably a malignant skin disease,[4] highly infectious and fatal in its character. As we gather from the context, Philistia consisted at that time of a federation of five "cities," or cantons, under the oligarchical rule of "lords," or princes, with this provision, that no great public measure (such as the removal of the ark, which had been placed at Ashdod by common decree) might be taken without the consent of all. Accordingly, on an appeal of the people of Ashdod, the lords of the Philistines ordered the removal of the ark to Gath, probably judging, that the calamities complained of were due rather to natural causes than to its presence. But in

---

[1] See the description and representation in Layard's *Nineveh and Babylon,* pp. 343, 350. Dagon was the male god of fertility.

[2] *Dagon* means the "fish-form," from *dag,* a fish.

[3] Comp. the quotations in Bochart, *Hieroz.* i., pp. 1017–1019.

[4] Judging from the derivation of the word, and from its employment (in Deut. xxviii. 27) in connection with other skin diseases, we regard it as a kind of pestilential boils of a very malignant character.

Gath the same consequences also followed; and when on its further transportation to Ekron the public sufferings were even greater and more sudden than before,[1] the cry became universal to return the ark to the land of Israel.

The experience of these seven months during which the ark had been in their land, not only convinced the lords of the Philistines of the necessity of yielding to the popular demand, but also made them careful as to the manner of handling the ark when returning it to its place. Accordingly they resolved to consult their priests and soothsayers on this question: "What shall we do in reference to the ark of Jehovah—instruct us with what we shall send it to its place?" The reply was to this effect, that if the ark were returned it should be accompanied by a "trespass-offering" (in expiation of their wrong (Lev. vi. 5; Num. v. 7),[2]—consisting, according to common heathen custom,[3] of votive offerings in gold, representing that wherein or whereby they had suffered. Never perhaps did superstition more truly appear in its real character than in the advice which these priests pressed upon their people. Evidently they were fully acquainted with the judgments which the God of Israel had executed upon the Egyptians when hardening their hearts, and with solemn earnestness they urge the return of the ark and a trespass-offering. And yet they are not quite sure whether, after all, it was not mere chance that had happened to them; and they propose a curious device by which to decide that question (1 Sam. vi. 7-9).

The advice of the priests was literally followed. The ark,

---

[1] From the text it appears that the Ekronites, immediately on the arrival of the ark, entreated its removal; but that before the necessary steps could be taken, they were visited with plagues similar to those in Ashdod and Gath, but more intense and widespread even than before. Thus the strokes fell quicker and heavier as the Philistines resisted the hand of God.

[2] The last clause of 1 Sam. vi. 3 should be rendered: "If ye shall then be healed, it will be known to you, why His hand is not removed from you," viz., not until you had returned the ark and brought a trespass-offering.

[3] This custom, it is well known, has since passed into the Roman Catholic Church.

with its trespass-offerings,[1] was placed on a new cart, which had never served profane purposes. To this were attached two milch cows, on whom never yoke of other service had been laid, and from whom their calves had just been taken. No force was to be used to keep them from returning to their calves; no guidance to be given what road to take. And, behold, it happened as the priests had suggested it would, if it were God Who had smitten them. "Though lowing as they went" for their calves, the kine took the straight road to the nearest Israelitish border-city, *Beth-shemesh* ("the house of the Sun"), followed by the wondering lords of the Philistines. The boundary was reached, and the Philistines waited to see what would happen.

About fourteen miles west of Jerusalem, on the northern boundary of the possession of Judah, about two miles from the great Philistine plain, and seven from Ekron, lay the ancient "sun-city," Beth-shemesh. It was one of those allotted by Joshua to the priests (Josh. xxi. 16), though, of course, not exclusively inhabited by them. To reach it from Ekron, the great plain has first to be traversed. Then the hills are crossed which bound the great plain of Philistia. Ascending these, and standing on the top of a steep ridge, a valley stretches beneath, or rather "the junction of two fine plains."[2] This is "the valley of Beth-shemesh," where on that summer afternoon they were reaping the wheat-harvest (1 Sam. vi. 13); and beyond it, on "the plateau of a low swell or mound," was the ancient Beth-shemesh itself.

A fit place this to which to bring the ark from Philistia, right in view of Zorah, the birth-place of Samson. Here, over

[1] In 1 Sam. vi. 4, we read of "five" golden mice as part of the trespass-offering, the priests computing the number according to that of the five Philistine capitals. But from ver. 18 we infer that, in point of fact, their number was *not* limited to five, but that these votive offerings were brought not only for the five cities, but also for all "fenced cities" and "country villages," the plague of the mice having apparently been much wider in its ravages than that of the pestilential boils.

[2] Comp. Robinson's *Bibl. Researches*, ii. pp. 223-225; iii. p. 153.

these ridges, he had often made those incursions which had carried terror and destruction to the enemies of Israel. The sound of the approaching escort—for, no doubt, the Philistine "lords" were accompanied by their retainers, and by a multitude eager to see the result—attracted the attention of the reapers below. As, literally, "they lifted up their eyes" to the hill whence it slowly wound down, the momentary fear at seeing the Philistine escort gave place first to astonishment and then to unbounded joy, as they recognised their own ark heading the strange procession. Now it had reached the boundary—probably marked by a "great stone" in the field of Joshua.[1] The Philistines had remained reverently within their own territory, and the unguided kine stood still by the first landmark in Israel. The precious burden they brought was soon surrounded by Beth-shemites. Levites were called to lift it with consecrated hands, and to offer first the kine that had been devoted by the Philistines to the service of the Lord, and then other "burnt-offerings and sacrifices" which the men of Beth-shemesh had brought. But even so, on its first return to the land, another lesson must be taught to Israel in connection with the ark of God. It *was* the symbol to which the Presence of Jehovah in the midst of His people attached. Alike superstition and profanity would entail judgment at His Hand. What the peculiar desecration or sin of the Beth-shemites may have been, either on that day of almost unbounded excitement, or afterwards, we cannot tell.[2]

[1] In vers. 14, 15 we read of a "great stone," while in ver. 18 it is called "the great Avel." Interpreters regard this as a clerical error of the copyist—אבל for אבן, AVeL for EVeN. But may it not be that this "great stone" obtained the name *Avel*, "mourning," as marking the boundary-line towards Philistia?

[2] The Authorised Version translates in ver. 19, "they had looked into the ark," following in this the Rabbis. But this view is scarcely tenable. Nor is the rendering of other interpreters satisfactory: "They looked (in the sense of curious gazing) at the ark," although this assuredly comes within the range of the warning, Num. iv. 20. But the whole text here seems corrupted. Thus in the statement that " He smote threescore and ten men," the addition " of the people, 50,000," has—judging it both on linguistic and

Suffice it that it was something which the people themselves felt to be incompatible with the "holiness" of Jehovah God (ver. 20), and that it was punished by the death of not less than seventy persons.[1] In consequence the ark was, at the request of the Beth-shemites, once more removed, up the heights at the head of the valley to the "city of forest-trees," *Kirjath-jearim*, where it was given in charge to *Abinadab*, no doubt a Levite; whose son *Eleazar* was set apart to the office of guardian, not priest, of the ark.[2] Here this sacred symbol remained, while the tabernacle itself was moved from Shiloh to Nob, and from Nob to Gibeon, till David brought it, after the conquest of Jerusalem, into his royal city (2 Sam. vi. 2, 3, 12). Thus for all this period the sanctuary was empty of that which was its greatest treasure, and the symbol of God's Personal Presence removed from the place in which He was worshipped.

---

rational grounds—unquestionably crept into the text by the mistake of a copyist. But Thenius points out other linguistic anomalies, which lead to the inference that there may be here some farther corruption of the text. Accordingly, he adopts the reading from which the LXX. translated: "And the sons of Jechonias rejoiced not among the men of Beth-shemesh, that they saw the ark of the Lord."

[1] See previous note.

[2] It is difficult to say why the ark was not carried to Shiloh. Ewald thinks that the Philistines had taken Shiloh, and destroyed its sanctuary; Keil, that the people were unwilling to restore the ark to a place which had been profaned by the sons of Eli; Erdmann, that it was temporarily placed at Kirjath-jearim for safety, till the will of God were known. The latter seems the most satisfactory explanation, especially as Kirjath-jearim was the first large town between Beth-shemesh and Shiloh, and the priesthood of Shiloh had proved themselves untrustworthy guardians of the ark.

CHAPTER IV.

Samuel as Prophet—The Gathering at Mizpeh—Battle of Eben-ezer; Its Consequences—Samuel's Administration—The Demand for a King.

(1 SAM. VII., VIII.)

PERHAPS the most majestic form presented, even among the heroes of Old Testament history, is that of Samuel, who is specially introduced to us as a man of prayer (Psa. xcix. 6). Levite, Nazarite, prophet, judge—each phase of his outward calling seems to have left its influence on his mind and heart. At Shiloh, the contrast between the life of self-denial of the young Nazarite and the unbridled self-indulgence of Eli's sons must have prepared the people for the general acknowledgment of his prophetic office. And Nazarite—God-devoted, stern, unbending, true to his calling, whithersoever it might direct him,—such was ever the life and the character of Samuel![1]

It needed such a man in this period of reformation and transition, when all the old had signally failed, not through inherent weakness, but through the sin of the people, and when the forms of the new were to be outlined in their Divine perfectness.[2] The past, the present, and the future of the people seemed to meet in his history; and over it the figure

---

[1] Second, probably, only to Moses, if such comparisons are lawful. But even so, Samuel seems at times more majestic even than Moses—more grand, unbending, and unapproachable. Ewald compares Samuel with Luther.

[2] In the New Testament dispensation the outward calling is the result of, or at least intimately connected with, the inner state. The reverse was the case under the Old Testament, where the outward calling seems to mould the men. Even the prophetic office is not quite an exception to this rule.

of the life-Nazarite cast its shadow, and through it the first voice from the prophetic order was heard in Israel.

The sanctuary, destitute of the ark, and tended by a decrepid priesthood, over which the doom had been pronounced, had apparently fallen into utter disregard. The ark, carried captive into Philistia, but having proved a conqueror there, had indeed been restored to Israel, but was rather a witness of the past than the symbol of present help. The only living hope of Israel centred in the person of Samuel. Although, since the death of Eli, no longer attached to the sanctuary, which indeed his mission to a certain extent set aside, his spiritual activity had not been interrupted. Known and owned as prophet, he closely watched, and at the proper time decisively directed the religious movement in Israel. That decisive hour had now come.

Twenty years had passed since the return of the ark—a period, as we gather from the subsequent history, outwardly of political subjection to the Philistine, and spiritually of religious depression, caused by the desolateness of their sanctuary, and the manifest absence of the Lord from among His people. It was no doubt due to the influence of Samuel that these feelings led them towards the Lord. In the language of Scripture, they " lamented after Jehovah."[1] But this was only preparatory. It was Samuel's work to direct to a happy issue the change which had already begun. His earnest message to all Israel now was : " If with all your hearts you are returning to Jehovah,"—implying in the expression that repentance was primarily of the heart, and by the form of the Hebrew verb, that that return had indeed commenced and was going on—"put away the strange gods (*Baalim*, ver. 4), and the Ashtaroth, and make firm your hearts towards Jehovah " —in opposition to the former vacillation and indecision—

[1] As Schmid puts it : " One who follows another, and lamentingly entreats till he obtains,"—as did the Syrophenician woman. Thenius imagines that there is a *hiatus* between vers. 2 and 3 ; while Ewald regards vers. 3, 4 as a later addition. Impartial students, however, will fail to perceive either, but will be content to leave these two assertions to refute one another.

"and serve Him alone."[1] To Israel so returning with their
whole heart, and repenting alike by the removal of their sin,
and by exercising lively faith, Jehovah would, as of old, prove
a Saviour—in the present instance, from the Philistines.

The words of Samuel produced the marks of at least full
outward repentance. The next step was to call the people to
one of those solemn national gatherings, in which, as on former
occasions (Josh. xxiii. 2, etc. ; xxiv. 1, etc.), they would confess
national sins and renew national obligations towards Jehovah.
On its mountain height,[2] *Mizpeh*, the "look out" of Benjamin,
was among those ancient sanctuaries in the land, where, as in
Shechem (Josh. xxiv. 26), in *Gilgal* (Josh. v. 2–12, 15), and in
Bethel (Judg. xx. 18, 23, 26 ; xxi. 2), the people were wont to
assemble for solemn deliberation (Judg. xi. 11 ; xx. 1). But
never before, since the days of Moses, had Israel so humbled
itself before the Lord in confession of sin.[3] It was thus that
Samuel would prepare for his grand act of intercession on their
behalf, and it was under such circumstances that he publicly
exercised, or more probably that he began his office of
"judge" (1 Sam. viii. 6), in its real meaning, by setting right
what was wrong within Israel, and by becoming the means
of their deliverance from the enemy.

The assembly had met in Mizpeh, not with any thought of
war, far less in preparation for it. In fact, when Israel in
Mizpeh heard of the hostile approach of the Philistines, "they
were afraid" (ver. 7). But as rebellion had caused their
desertion, so would return bring them help from the Lord. As

[1] So 1 Sam. vii. 3, rendered literally.

[2] The ancient Mizpeh, as we have identified it, lay about 2848 feet
above the level of the sea. It seems to us impossible, from the localisation
of this assembly and of the battle which followed, to identify Mizpeh
with the hill Scopus, close to Jerusalem.

[3] The ceremony of drawing and pouring out water, which accompanied
Israel's fast and confession, has been regarded by most interpreters as a
symbol of their sorrow and contrition. But may it not have been a
ceremonial act, indicative not only of penitence, but of the purification
and separation of the service of Jehovah from all foreign elements around?
Comp. here also the similar act of Elijah (1 Kings xviii. 33–35).

so generally in this history, all would happen naturally in the ordinary succession of cause and effect ; and yet all would be really and directly of God in the ordering and arrangement of events. Israel must not go to war, nor must victory be due to their own prowess. It must be all of God, and the Philistines must rush on their own fate. Yet it was quite natural that when the Philistines heard of this grand national gathering at Mizpeh, after twenty years of unattempted resistance to their rule, they should wish to anticipate their movements ; and that, whether they regarded the assembly as a revival of distinctively national religion or as preparatory for war. Similarly, it was natural that they would go on this expedition not without serious misgivings as to the power of the God of Israel, which they had experienced during the stay of the ark in their land ; and that in this state of mind they would be prepared to regard any terrible phenomenon in nature as His interposition, and be affected accordingly.

All this actually took place, but its real causes lay deeper than appeared on the surface. While Israel trembled at the approach of the Philistines, Samuel prayed,[1] and " Jehovah answered him." The great thunder-storm on that day, which filled the Philistines with panic, was really the Lord's thundering. It was a wild mass of fugitives against which Israel went out from Mizpeh, and whom they pursued and smote until under the broad meadows of Beth-car, "the house of the lamb." And it was to mark not only the victory, but

[1] In the text we read : " And Samuel took a *sucking* lamb, and offered it for a burnt-offering *wholly* unto Jehovah : and Samuel cried unto Jehovah for Israel " (1 Sam. vii. 9). The two words which we have italicised require brief comment. The " sucking lamb" would, according to Lev. xxii. 27, be, of course, seven days old. It was chosen so young as symbol of the new spiritual life among Israel. The expression, "a burnt-offering wholly unto Jehovah," is regarded by Keil as implying that the sacrifice was not, as ordinarily, cut up, but laid undivided on the altar. But this view is, on many grounds, untenable ; and the expression, which is also otherwise used (Lev. vi. 22 ; Deut. xxxiii. 10 ; Psa. li. 19) is probably intended to point to the symbolical meaning of the burnt-offering, as wholly consumed (Lev. i. 9).

its cause and meaning, that Samuel placed the memorial-
stone on the scene of this rout, between "the look out"
and *Shen,* "the tooth," probably a rocky crag on the heights
down which the Philistines were hurled in their flight. That
stone he named "Eben-ezer, saying, Hitherto hath Jehovah
helped us."

Helped—but only "hitherto!" For all Jehovah's help
is only "hitherto"—from day to day, and from place to
place — not unconditionally, nor wholly, nor once for all,
irrespective of our bearing. But even so, the outward consequences of this Philistine defeat were most important.
Although their military possession of certain posts, and their
tenure of these districts still continued (comp. 1 Sam. x. 5;
xiii. 4, 11–21; xiv. 21), yet the advancing tide of their incursions was stemmed, and no further expeditions were attempted such as that which had been so signally defeated.[1]
More than that. In the immediate vicinity of the field of
battle, all the cities which the Philistines had formerly taken
from Israel, "with the coasts thereof,"—that is, with their
surroundings—were restored to Israel, along the whole line
extending north and south from Ekron to Gath.[2] Moreover,
"the Amorites," or Canaanitish tribes in that neighbourhood,
had withdrawn from their alliance with the Philistines : "And
there was peace between Israel and the Amorites."

Similarly, order was introduced into the internal administration of the land, at least so far as the central and the southern
portions of it were concerned. Samuel had his permanent
residence in Ramah, where he was always accessible to the
people. But, besides, "he went from year to year in circuit"

---

[1] It is thus that we understand 1 Sam. vii. 13. Indeed, the expression :
"the hand of Jehovah was against (or rather, upon) the Philistines all the
days of Samuel," implies that the hostilities between the two parties continued, although no further incursions were attempted, and the Philistines
stood on the defensive rather than took the offensive.

[2] Of course, *outside* these two cities. The expression, "with the coasts
thereof, " refers to the towns restored to Israel, and not to Ekron or Gath.

—to Bethel, thence to Gilgal,[1] returning by Mizpeh to his own home. In each of these centres, sacred, as we have seen, perhaps from time immemorial, he "judged Israel,"—not in the sense of settling disputes between individuals, but in that of the spiritual and national administration of affairs, as the centre and organ of the religious and political life of the people.

We have no means of judging how long this happy state of things lasted. As usually, Holy Scripture furnishes not details even of the life and administration of a Samuel. It traces the history of the kingdom of God. As we have no account of events during the twenty years which preceded the battle of Eben-ezer (1 Sam. vii. 2), so we are left in ignorance of those which followed it. From the gathering at Mizpeh, with its consequences, we are at once transported to Samuel's old age.[2] He is still "the judge;" the same stern, unbending, earnest, God-devoted man as when in the full vigour of manhood. But he has felt the need of help in matters of detail; and his two sons are now made "judges," with residence in Beer-sheba,[3] the ancient "well of the seven," or "of the oath," on the southern boundary of the land. Their office seems to have been chiefly, if not exclusively, that of civil administration, for which in the border district, and so near a nomadic or semi-nomadic population, there must have been ample need. Unfortunately, they were quite unlike their father. Although not guilty of the wicked practices of Eli's sons, yet among a pastoral and nomadic population there would be alike frequent opportunity for, and abundant temptation to, bribery; nor would any other charge against a judge so quickly spread, or be so keenly

[1] Of course, not the Gilgal in the Jordan-valley, but that formerly referred to in Josh. xii. 23.

[2] According to Jewish tradition, Samuel, like Solomon, died at the age of fifty-two. He is said to have become prematurely old.

[3] Josephus adds "Bethel" (*Ant.*, vi. 3, 2), implying that one of the two sons "judged" at Bethel, the other at Beersheba. But this suggestion— for it amounts to no more than that—is wholly unsupported.

resented as this.[1]   Soon the murmurs became a complaint ;
and that loud enough to bring about a meeting of that most
ancient and powerful institution in Israel, "the eldership,"
or local and tribal oligarchy.   Probably it was not merely
discontent with this partial administration of justice that led
to the proposal of changing the form of government from a
pure theocracy to hereditary monarchy.   Other causes had long
been at work.   We know that a similar proposal had been
made to Gideon (Judg. viii. 22), if not to Jephthah (Judg.
xi. 6).   Although in both instances these overtures had
been declined, the feeling which prompted it could only have
gained strength.   An hereditary monarchy seemed the only
means of combining the tribes into one nation, putting an end
to their mutual jealousies, and subordinating tribal to national
interests.   All nations around had their kings ; and whether
for war or in peace, the want of a strong hand wielding a
central power for the common good must have been increasingly felt.

Moreover, the ancient God-given constitution of Israel had
distinctly contemplated and provided for a monarchy, when
once the people had attained a settled state in the land.   It
must be admitted that, if ever, circumstances now pointed to
this as the proper period for the change.   The institution of
"judges," however successful at times and in individuals, had
failed as a whole.   It had neither given external security nor
good government to the people.   Manifestly, it was at an end.
Samuel must soon die ; and what after him ?   Would it not be
better to make the change under his direction, instead of
leaving the people in charge of two men who could not even
keep their hands from taking bribes?   Many years had elapsed
since the battle of Mizpeh, and yet the Philistines were not
driven out of the land.   In fact, the present administration
held out no prospect of any such result.   This then, if ever,

---

[1] The rendering of the Authorised Version, they "perverted judgment,"
is stronger than the original, which means, "they inclined," or "bent,"
judgment.

was the proper time to carry out the long-desired and much-needed reform.

It cannot be denied that there was much force in all these considerations ; and yet we find that not only Samuel resented it, but that God also declared it a virtual rejection of Himself. The subject is so important as to require careful consideration.

First, as to the facts of the case. The " elders of Israel " having formally applied to Samuel : " Make us now a king to judge us, like all the nations," on the ground of his own advanced age and the unfitness of his sons, "the thing was evil in the eyes of Samuel as they spake *it*,[1] Give us a king to judge us." But instead of making an immediate reply, Samuel referred the matter to the Lord in prayer. The view which Samuel had taken was fully confirmed by the Lord, Who declared it a rejection of Himself, similar to that of their fathers when they forsook Him and served other gods. Still He directed His prophet to grant their request, with this twofold proviso : to " bear strong testimony against them "[2] in reference to their sin in this matter, and to "declare to them the right of the king,"—not, of course, as God had fixed it, but as exercised in those heathen monarchies, the like of which they now wished to inaugurate in Israel. Samuel having fully complied with the Divine direction, and the people still persisting in their request, the prophet had now only to await the indication from on high as to the person to be appointed king—till which time the deputies of Israel were dismissed to their homes.

Keeping in view that there was nothing *absolutely* wrong in Israel's desire for a monarchy (Deut. xvii. 14, etc. ; comp. even Gen. xvii. 6, 16; xxxv. 11), nor yet, so far as we can judge, *relatively*, as concerned the time when this demand was made, the explanation of the difficulty must lie in the motives

---

[1] The word "it" seems necessary to give the sense of the Hebrew correctly.

[2] This is the nearest approximation to a full rendering of the Hebrew expression.

and the manner rather than in the fact of the "elders," request. In truth, it is precisely this—the "*wherefore*" and the "*how*," not the thing itself,—not *that* they spake it, but "*as* they spake it," which was "evil in the eyes of Samuel."[1] Israel asked "a king" to "judge" them, such as those of all the nations. We know what the term "judge" meant in Israel. It meant implicit reliance for deliverance from their enemies on an individual, specially God-appointed—that is, really on the unseen God. It was this to which the people had objected in the time of Gideon, and which they would no longer bear in the days of Samuel. Their deliverance was *unseen*, they wanted it seen; it was only certain to *faith*, but quite uncertain to them in their state of mind; it was in heaven, they wanted it upon earth; it was of God, they wanted it visibly embodied in a man. In this aspect of the matter, we quite understand why God characterised it as a rejection of Himself, and that in reference to it He directed Samuel to "bear strong testimony against them."

But sin is ever also folly. In asking for a monarchy like those around them, the people were courting a despotism whose intolerable yoke it would not be possible for them to shake off in the future (1 Sam. viii. 18). Accordingly, in this respect Samuel was to set before them "the right of the king" (vers. 9, 11),[2] that is, the royal rights, as claimed by heathen monarchs. But whether from disbelief of the warning, or the thought that, if oppressed, they would be able to right themselves, or, as seems to us, from deliberate choice in view of the whole case, the "elders" persisted in their demand. And, truth to say, in the then political circumstances of the land, with the bond of national unity al-

---

[1] It is noteworthy that Samuel introduces no personal element, nor complains of their charges against his sons. If I have not remarked in the text on the absence of all prayer before making such an application, as contrasted with the conduct of Samuel, it is not that I am insensible to it, but that I wish to present the matter in its objective rather than its subjective aspect.

[2] Not the manner of the king.

most dissolved, and in the total failure of that living reali-
sation of the constant Presence of the Divine "Judge,"
which, if it had existed, would have made His "reign" seem
the most to be desired, but, when wanting, made the present
state of things appear the most incongruous and undesirable,
their choice seems to us only natural. In so doing, however,
they became openly unfaithful to their calling, and renounced
the principle which underlay their national history. Yet even
so, it was but another phase in the development of this history, another stage in the progress towards that end which had
been viewed and willed from the first.[1]

CHAPTER V.

*The Calling of Saul—Occasion of his Interview with Samuel—Samuel
Communes with Saul—Saul is Anointed King—The Three "Signs"—
Their Deeper Significance.*

(1 Sam IX.—X. 16.)

THE Divine direction for which prophet and people were
to wait was not long withheld. It came, as so often,
through a concurrence of natural circumstances, and in the
manner least expected. Its object, if we may venture to
judge, was to embody in the person of the new king the

---

[1] This account of the origin of monarchy in Israel seems to us to have
also another important bearing. It is impossible to regard it as either
unauthentic or of much later origin. For the manifest tendency of the
Jewish mind in later periods increasingly was to surround existing institutions with a halo of glory in their origin. This would especially be the
case in reference to the origin of monarchy, associated as it was in later
times with the house of David. Of anti-monarchical tendencies we discover
no real trace. An account so disparaging to royalty would never have
been *invented*, least of all in later times. The thoughtful reader will find
in what we have just marked a principle which has a wide application in
the criticism of Old Testament history.

ideal which Israel had had in view in making their demand for a monarchy.   He should possess all the natural attractions and martial qualities which the people could desiderate in their king; he should reflect their religious standpoint at its best; but he should also represent their national failings and the inmost defect of their religious life : that of combining zeal for the religion of Jehovah, and outward conformity to it, with utter want of real heart submission to the Lord, and of true devotedness to Him.

Thus viewed, we can understand alike the choice of Saul at the first, his failure afterwards, and his final rejection.   The people obtained precisely what they wanted ; and because he who was their king so corresponded to their ideal, and so reflected the national state, he failed.   If, therefore, it is with a feeling of sadness that we follow this story, we must remember that its tragic element does not begin and end with Saul ; and that the meaning of his life and career must be gathered from a deeper consideration of the history of his people.   In truth, the history of Saul is a summary and a reflection of that of Israel.   A monarchy such as his must first succeed, and finally fail when, under the test of trials, its inmost tendencies would be brought to light.   Such a reign was also necessary, in order to bring out what was the real meaning of the people's demand, and to prepare Israel for the king of God's election and selection in the person of David.

Of all the tribes in Israel perhaps the most martial, although the smallest, was that of Benjamin.   The " family " of Abiel[1] was, indeed, not famous for wealth or influence.   But it must have occupied a prominent place in Benjamin for the manly qualities and the military capacity of its members, since within a narrow circle it numbered such men as Saul, Jonathan,

---

[1] It is only such a view of the character of Saul which, I venture to think, satisfactorily accounts for his choice in the first instance, and then for his fall and final rejection.   But thus read, there is a strict unity about his whole history, and his outward religiousness and the deeper defects of this religion appear consistent with each other.

and Abner.[1] The whole of this history gives such sketches of primitive life in Israel as to prove that it was derived from early and authentic sources. Kish, the father of Saul, and Ner, the father of Abner, were brothers, the sons of Abiel.[2] The former is described in the text as "a hero of might," by which, as in the case of Boaz, who is similarly designated (Ruth ii. 1), were meant in those times men stalwart, strong, and true, worthy representatives and, if need were, defenders of their national rights and of their national religion. Such, no doubt, was also the father of Abner. And yet there was exquisite simplicity about the family-life of these great, strong men. Kish had lost his she-asses—a loss of some consequence in times of such poverty that a man would consider "the fourth part of a shekel," or a *sus*—about $6\frac{1}{2}d.$ of our money—as quite an adequate gift to offer a "seer" in return for consulting him (1 Sam. ix. 8). To find, if possible, the straying ani-mals, Saul, the only son of Kish,[3] as we infer from the text, was sent in company with a servant. Saul, "the asked-for," was not only "choice[4] and goodly," like all his race, but apparently as handsome as any man in the land, and taller than any by head and shoulders. In any country and age this would tell in favour of a popular leader, but especially in ancient times,[5] and more particularly in Israel at that period.

---

[1] 1 Sam. ix. 1; comp. xiv. 51. The notice, therefore, in 1 Chron. viii. 33, ix. 39, must probably be a clerical error, though Keil suggests that, as in other places, the reference is to a "grandfather," or even more remote ancestor.

[2] Comp. 1 Sam. xiv. 51.

[3] Critics infer from the name *Shaul*—"the asked for"—that he was the *firstborn*. But I rather conclude from the use of the term in such passages as Gen. xlvi. 10, 1 Sam. i. 17. 27, that Kish had long been childless, and that Saul was the child of prayer; while from the absence of the mention of any other children, I would infer that he was the only son of Kish.

[4] Most critics render the term by "young." But I prefer the rendering "choice"—not, however, in the sense of the *Vulgate: electus*, chosen. From xiii. 1–3 we know that Jonathan was at the time capable of taking a command, so that Saul his father must have been at least forty years old.

[5] For quotations from the Classics, see the Commentaries.

From his home at Gibeah[1] Saul and his servant passed in a north-westerly direction over a spur of Mount Ephraim. Thence they turned in their search north-eastward to "the land of *Shalishah*," probably so called from the circumstance that three *Wadys* met there,[2] and then eastwards to the land of *Shaalim*—probably "the hollow," the modern *Salem*. Having traversed another district, which is called "the land of *Yemini*,"—either "the right hand," or else "of Benjamin," though apparently not within the territory of Benjamin—they found themselves in the district of *Zuph*, where Samuel's home at Ramah was.[3]

For three days had the two continued their unsuccessful search, when it occurred to Saul that their long absence might cause his father more anxiety than the straying of the she-asses. But before returning home, Saul's servant suggested that since they were just in view of the city where "the seer" lived, they might first consult him as to "the way" they "should go" in order to find the she-asses.[4] Having ascer-

---

[1] Our Authorised Version renders 1 Sam. x. 5, "the hill of God," and again, ver. 10, "the hill." In both cases it is Gibeah; and, as we infer from the familiarity of the people with Saul (ver. 11), either the place where Saul lived or quite close by it.

[2] The modern Wady Kurawa (see Keil, p. 66).

[3] "The land *Yemini*" could not have been intended to designate the tribal territory of Benjamin. It is never so employed, and the analogy of the expressions "land Shalishah," "land Shaalim," "land Zuph," forbids us to regard it as other than *a district*. Again, it is said, "he passed through the land of Benjamin." From where, and whither? Certainly not into Ephraim, for he came thence; and as certainly not into Judah. But the whole question of the localisation of the *Ramah* of Samuel and of the journey of Saul is amongst the most difficult in Biblical geography. There is another important consideration in regard to this subject to which we shall refer in a subsequent Note.

[4] There can be no reasonable doubt that this "city" was Ramah, the ordinary residence of Samuel. The question and answer in vers. 10 and 11 imply this; so does the circumstance that Samuel had a house there. Lastly, how could Saul's servant have known that the "seer" was in that city, if it had not been his ordinary residence? These two points, then, seem established: Saul's residence was at Gibeah, and he first met Samuel in Ramah. But if so, it seems impossible, in view of 1 Sam. x. 2,

tained that the seer was not only in the city, but that the people had had "a sacrifice" on the "height" outside, where, as we know (1 Sam. vii. 17), Samuel had built an altar, the two hastened on, in the hope of finding him in the city itself, before he went up "to bless," or speak the prayer of thanksgiving, with which the sacrificial meal would begin. For, amidst the guests gathered there, the two strangers could have little expectation of finding access to the president of the feast. They had just entered the city itself, and were "in the gate," or wide place inside the city-entrance, where the elders used to sit and popular assemblies gathered, when they met Samuel coming from an opposite direction on his way to the "*Bamah*," or sacrificial "height." To Saul's inquiry for "the seer's house," Samuel replied by making himself known.[1] He had expected him—for the day before the Lord had expressly intimated it to him. Indeed, Samuel had prepared for it by ordering the choicest piece of that which was to be eaten of the sacrifice to be set aside for his guest—so sure was he of his arrival. And now when he saw before him in the gate the stateliest and finest-looking man in all Israel, the same voice which had led him to expect, indicated that this was the future leader of God's people.

---

to identify the Ramah of Samuel with the Ramah of Benjamin, or to regard it as the modern *Neby Samuel*, four miles north-west of Jerusalem.

[1] We may here give a curious extract from *Siphre*, all the more readily that this commentary on Numbers and Deuteronomy, which is older than the Mishnah, is so little quoted even by those who make Rabbinical literature their study. In *Siphre* 69a, by way of enforcing the duty of modesty, the expression of Samuel, "I am the seer" (1 Sam. ix. 19), is thus commented on : "The Holy One, blessed be He, said to him, Art thou the seer? by thy life, I shall shew thee that thou art not a seer. And how did He shew it to him ? At the time when it was said : Fill thy horn with oil, and go, I will send thee to Jesse, the Bethlehemite," etc. Upon which 1 Sam. xvi. 6 is quoted, when the Holy One reminded Samuel that he had said : "I am a seer," while nevertheless he was entirely mistaken on the subject of the choice of Eliab !

The bearing of Samuel towards Saul was precisely such as the circumstances required. Moreover, it was consistent throughout, and dignified. An entirely new office, involving the greatest difficulties and responsibilities, was most unexpectedly to be almost thrust upon Saul; an office, besides, the reality of which would not only be soon tested by such enemies as the Philistines, but to which he had neither family nor personal claims, and which would be sure to excite tribal jealousies and personal envies. To prepare Saul, it was necessary to call forth in him expectations, it might be vague, of great things; to inspire him with absolute confidence in Samuel as the medium through whom God spake; and finally, by converse on the deepest concerns of Israel, to bring out what lay inmost in his heart, and to direct it to its proper goal. Accordingly, Samuel invited Saul first to the feast and then to his house, at the outset intimating that he would tell him all that was in his heart (ver. 19). This assuredly could not have reference to the finding of the she-asses, since he immediately informed Saul about them, as evidence that he was "a seer," whose words must, therefore, be received as a message coming from God. Mysterious as was the allusion to what was in Saul's heart, the remark which accompanied his intimation of the finding of the she-asses sounded even more strange. As if treating such a loss as a very small matter, he added (ver. 20): "And whose is all that is desirable in Israel? Is it not thine and thy father's house?"[1] The remark was so strange both in itself and as coming from "the seer," that Saul, feeling its seeming incongruity, could only answer by pointing to the fact that Benjamin was the smallest tribe, and his own family among the least influential in it. Saul was undoubtedly aware that Israel had demanded and were about to receive from Samuel a king. His reply leaves the impression on us, that, although probably he did not exactly formulate it in his own mind, yet Samuel's words had called up in him thoughts of the

[1] This is the correct rendering.

kingdom. Else why the reference to the size of his tribe and the influence of his family? And this was exactly what Samuel had wished : gradually to prepare him for what was coming.

Apparently the "seer" made no answer to what Saul had said. But at the sacrificial feast he pursued the same course towards his guest. To the Ephraimites there assembled he was, of course, unknown. But even they must have been surprised at finding that, while the mass of the people feasted outside, among the thirty principal guests who were bidden into "the parlour," not only was the chief place given to this stranger, but that the principal portion of the sacrifice had, as a mark of special honour, been reserved for him.

The feast was past, and Saul followed his host to his house. There on the flat roof,[1] so often the scene of private converse in the East, Samuel long "communed" with Saul, no doubt of "all that was in his heart;" not, indeed, of the office about to be conferred on him, but of the thoughts which had been called up in Saul that day : of Israel's need, of Israel's sin, of Israel's help, and of Israel's God. After such "communing," neither of them could have found much sleep that night. It was grey dawn when they rose; and as the morning broke, Samuel called up to Saul on the roof that it was time to depart. He himself convoyed him through the town ; then, sending forward the servant, he stopped to deliver the message of God. Taking a vial of oil,[2] he "anointed" Saul, thus placing the institution of royalty on the same footing as that of the sanctuary and the priesthood (Ex. xxx. 23, etc., Lev. viii. 10, etc), as appointed and consecrated by God and for God, and intended to be the medium for receiving and transmitting

---

[1] The LXX. translators in this, as in several other passages in this section, either had a Hebrew text somewhat varying from ours or else altered it in their translation. Notwithstanding the views of some critics (notably Thenius), we have seen no reason to depart from the *textus receptus.*

[2] The Hebrew word indicates a narrow-necked vessel from which the oil would come by drops.

blessing to His people. And with this, a kiss, in token of homage (Psa. ii. 12), and the perhaps not quite unexpected message : " Is it not that Jehovah hath anointed thee to be prince over His inheritance ?" Saul was appointed the first king in Israel.

In order to assure Saul of the Divine agency in all this, Samuel gave him three signs. Each was stranger than the other, and all were significant of what would mark the path of Israel's king. After leaving Samuel, coming from Ephraim, he would cross the northern boundary of Benjamin by the grave of Rachel.[1] There he would meet two men who would inform him of the finding of the she-asses and of his father's anxiety on his account. This, as confirming Samuel's words, would be a pledge that it was likewise by God's appointment he had been anointed king. Thus the first sign would convey that *his royalty was of God.* Then as he passed southwards, and reached " the terebinth Tabor,"[2] three men would meet him, coming from an opposite direction, and "going up to God, to Bethel," bearing sacrificial gifts. These would salute him, and, unasked, give him a portion of their sacrificial offerings—two loaves, probably one for himself, another for his servant. If, as seems likely, these three men belonged to " the sons of the prophets," the act was even more significant. It meant homage on the part of the godly in Israel, yet such as did not supersede nor swallow up the higher homage due to God—only two loaves out of all the sacrificial gifts being presented to Saul. To Saul this, then, would indicate *royalty in subordination to God.* The last was the strangest, but, rightly understood, also the most significant sign of all. Arrived at *Gibeah Elohim,* his own city, or else the hill close by, where the Philistines kept a garrison,[3] he would, on entering the city, meet " a band of prophets" coming down

---

[1] The traditional site of Rachel's grave near Bethlehem must be given up as wholly incompatible with this passage. The reasons have been fully explained in my *Sketches of Jewish Social Life,* p. 60.

[2] The locality cannot be identified. The suggestion of Thenius and Ewald, who regard *Tabor* as equivalent for *Deborah,* is scarcely tenable.

[3] Thenius and Böttcher render it, " a pillar ; " Ewald, " a tax-collector." But the rendering in the text seems the correct one (comp. xiii. 3, 4).

from the *Bamah*, or sacrificial height, in festive procession, preceded by the sound of the *nevel*, lute or guitar, the *thof*, or tambourine (Ex. xv. 20), the flute, and the *chinnor*,[1] or hand-harp, themselves the while " prophesying." Then " the Spirit of Jehovah " would " seize upon him," and he would " be turned into another man." The obvious import of this " sign," in combination with the others, would be : royalty not only *from* God and *under* God, but *with* God. And all the more significant would it appear, that Gibeah, the home of Saul, where all knew him and could mark the change, was now held by a garrison of Philistines ; and that Israel's deliverance should there commence [2] by the Spirit of Jehovah mightily laying hold on Israel's new king, and making of him another man. When all these " signs happen to thee," added the prophet, " do to thyself what thy hand findeth " (as circumstances indicate, comp. Judg. ix. 33) ; concluding therefrom : " for God is with thee."

The event proved as Samuel had foretold. Holy Scripture passes, indeed, lightly over the two first signs, as of comparatively less importance, but records the third with the more full detail. It tells how, immediately on leaving Samuel, " God turned to Saul another heart " (ver 9) ; how, when he met the band of prophets at Gibeah (ver. 10, not " the hill," as in our Authorised Version), " the Spirit of Elohim " " seized " upon him, and he " prophesied among them ;" so that those who had so intimately known him before exclaimed in astonishment : " What is this that has come unto the son of Kish ? Is Saul also among the prophets ?" Upon which " one from thence," more spiritually enlightened than the rest, answered : " And who is their father ?" implying that, in the case of the other prophets also, the gift of prophecy was not of

---

[1] The difference between the *nevel* and the *chinnor* is explained in my volume on *The Temple*, etc., p. 55. The *chinnor* differed from our harp in that it was carried in the hand (comp. 2 Sam. vi. 5).

[2] In the original the clause—" which there a garrison of the Philistines " —reads like an emphatic parenthesis, altogether meaningless except for the purpose indicated in the text.

hereditary descent.[1] Thus the proverb arose: "Is Saul also among the prophets?" to indicate, according to circumstances, either a sudden and almost incredible change in the outward religious bearing of a man, or the possibility of its occurrence.

But there are deeper questions here which must, at least briefly, be answered. Apparently, there were already at that time prophetic associations, called "schools of the prophets." Whether these owed their origin to Samuel or not, the movement received at least a mighty impulse from him, and henceforth became a permanent institution in Israel. But this "prophesying" must not be considered as in all cases prediction. In the present instance it certainly was not such, but, as that of the "elders" in the time of Moses (Num. xi. 25), an ecstatic state of a religious character, in which men unreservedly poured forth their feelings. The characteristics of this ecstatic state were entire separation from the circumstances around, and complete subjection to an extraordinary influence from without, when thoughts, feelings, words, and deeds were no longer under personal control, but became, so to speak, passive instruments. Viewing it in this light, we can understand the use made of music, not only by true prophets, but even among the heathen. For the effect of music is to detach from surrounding circumstances, to call forth strong feelings, and to make us yield ourselves implicitly to their influence. In the case of the prophets at Gibeah and in that of Saul, this ecstatic state was under the influence of the "Spirit of Elohim."[2] By this, as in the case of the judges,[3] we are, however, not to understand the abiding and sanctifying Presence of the Holy Ghost dwelling in the heart as His temple. The Holy Ghost was peculiarly "the gift of the Father" and "of the Son," and only granted to the Church

[1] This is the view of Bunsen, and especially of Oehler, and seems to afford the only correct interpretation of the saying.

[2] Samuel speaks of "the Spirit of Jehovah," while in the actual narrative we read of the "Spirit of Elohim." Can the change of term have been intentional?

[3] See Vol. III. of this History, p. 115.

in connection with, and after the Resurrection of our Blessed Lord. Under the Old Testament, only the manifold influences of the Spirit were experienced, not His indwelling as the Paraclete. This appears not only from the history of those so influenced, and from the character of that influence, but even from the language in which it is described. Thus we read that the Spirit of Elohim "seized upon" Saul, suddenly and mightily laid hold on him,—the same expression being used in Judg. xiv. 6, 19 ; xv. 14 ; 1 Sam. xvi. 13 ; xviii. 10.

But although they were only "influences" of the Spirit of Elohim, it need scarcely be said that such could not have been experienced without deep moral and religious effect. The inner springs of the life, thoughts, feelings, and purposes must necessarily have been mightily affected. It was so in the case of Saul, and the contrast was so great that his fellow-townsmen made a proverb of it. In the language of Holy Scripture, his "heart," that is, in Old Testament language, the spring of his feeling, purposing, and willing, was "turned into another" from what it had been, and he was "turned into another man," with quite other thoughts, aims, and desires than before. The difference between this and what in the New Testament is designated as "the new man," is too obvious to require detailed explanation. But we may notice these two as important points : as in the one case it was only an overpowering influence of the Spirit of Elohim, not the abiding Presence of the Paraclete, so the moral effects produced through that influence were not primary, but secondary, and, so to speak, reflex, while those of the Holy Ghost in the hearts of God's people are direct, primary, and permanent.[1]

The application of these principles to "the spiritual gifts" in the early Church will readily occur to us. But perhaps it is more important to remember that we are always—and now more than ever—prone to confound the influences of

---

[1] If I may express it by a play upon two Latin words : In the one case it is *affectus* ab *effectu ;* in the other, if there is *effectus*, it is *effectus* ab *affectu.*

the Spirit of God with His abiding Presence in us, and to mistake the undoubted moral and religious effects, which for a time may result from the former, for the entire inward change, when "all old things have passed away," and "all things have become new," and are "of Christ." Yet the one is only the reflex influence of the spirit of man, powerfully influenced by the Spirit of Elohim ; the other the direct work of the Holy Ghost on the heart.

One of the effects of the new spiritual influence which had come upon Saul was, that when his uncle, Ner, met him upon the *Bamah,* or high place (ver. 14), probably joining him in his worship there to find out the real meaning of a change which he must have seen more clearly than any other, and which it would readily occur to him to connect with the visit to Samuel, he forbore to gratify a curiosity, probably not unmixed with worldly ambition and calculations.

But yet another charge had Samuel given to Saul before parting (ver. 8), and that not only a charge, but a life-direction, a warning, and a test of what was in him. That he understood it, is evident from 1 Sam. xiii. 7, 8. But would he submit to it, or rather to God? That would be to him the place and time when the two ways met and parted—and his choice of either one or the other would be decisive, both so far as his life and his kingdom were concerned.

CHAPTER VI.

Saul Chosen King at Mizpeh—His Comparative Privacy—Incursion of Nahash — Relief of Jabesh-gilead — Popular Assembly at Gilgal— Address of Samuel.

(1 Sam. x. 17—xii. 25.)

IN answer to the people's demand, Saul had been selected as their king. The motives and views which underlay their application for a king were manifest. They had been clearly set before the representatives of Israel by Samuel; and they had not gainsaid the correctness of his statement. They wanted not only a king, but royalty like that of the nations around, and for the purpose of outward deliverance; thus forgetting God's dealings in the past, disclaiming simple trust in Him, and disbelieving the sufficiency of His leadership. In fact, what they really wanted was a king who would reflect and embody their idea of royalty, not the ideal which God had set before them. And no better representative of Israel could have been found than Saul, alike in appearance and in military qualification; nor yet a truer reflex of the people than that which his character and religious bearing offered. He was the typical Israelite of his period, and this neither as regarded the evil-disposed or "sons of Belial," nor yet, of course, the minority of the truly enlightened, but the great body of the well-disposed people. If David was the king "after God's own heart," Saul was the king after the people's own heart. What they had asked, they obtained; and what they obtained, must fail; and what failed would prepare for what God had intended.

But as yet the choice of Saul had been a secret between the messenger of the Lord and the new king. As in every other case, so in this,[1] God would give the person called to most difficult work every opportunity of knowing His will, and every encouragement to do it. For this purpose Samuel had first called up great thoughts in Saul; then "communed" with him long and earnestly; then given him undoubted evidence that the message he bore was God's; and, finally, embodied in one significant direction alike a warning of his danger and guidance for his safety. All this had passed secretly between the two, that, undisturbed by influences from without, Saul might consider his calling and future course, and this in circumstances most favourable to a happy issue, while the transaction was still, as it were, between God and himself, and before he could be led astray by the intoxicating effect of success or by popular flattery.

And now this brief period of preparation was past, and what had been done in secret must be confirmed in public.[2] Accordingly Samuel summoned the people—no doubt by their representatives—to a solemn assembly "before Jehovah" in Mizpeh. Here the first great victory over the Philistines had been obtained by prayer (vii. 5), and here there was an "altar unto Jehovah" (ver. 9). As so often before, the lot was solemnly cast to indicate the will of God. But before so doing, Samuel once more presented to the people what the leadership of the Lord had been in the past, and what their choice of another leadership implied. This not with the view of annulling the proposed establishment of royalty, but with that of leading the people to repentance of their sin in connection with it. But the people remained unmoved. And now the lot was drawn.[3]

[1] Thus, for example, in the case of Balaam, and even of Pharaoh.

[2] Thenius and other writers regard this account of the election of Saul as incompatible with that of the previous interview between him and Samuel. They accordingly speak of two different accounts here incorporated into one narrative. But the thoughtful reader will agree with Ewald that closer consideration will convince us that Saul's appointment would have been incomplete without the public selection at Mizpeh.

[3] We note that the lot was, in this instance, not cast but drawn, evidently out of an urn. This is implied in the expression "taken," or rather "taken out," vers. 20, 21 (comp. Lev. xvi. 8; Numb. xxxiii. 54;

It fell on Saul, the son of Kish. But although he had come to Mizpeh, he could not be found in the assembly. It was a supreme moment in the history of Israel when God had indicated to His people, gathered before Him, their king by name. In circumstances so urgent, inquiry by the *Urim* and *Thummim* seemed appropriate. The answer indicated that Saul had concealed himself among the baggage on the out-skirts of the encampment. Even this seems characteristic of Saul. It could have been neither from humility nor modesty [1] —both of which would, to say the least, have been here mis-placed. It is indeed true that this was a moment in which the heart of the bravest might fail,[2] and that thoughts of what was before him might well fill him with anxiety.[3] Saul must have known what would be expected of him as king. Would he succeed in it? He knew the tribal and personal jealousies which his election would call forth. Would he be strong enough to stand against them? Such questions were natural. The only true answer would have been a *spiritual* one. Unable to give it, Saul withdrew from the assembly. Did he wonder whether after all it would come to pass or what would happen, and wait till a decision was forced upon him? The people, at any rate, saw nothing in his conduct that seemed to them strange; and so we may take it that it was just up to the level of their own conceptions, though to us it appears very different from what a hero of God would have done.[4]

And so the newly-found king was brought back to the

Josh. vii. 14). The election was evidently first of tribes, then of clans, (here that of Matri), then of families, and lastly of individuals in the family selected. As the name of *Matri* does not otherwise occur, Ewald suggests that it is a copyist's error for *Bichri*, 2 Sam. xx. 1.

[1] So Keil.

[2] This is the suggestion of Nägelsbach.

[3] This is Ewald's view.

[4] The reluctance of Moses and of Jeremiah in similar circumstances afford no parallel, although that of the former, at least, was the result of weakness in faith. But their hesitation was before God, not before men.

E

assembly. And when Samuel pointed to him as he stood there, "from his shoulders upward" overtopping every one around, the people burst into a shout: "Let the king live!" For thus far Saul seemed the very embodiment of their ideal of a king. The transaction was closed by Samuel explaining to the people, this time not "the right of the king" (1 Sam. viii. 9, 11), as claimed among other heathen nations whom they wished to imitate, but "the right of the kingdom"[1] (x. 25), as it should exist in Israel in accordance with the principles laid down in Deut. xvii. 14–20. This was put in writing, and the document solemnly deposited in the tabernacle.

For the moment, however, the establishment of the new monarchy seemed to bring no change. Saul returned to his home in Gibeah, attended indeed on his journey, by way of honour, by "a band whom Elohim had touched in their hearts," and who no doubt "brought him presents" as their king. But he also returned to his former humble avocations. On the other hand, "the sons of Belial" not only withheld such marks of homage, but openly derided the new king as wanting in tribal influence and military means for his office. When we bear in mind that these represented a party, possibly belonging to the great tribes of Judah and Ephraim, so strong as openly to express their opposition (1 Sam. xi. 12), and sufficiently numerous not to be resisted by those who thought otherwise, the movement must have been formidable enough to dictate as a prudential measure the retirement of Saul till the time when events would vindicate his election. And so complete was that privacy, that even the Philistine garrison in Gibeah remained in ignorance of the fact of Saul's new office, and of what it implied; and that in the east, across the Jordan, the Ammonite king who waged war with Israel was

---

[1] Our Authorised Version translates, both here and 1 Sam. viii. 9, 11, "the manner;" but the word can only mean "right," in the sense of right belonging to, or claimed by, any one. Thenius speaks of this as the establishment of a *constitutional* monarchy. But if "constitution" there was, it was God-given, not man-made.

apparently wholly unaware of any combined national movement on the part of the people, or of any new centre of union and resistance against a common enemy.

This expedition on the part of Nahash, king of the Ammonites, to which we have just referred, is otherwise also of interest, as showing that the desire of Israel after a king must have sprung from other and deeper motives than merely the age of Samuel, or even the conduct of his sons. From 1 Sam. xii. 12 it appears that the invasion by Nahash commenced before Israel's demand for a king, and was, indeed, the cause of it; thus proving that, as Samuel charged them, distrust of their heavenly Leader was the real motive of their movement. The expedition of Nahash had no doubt been undertaken to renew the claims which his predecessor had made, and to avenge the defeat which Jephthah had inflicted upon him (Judg. xi. 13, 33). But Nahash had penetrated much farther into Israelitish territory than his predecessor. His hordes had swarmed up the lovely rich valley of the Jabesh, laying bare its barley-fields and olive plantations, and wasting its villages; and they were now besieging the capital of Gilead—Jabesh-gilead—which occupied a commanding position on the top of an isolated hill overhanging the southern crest of the valley. In their despair, the people of Jabesh offered to surrender, but Nahash, in his insolence, insisted that he would thrust out their right eyes, avowedly to "lay it as a shame upon all Israel." Terrible as these conditions were, the "elders" of Jabesh saw no means of resisting, and only begged seven days' respite, to see whether any were left in Israel able and willing to save them. In the foolhardiness of his swagger, Nahash consented, well assured that if Israel were, as he fully believed, incapable of a combined movement for the relief of Jabesh, the whole land would henceforth be at his mercy, and between Philistia in the west and Ammon in the east, Israel—their land and their God —would lie helpless before the heathen powers.

It is, to say the least, a curious coincidence that Jabesh was the only town in Israel which had not taken part in the exterminating warfare against the tribe of Benjamin (Judg. xxi. 9). But it was not on that ground, but because tidings had no doubt reached them of the new royal office in Israel,[1] that their messengers went straight to Gibeah. It was evening when Saul returned home "behind the oxen," with which he had been working,[2] to find Gibeah strangely moved. The tidings which the men of Jabesh had brought had filled the place with impotent lamentation, not roused the people to action. So low had Israel sunk! But now, as he heard it, once more "the Spirit of Elohim seized upon Saul." He hewed in pieces the "yoke of oxen" with which he had just returned, and sent —probably by the messengers from Jabesh—these pieces throughout the land, bidding those know who had no higher thoughts than self, that thus it would be done to their oxen who followed not after Saul and Samuel in the general war against Ammon.

This, if ever, was the time when the Divine appointment of Saul must be vindicated; and to indicate this he conjoined with himself Samuel, the venerated prophet of God, so long the judge of Israel. It is said that "the terror of Jehovah" fell upon the people.[3] From all parts of the land armed men trooped to the trysting-place at Bezek, within the territory of Issachar, near to Bethshan, and almost in a straight line to Jabesh. Three hundred thousand from Israel, and thirty

---

[1] Most critics seem to imagine that they had first gone all round Israel, and only ultimately arrived at Gibeah, where they addressed themselves to the people, and not to Saul. But this account is in no way borne out by the text, nor would it leave sufficient time for the measures taken by Saul (ver. 7). The statement of the elders of Jabesh (ver. 3) was evidently intended to mislead Nahash.

[2] This is evidently the meaning, and not that conveyed in our Authorised Version.

[3] Curiously enough, Keil seems to have overlooked that the Hebrew word here used is that for "terror," or "awe," not fear. The sacred text ascribes the origin of this terror to the agency of Jehovah—not in the sense of a miracle, but because it always traces up effects to Him as their first cause.

thousand from Judah [1] (for that territory was in part held by the Philistines), had obeyed the summons of Saul. It was not an army, but a ban—a *landsturm*—an armed rising of the people. From the brow of the hill on which Bethshan lay, in the plain of Jezreel, you might look across Jordan and see Jabesh-gilead on its eminence. A very few hours would bring relief to the beleaguered city, and so they bade them know and expect. A feigned promise of subjection on the morrow made Nahash and his army even more confident than before. And what, indeed, had they to fear when all Israel lay so helplessly prostrate?

It was night when Saul and the armed multitude which followed him broke up from Bezek. Little did he know how well the brave men of Jabesh would requite the service; how, when on that disastrous day on Mount Gilboa he and his sons would fall in battle, and the victorious Philistines fasten their dead bodies to the walls of Bethshan, these brave men of Jabesh would march all night and rescue the fallen heroes from exposure (1 Sam. xxxi. 8–13). Strange that Saul's first march should have been by night from Bethshan to Jabesh, the same route by which at the last they carried his dead body at night.

But no such thoughts disturbed the host as they crossed the fords of the Jordan, and swarmed up the other bank. A few hours more, and they had reached the valley of the Jabesh. Following the example of Gideon (Judg. vii. 16), Saul divided the people "into three companies." From the rear and from either flank they fell upon the unsuspecting Ammonites when most secure—"in the morning watch," between three and six o'clock. A general panic ensued; and before the rout was ended not two of the enemy were left together. The revulsion of popular feeling toward Saul was complete. They would even have killed those who had formerly derided the new

---

[1] It almost appears as if we here met the first traces of a separation of the people into Israel and Judah. Similarly xvii. 52 ; xviii. 16 ; 2 Sam. ii. 9 ; iii. 10 ; v. 1–5 ; xix. 41, etc. ; xx. 2, 4.

monarchy.   But Saul refused such counsel.   Rather did
Samuel make different use of the new state of feeling.   On
his proposal the people followed him and Saul to Gilgal, to
which place so many sacred memories clung.   Here they
offered thank and peace-offerings, and greatly rejoiced as they
renewed "the kingdom," and, in the sense of real and universal
acknowledgment, "made Saul king before Jehovah."[1]

Although all his lifetime Samuel never ceased to judge
Israel, yet his official work in that capacity had now come to
an end.   Accordingly he gave a solemn and public account of
his administration, calling alike the Lord and His anointed to
witness of what passed between him and the people.   Leaving
his sons to bear the responsibility[2] of their own doings, he
challenged any charge against himself.   But, as a faithful
servant of the Lord, and ruler in Israel, he went further.
Fain would he bring them to repentance for their great sin
in the manner wherein they had demanded a king.[3]   One by
one he recalled to them the "righteous doings" of Jehovah
in the fulfilment of His covenant-promises in the past.[4]   In
contrast to this never-failing help, he pointed to their unbelief,
when, unmindful of what God had done and distrustful of what
He would do, they had, on the approach of serious danger,
virtually said concerning His leadership, "Nay, but a king
shall reign over us."   And God had granted their desire.   But
upon their and their king's bearing towards the Lord, not upon
the fact that they had now a king, would the future of Israel
depend.   And this truth, so difficult for them to learn, God

---

[1] Some writers have imagined that Saul was anointed a second time.
But for this there is no warrant in the text.

[2] It is thus that I understand I Sam. xii. 2: "And, behold, my sons,
they are with you."

[3] That Samuel did not blame Israel for wishing a king, but for the
views and motives which underlay their application, appears (as Hengstenberg has shown) from the circumstance that when the people are repentant (ver. 19), he does not labour to make them recall what had been
done, but only to turn unto the Lord (vers. 20–25).

[4] In the list of the judges mentioned by Samuel we find the name of
Bedan (ver. 11). In all probability this is a copyist's mistake for *Barak*.

would now, as it were, *prove* before them in a symbol. Did they think it unlikely, nay, well-nigh impossible, to fail in their present circumstances? God would bring the unlikely and seemingly incredible to pass in a manner patent to all. Was it not the time of wheat-harvest,[1] when in the east not a cloud darkens the clear sky? God would send thunder and rain to convince them, by making the unlikely real, of the folly and sin of their thoughts in demanding a king.[2] So manifest a proof of the truth of what Samuel had said, and of the nearness of God and of His personal interposition, struck terror into the hearts of the people, and led to at least outward repentance. In reply to their confession and en-treaty for his continued intercession, Samuel assured them that he would not fail in his duty of prayer for them, nor yet God, either in His faithfulness to His covenant and promises, or in His justice and holiness if they did wickedly.

And so the assembly parted—Israel to their tents, Saul to the work of the kingdom which lay to his hands, and Samuel to the far more trying and difficult duty of faithfully representing and executing the will of God as His appointed messenger in the land.

[1] That is—the months of May and June.

[2] We have ventured to suggest this explanation of the miraculous occurrence, because it meets all the requirements of the case, and because, even during the preparatory dispensation of the Old Testament, miracles were not mere exhibitions of *power* without moral purpose or meaning. At the same time, we fully and frankly accept the fact that in Biblical times, and till after the outpouring of the Holy Ghost, personal interposition on the part of God—miracle and prophetic inspiration—was the rule, not the exception, in God's dealings with His people.

CHAPTER VII.

Saul Marches against the Philistines—Position of the two Camps—Jonathan's Feat of Arms—Saul Retreats to Gilgal—Terror among the People—Saul's Disobedience to the Divine Command, and Rejection of his Kingdom.

(1 SAM. XIII.)

A T Gilgal Saul had been accepted by the whole people as their king,[1] and it now behoved him to show himself such by immediately taking in hand as his great work the liberation of the land from Israel's hereditary enemy the Philistines. For this purpose he selected from the armed multitude at Gilgal three thousand men, of whom two thousand under his own command were posted in Michmash and in Mount Bethel, while the other thousand advanced under Jonathan to Gibeah of Benjamin (or Gibeah of Saul). Close to this, a little

---

[1] Accordingly the commencement of Saul's reign was dated from Gilgal. Hence 1 Sam. xiii. 1 had opened, as the history of all other kings (comp. 2 Sam. ii. 10; v. 4; 1 Kings xiv. 21; xxii. 42; 2 Kings viii. 26; etc.), with the statistical data of his age at the commencement, and the duration of his reign. But unfortunately the numeral letters have wholly fallen out of the first, and partially out of the second clause of ver. 1, which, as they stand in our present Hebrew text, may be thus represented: "Saul was . . . years old when he was made king, and he reigned two . . . years over Israel." All other attempts at explanation of this verse— notably that of our Authorised Version—are incompatible with the Hebrew and with history. According to Jewish tradition (Jos., *Antiq.*, vi. 14, 9), Saul reigned for forty years. This is also the time mentioned by St. Paul (Acts xiii. 21). There is no sufficient reason for the view of certain critics that the "original narrative" is here resumed from x. 16. In fact, if such were the case, we would require some explanation of the phrase: "Saul chose him three thousand men of Israel" (xiii. 2). Whence and where did he choose them, if not from the assembly at Gilgal? Certainly, more unlikely circumstances for this could not be found than those in which Saul is left in x. 16, when, so far from selecting three thousand men, he ventures not to confide the secret of his elevation even to his uncle!

to the north, at Geba, the Philistines had pushed forward an advanced post, perhaps from Gibeah, to a position more favourable than the latter. Unable, with the forces at his disposal, to make a regular attack, it seems to have been Saul's purpose to form the nucleus of an army, and meanwhile to blockade and watch the Philistines in Geba. So far as we can judge, it does not appear to have lain within his plan to attack that garrison, or else the enterprise would have been undertaken by himself, nor would it have caused the surprise afterwards excited by Jonathan's success.

As it is of considerable importance for the understanding of this history to have a clear idea of the scene where these events took place, we add the most necessary details. Geba, the post of the Philistines, lay on a low conical eminence, on the western end of a ridge which shelves eastwards towards the Jordan. Passing from Geba northwards and westwards we come to a steep descent, leading into what now is called the Wady-es-Suweinit. This, no doubt, represents the ancient "passage of Michmash" (1 Sam. xiii. 23). On the opposite steep brow, right over against Geba, lies Michmash, at a distance of barely three miles in a north-westerly direction. This Wady-es-Suweinit is also otherwise interesting. Running up in a north-westerly direction towards Bethel, the ridge on either side the wady juts out into two very steep rock-covered eminences—one south-west, towards Geba, the other north-west, towards Michmash. Side wadys, trending from north to south behind these two eminences, render them quite abrupt and isolated. These two peaks, or "teeth," were respectively called *Bozez*, "the shining," and *Seneh*, either "the tooth-like," "the pointed," or perhaps "the thorn," afterwards the scene of Jonathan's daring feat of arms (1 Sam. xiv. 1–13). Bethel itself lies on the ridge, which runs in a north-westerly direction from Michmash. From this brief sketch it will be seen that, small as Saul's army was, the Philistine garrison in Geba was, to use a military term, completely *enfiladed* by it, since Saul with his two thousand men occupied Michmash and Mount Bethel to the north-east, north, and north-west, threatening their communications through the Wady-es-Suweinit with Philistia, while Jonathan with his thousand men lay at Gibeah to the south of Geba.

But the brave spirit of Jonathan could ill brook enforced idleness in face of the enemy. Apparently without consultation with his father, he attacked and "smote" the Philistine garrison in Geba. The blow was equally unexpected by Philistine and Israelite. In view of the preparations made by the enemy, Saul now retired to Gilgal—probably not that in which the late assembly had been held, but the other Gilgal near Jericho.[1] Hither "the people were called together after Saul." But the impression left on us is, that from the first the people were depressed rather than elated, frightened rather than encouraged by Jonathan's feat of arms. And no wonder, considering not only the moral unpreparedness of the people, but their unfitness to cope with the Philistines, alike so far as arms and military training were concerned. The hundreds of thousands who had followed Saul to Jabesh were little better than an undisciplined mob that had seized any kind of weapons. Such a multitude would be rather a hindrance than a help in a war against disciplined infantry, horsemen, and war-chariots. In fact, only three thousand of them were fit to form the nucleus of an army, and even they, or what at last remained of them to encounter the Philistines, were so badly equipped that they could be truthfully described as without either "sword or spear" (xiii. 22).[2]

[1] I have put this hypothetically, for I feel by no means sure that it was not the other Gilgal. The argument of Keil, that in that case Saul would have had to attack the Philistines at Michmash before reaching Gibeah (ver. 15), is not convincing, since there was a road to the latter place to the west of Michmash. On the other hand, however, the Gilgal near Jericho was no doubt a more safe place of retreat where to collect an army, and the wadys open directly upon it from Geba and Gibeah; while, lastly, the remark, that "Hebrews went over Jordan to the land of Gad and Gilead" (ver. 7), seems to point to a camp in the immediate neighbourhood of that river.

[2] Of course, the expression must be taken in a general sense, and not absolutely, and refers to the total want of regular armament.

The army with which the Philistines now invaded the land was the largest and best appointed[1] which they had yet brought into the field. Avoiding the former mistake of allowing their opponents to take them in flank by camping in Michmash, the Philistines now occupied that post themselves, their line extending thither from Beth-aven.[2] From their position at Gilgal the Israelites could see that mighty host, and under the influence of terror rapidly melted away. Some passed across the Jordan, the most part hid themselves in the caves and pits and rocks with which the whole district around the position of the Philistines abounds. The situation was indeed becoming critical in the extreme. Day by day the number of deserters increased, and even those who yet remained " behind him," " were terrified." [3] And still Saul waited from day to day for that without which he had been told he must not move out of Gilgal, and which now was so unaccountably and, as it would seem to a commander, so fatally delayed !

It will be remembered that on parting from Saul, immediately after his anointing, Samuel had spoken these somewhat mysterious words (1 Sam. x. 7, 8): " And it shall be when these signs shall come unto thee, do for thyself as thine hand shall find, for Elohim is with thee. And when thou goest down before me to Gilgal,—and behold I am going down to thee,[4]—to offer burnt-offerings and to sacrifice sacrifices of peace-

---

[1] Our Hebrew text has " thirty thousand chariots."—a number not only disproportionate to the horsemen but unheard of in history. The copyist's mistake evidently arose in this manner. Writing, " And the Philistines gathered themselves together to fight with Israel," the copyist by mistake repeated the letter *l*, which in Hebrew is the numeral sign for 30, and so wrote what reads " *thirty* thousand chariots," instead of " one thousand chariots," as had been intended.

[2] This Beth-aven is mentioned in Josh. vii. 2, and must not be confounded with Bethel, east of which it evidently lay, between Bethel and Michmash. At the same time the word rendered "*eastward* from Beth-aven" (ver. 5) does not *necessarily* mean " eastwards," but might also be rendered " in front of," or " over against."

[3] So ver. 7 literally.

[4] I have so punctuated in accordance with most critics, to indicate that the offering of sacrifices refers to *Saul's* purpose in going to Gilgal,

offerings, seven days shalt thou tarry till I come to thee, and shew thee what thou shalt do." The first part of Samuel's injunction—to do as his hand should find—Saul had followed when making war against Nahash. It is the second part which sounds so mysterious. It will be remembered that, immediately after the defeat of Nahash, Saul and the people had, on the suggestion of Samuel, gone to Gilgal, there to "renew the kingdom." Manifestly that visit to Gilgal could not have been meant, since, so far from having to wait seven days for the arrival of Samuel, the prophet had accompanied Saul thither. It can, therefore, only have been intended to apply to this retreat of Saul upon Gilgal in preparation for his first great campaign against the Philistines.[1] And what to us sounds so mysterious in the language of Samuel may not have been so at the time to Saul. During that communing on the roof of Samuel's house, or afterwards, the two may have spoken of a great war against the Philistines, and of the necessity of gathering all Israel in preparation for it to Gilgal, not only for obvious military reasons, but as the place where the reproach of Israel had first been rolled away (Josh. v. 9), and whence appro-

---

and that the sentence about Samuel's coming down is intercalated. But on this point I do not feel sure. It would make no difference, however, so far as regards the meaning of Samuel, whose injunction was intended to warn Saul not to interfere with the functions of the priestly office. I have, of course, translated the passage literally. The rendering of our Authorised Version, "and thou shalt go down," is impossible. We have our choice between the imperative and the conditional mood, and the balance of argument is strongly in favour of the latter.

[1] Of course, two other theories are possible. The one, a suggestion that the verse 1 Sam. x. 8 may be displaced in our Hebrew text, and should stand somewhere else, is a wild and vague hypothesis. The other suggestion, that all between x. 17 and xiii. 2 is intercalated from another narrative will not bear investigation. If the reader tries to piece ch. x. 16 to xiii. 3, he will at once perceive that there would be a felt gap in the narrative. Besides, how are we to account for the selection of three thousand men, and the going to war against the Philistines on the part of a man who is made the target of wit in his own place, and who dares not tell even his own uncle of his secret elevation to the royal office?

priately the re-conquest of the land should commence by sacrifices and seeking the direction of the Lord.

But even if at the time when first uttered by Samuel it had seemed mysterious to Saul, there could be no doubt that the injunction applied to the circumstances in which the king and his followers now found themselves. What should he do? Day by day passed without tidings of Samuel, and still his followers decreased, and the hearts of those who remained waxed more feeble. Yet Saul *did* wait the full seven days which Samuel had appointed. But when the seventh day was drawing to a close[1] he forbore no longer; and although, as he said, most reluctantly, he had the sacrifices offered, no doubt by the regular priesthood (comp. 2 Sam. xxiv. 25 ; 1 Kings iii. 4 ; viii. 63). No sooner had the sacrifices been offered, than on a sudden Samuel himself appeared—as we understand it, before the full term which he had set for his arrival had actually been passed. Whether simply to brave it, or, as seems to us more likely, from real ignorance of the import of what he had done, Saul went to meet and salute Samuel. But the prophet came as God's messenger. He denounced the *folly* of Saul, and his *sin* in disobeying the express command of the Lord, and intimated that, had he stood the test, his kingdom, or royal line, would have been established, whereas now his throne would pass to a worthier successor. Not, therefore, his personal rejection, nor even that of his title to the throne, but only that of his "kingdom," or line, as unfit to be "captains" over "Jehovah's people"—such was the sentence which Samuel had to announce on that day.

The "folly" of Saul's conduct must, indeed, have been evident to all. He had not waited long enough, and yet too long, so far as his following was concerned, which, after the sacrifice, amounted to only about six hundred men (1 Sam. xiii. 15). On the other hand, the only motive which, even politically speaking, could have brought numbers to his ranks

---

[1] The context seems to imply that Saul offered his sacrifice and Samuel came before the actual termination of the seven days.

or fired them with courage, was a religious belief in the help
of Jehovah, of which Saul's breach of the Divine command and
the defection of Samuel would threaten to deprive Israel.   But
still there are questions involved in the Divine punishment of
Saul which require most earnest attention, not only for the
vindication, but even for the proper understanding of this history.

To the first question which arises, why Samuel thus unduly
delayed his journey to Gilgal, apparently without necessary
reason, we can, in fairness, only return the answer, that his
delay seems to have been *intentional*, quite as much as that of
our blessed Lord, after He had heard of the sickness of Lazarus,
and when He knew of his death (John xi. 6, 14, 15).   But if
intentional, its object can only have been to test the character
of Saul's kingdom.   Upon this, of course, the permanency of
that kingdom would depend.   We have already seen that Saul
represented the kind of monarchy which Israel wished to have
established.   Saul's going down to Gilgal to offer sacrifices,
and yet not offering them properly ; his unwillingness to enter
on the campaign without having entreated the face of Jehovah,
and yet offending Him by disobedience ; his waiting so long,
and not long enough ; his trust in the help of Jehovah, and yet
his distrust when his followers left him ; his evident belief in
the absolute efficacy of sacrifices as an outward ordinance
irrespective of the inward sacrifice of heart and will—are all
exactly representative of the religious state of Israel.   But
although Israel had sought, and in Saul obtained a monarchy
"after *their own* heart," yet, as Samuel had intimated in
Gilgal (xii. 14, 20-22, 24), the Lord, in His infinite mercy,
was willing to forgive and to turn all for good, if Israel would
only "fear the Lord and serve Him in truth."   Upon this
conversion, so to speak, of Israel's royalty into the kingdom of
God the whole question turned.   For, either Israel must cease
to be the people of the Lord, or else the principle on which its
monarchy was founded must become spiritual and Divine ;
and consequently any government that contravened this must
be swept away to give place to another.   If it be asked, what

this Divine principle of monarchy was to be, we have no hesitation in answering, that it was intended to constitute a kingdom in which *the will of the earthly should be in avowed subjection to that of the heavenly King.* This was right in itself; it was expressive of the covenant-relationship by which Jehovah became the God of Israel, and Israel the people of Jehovah; and it embodied the typical idea of the kingdom of God, to be fully realised in the *King* of the Jews, Who came not to do His own will, but that of His Father in heaven, even to the bitter agony of the cup in Gethsemane and the sufferings of Golgotha. *Saul was the king after Israel's own heart* (1 Sam. xii. 13); *David the king after God's own heart,* not because of his greater piety or goodness, but because, despite his failings and his sins, he fully embodied the Divine idea of Israel's kingdom; and for this reason also he and his kingdom were the type of our Lord Jesus Christ and of His kingdom.

In what has been said the second great difficulty, which almost instinctively rises in our minds on reading this history, has in part been anticipated. It will easily be understood that this great question had, if ever, to be tested and decided at the very commencement of Saul's reign, and before he engaged in any great operations, the success or failure of which might divert the mind. If to be tried at all, it must be on its own merits, and irrespective of results. Still, it must be admitted, that the first feeling with most of us is that, considering the difficulties of Saul's position, the punishment awarded to him seems excessive. Yet it only seems, but is not such. Putting aside the idea of his personal rejection and dethronement, neither of which was implied in the words of Samuel, the sentence upon Saul only embodied this principle, that no monarchy could be enduring in Israel which did not own the supreme authority of God. As Adam's obedience was tested in a seemingly small matter, and his failure involved that of his race, so also in the case of Saul. His partial obedience and his anxiety to offer the sacrifices as, in his mind, in themselves efficacious, only rendered it the more necessary to bring to the foreground the great question of absolute, unquestioning, and believing submission to the will of the Heavenly King. Saul's kingdom had shown itself not to be God's kingdom, and its continuance was henceforth impossible. However different their circumstances, *Saul was as unfit for the inheritance of the kingdom*, with the promises which this implied and the typical meaning it bore, *as Esau had been* for the inheritance of the first-born, with all that it conveyed in the present, in the near, and in the distant future.

⁓⁓⁓

CHAPTER VIII.

Camps of Israel and of the Philistines—Jonathan and his Armour-bearer —Panic among the Philistines, and Flight—Saul's Rash Vow—The "Lot " cast at Ajalon—Cessation of the War.

(1 SAM. XIII. 15—XIV. 46.)

WHEN, after Samuel's departure, Saul with his six hundred men marched out of Gilgal, he found the Philistines occupying the range at Michmash which he had formerly held. With such weak following as he could command, it was wise on his part to take up a position in the "uttermost part of Gibeah" (xiv. 2), that is, as we gather from the context, to the north of the town itself, and on the outskirts of Geba[1] and its district (xiii. 16). Geba is only about an hour and a quarter north of Gibeah. We may therefore suppose Saul's camp to have been about two miles to the north of the latter city, and to have extended towards Geba. His head-quarters were under a pomegranate tree at a place called Migron—probably a "land-slip;" and there, besides his principal men, he had the then

---

[1] Our Authorised Version erroneously corrects, "*Gibeah*," apparently following the LXX.

occupant of the high-priesthood, Ahiah,[1] the son of Ahitub, an elder brother of I-chabod, "wearing an ephod," or discharging the priestly functions. From Geba itself Michmash, which lay on the opposite ridge, was only divided by the intervening Wady-es-Suweinit. How long the Israelites had lain in that position we are not informed. But we are told that "the spoilers," or rather "the destroyers," "went out of the camp of the Philistines in three bands" (xiii. 17),—one "facing" in a north-easterly direction by Ophrah towards the district of Shual, the "fox-country," the other "facing" westwards towards Beth-horon, and the third south-eastwards, "the way to the district that overlooketh the valley of Zeboim" ("raveners,"[2] viz., wild beasts) "toward the wilderness" (of Judah). Thus the only direction left untouched was south and south-west, where Saul and Jonathan held the strong position of Gibeah-Geba. If the intention had been to draw them thence into the open, it failed. But immense damage must have been inflicted upon the country, while a systematic raid was made upon all smithies, so as to render it impossible not only to prepare weapons, but so much as to have the means of sharpening the necessary tools of husbandry.

In these circumstances it is once more the noble figure of Jonathan which comes to the foreground. Whatever fitness he might have shown for "the kingdom," had he been called to it, a more unselfish, warm-hearted, genuine, or noble character is not presented to us in Scripture than that of Jonathan. Weary of the long and apparently hopeless inactivity, trustful in Jehovah, and fired by the thought that with Him there was "no hindrance to save, by much or by little," he planned single-handed an

---

[1] This Ahiah, or rather *Achijah* ("brother," "friend of Jehovah"), is supposed to be the same as *Achimelech* ("brother," "friend of the King," viz., Jehovah), 1 Sam. xxii. 9, etc. Ewald (*Gesch.*, ii., 585, Note 3) regards the two names as interchangeable, like Elimelech and Elijahu. Keil suggests that Achimelech may have been a brother of Achijah.

[2] The Chaldee paraphrast has "serpents"—this valley being supposed to have been their lurking-place. But I have taken the more general meaning of the term.

expedition against the Philistine outpost at Michmash. As he put it, it was emphatically a deed of faith, in which he would not take counsel either with his father or with any of the people, only with God, of Whom he would seek a sign of approbation before actually entering on the undertaking. The sole companion whom he took was, as in the case of Gideon (Judg. vii. 9, 10), his armour-bearer, who seems to have been not only entirely devoted to his master, but like-minded. In the Wady-es-Suweinit, which, as we have seen, forms "the passage" between the ridge of Geba, where Jonathan was, and that of Michmash, now occupied by the Philistines, were the two conical heights, or "teeth of rock," called Bozez and Seneh. One of these, as we gather from the text, faced Jonathan and his armour-bearer toward the north over against Michmash. This we suppose to have been *Bozez*, "the shining one," probably so called from its rocky sides and top. It is figuratively described in the text as cast [1] like metal. Here, on the top of a sharp, very narrow ledge of rock, was the Philistine outpost. The "tooth of rock" opposite, on which Jonathan and his armour-bearer "discovered" themselves to their enemies, was *Seneh*, "the thornlike," or "pointed," or else "the tooth." [2] All around there was thick wood, or rather forest (xiv. 25), which stretched all the way towards Bethel (2 Kings ii. 23, 24). Standing on the extreme point of Seneh, the Philistines would probably only see Jonathan, with, at most, his armour-bearer; but they would be ignorant what forces might lurk under cover of the trees. And this was to be the sign by which Jonathan and his companion were to discern whether or not God favoured their enterprise. If, when they "discovered" themselves to the Philistines, these would challenge them to stay and await their coming over to fight, then Jonathan and his companion would forbear,

---

[1] 1 Sam. xiv. 5, literally, "the one tooth poured"—"or a pillar"—"towards the north before" (or "over against") "Michmash."

[2] Dean Stanley supposes the name to be derived from a thorn-bush on the top of the eminence. But it may simply mean the "thorn-like," or more probably, "the pointed."

while, if the challenge were the other way, they would infer
that Jehovah had delivered them into their hand. The one, of
course, would argue courage on the part of the Philistines, the
other the want of it. What followed is graphically sketched in
the sacred text. From the point of "the thorn," or "tooth of the
rock," Jonathan "discovered" himself to the Philistines. This
open appearance of the Hebrews was as startling as unexpected,
nor could the Philistines have imagined that two men alone
would challenge a post. Manifestly the Philistine post had no
inclination to fight an unknown enemy; and so with genuine
Eastern boastfulness they heaped abuse on them, uttering the
challenge to come up. This had been the preconcerted signal;
and, choosing the steepest ascent, where their approach would
least be looked for, Jonathan and his armour-bearer crept up
the ledge of the rock on their hands and feet. Up on the top
it was so narrow that only one could stand abreast. This we
infer not only from the language of the text, but from the
description of what ensued. As Jonathan reached the top, he
threw down his foremost opponent, and the armour-bearer,
coming up behind, killed him. There was not room for two to
attack or defend in line. And so twenty men fell, as the text
expresses it, within "half a furrow of a yoke of field," [1]—that is,
as we understand it, within the length commonly ploughed by
a yoke of oxen, and the width of about half a furrow, or more
probably half the width that would be occupied in ploughing a
furrow. All this time it would be impossible, from the nature of
the *terrain*, to know how many assailants were supporting Jonathan and his armour-bearer. This difficulty would be still more
felt in the camp and by those at a little farther distance, since it
would be manifestly impossible for them to examine the steep
sides of Bozez, or the neighbouring woods. The terror, probably
communicated by fugitives, who would naturally magnify the

---

[1] Both Keil and Erdmann refer for a similar feat to Sallust, *Bell. Jugurth.*
c. 89, 90. The quotation is so far erroneous that the story is told in c. 93,
94; but the feat of the Ligurian, however magnificent, was scarcely equal to
that of Jonathan. Still, the one story is certainly parallel to the other.

danger, perhaps into a general assault, soon became a panic, or, as the text expresses it, a " terror of Elohim." Presently the host became an armed rabble, melting away before their imaginary enemy, and each man's sword in the confusion turned against his neighbour.   At the same time the Hebrew auxiliaries, whom cowardice or force had brought into the camp of the Philistines, turned against them, and the noise and confusion became indescribable.

From the topmost height of Gibeah the outlook, which Saul had there posted, descried the growing confusion in the Philistine camp.   Only one cause could suggest itself for this. When Saul mustered his small army, he found that only Jonathan and his armour-bearer were missing.   But the king sufficiently knew the spirit of his son not to regard as impossible any undertaking on his part, however seemingly desperate. What was he to do ?   One thing alone suggested itself to him.   He would take counsel of the Lord by the well-known means of the Urim and Thummim.[1]   But while preparations were making for it, the necessity of its employment had evidently ceased.   It was not a sudden commotion, but an increasing panic among the Philistines that was observed. Presently Saul and his men, as they came to battle, found that the enemy himself had been doing their work.   And now it became a rout.   The Hebrews from the Philistine camp had joined the pursuers, and, as the well-known notes of the trumpet wakened the echoes of Mount Ephraim, the men who were in hiding crept out of their concealment. and followed in the chase. And so the tide of battle rolled as far as Beth-aven.

---

[1] Our present *textus receptus* has, in 1 Sam. xiv. 18, two copyist's errors. The one is emendated in our Authorised Version, which reads, "*with* the children of Israel," instead of, as in the *textus receptus*, "*and* the children of Israel," which would give no meaning.   The second error is emendated in the LXX., who seem to have had the correct text, according to which the word " Ephod " should be substituted for "ark."   The letters of these two words in the Hebrew are somewhat like each other, whence the error of the copyist.   The ark was at Kirjath Jearim, nor was it "brought hither" to ascertain the will of God.

But, though the battle was chiefly pursuit of the fleeing foe, already " the men of Israel were distressed," or rather " pressed," by weariness and faintness. For quite early in the day, and in the absence of Jonathan, Saul had yielded to one of his characteristic impulses. When he ascertained the real state of matters as regarded the Philistines, he put the people under a vow—to which, either by an " Amen," or else by their silence they gave assent—not to taste food until the evening, till he had avenged himself of his enemies. It need scarcely be said, that in this Saul acted without Divine direction. More than that, it is difficult to discern in it any religious motive, unless it were, that the enemies on whom Saul wished personally to be avenged were also the hereditary foes of Israel. And yet in the mind of Saul there was no doubt something religious about this rash vow. At any rate the form in which his impetuous Eastern resolve was cast, was such, and that of a kind which would peculiarly commend itself to an Israelite like Saul. Foolish and wrong as such a vow had been, still, as Israel had at least by their silence given consent, it lay as a heavy obligation upon the people. However faint, none dared break the fast during that long and weary day, when they followed the enemy as far as the western passes of Ajalon that led down into the Philistine plains. But Jonathan had not known it, till one told him of his father's vow after he had paused in the forest to dip his staff into honey that had dropped from the combs of wild bees. For such an offence Jonathan was certainly not morally responsible. Considering how small an amount of nourishment had helped him in his weariness, he could only deplore the rashness of his father, whose vow had, through the faintness which it entailed on the people, defeated the very object he had sought.

At last the weary day closed in Ajalon, and with it ended the obligation upon the people. The pursuit was stopped ; and the people, ravenous for food, slew the animals " on the ground," felling them down, and eating the meat without being careful to remove the blood. It is true that, when Saul heard of it, he reproved the people for the sin which this involved, and took immediate steps to provide a proper slaughtering-place. Still this breach of an express Divine command (Lev. xix. 26) must in fairness be laid to the charge of Saul's rash vow. Nor could the building of a memorial-altar on the spot be regarded as altering the character of what had taken place that day.

Night was closing around Ajalon. The place, the circumstances, nay, his very vow, could not but recall to Saul the story of Joshua, and of his pursuit of the enemies of Israel (Josh. x. 12, 13). His proposal to follow up the Philistines was willingly taken up by the people, who had meanwhile refreshed themselves and were eager for the fray. Only the priests would first ask counsel of God. But no answer came, though sought by Urim and Thummim. Some burden must lie upon Israel, and Saul with his usual rashness would bring it to the test with whom lay the guilt, at the same time swearing by Jehovah that it should be avenged by death, even though it rested on Jonathan, the victor of that day, who had "wrought this great salvation in Israel," nay, who "had wrought with God" that day. But the people, who well knew what Jonathan had done, listened in dull silence. It must have been a weird scene as they gathered around the camp fire, and the torches cast their fitful glare on those whose fate the lot was to decide. First it was to be between all the people on the one side, and Saul and Jonathan on the other. A brief, solemn invocation, and the lot fell upon Saul and his son. A second time it was cast, and now it pointed to Jonathan. Questioned by his father, he told what he had done in ignorance. Still Saul persisted that his vow must be fulfilled. But now the people interposed. He whom God had owned, and who had saved Israel, must not die. But the pursuit of the Philistines was given up, and the campaign abruptly closed. And so ended in sorrow and disappointment what had been begun in self-willed disobedience to God and distrustfulness of Him.

CHAPTER IX.

The War against Amalek—Saul's Disobedience, and its Motives—Samuel commissioned to announce Saul's Rejection—Agag Hewn in Pieces.

(1 SAM. XIV. 47-52; XV.)

THE successful war against the Philistines had secured Saul in possession of the throne.[1] Henceforth his reign was marked by wars against the various enemies of Israel, in all of which he proved victorious.[2] These expeditions are only indicated, not described, in the sacred text, as not forming constituent elements in the history of the kingdom of God, however they may have contributed to the prosperity of the Jewish state. The war against Amalek alone is separately told (ch. xv.), alike from its character and from its bearing on the kingdom which God would establish in Israel. Along with these outward successes the sacred text also indicates the seeming prosperity of Saul, as regarded his family-life.[3] It almost appears as if it had been intended to place before us, side by side in sharp contrast, these two facts: Saul's prosperity

[1] We take this to be the meaning of the expression: "So Saul took the kingdom" (xiv. 47).

[2] The sacred text has it (vers. 47, 48): "and whithersoever he turned himself, he vexed them"—the latter word being used of sentences pronounced by a judge,—"and he wrought might," that is, he displayed power.

[3] Only those three sons are mentioned whose story is identified with that of Saul himself, and who fell with him in the fatal battle of Gilboa (xxxi. 2). "*Ishui*" is evidently the same as *Abinadab*. We will not venture on any conjecture of the reason of the interchange of these two names (comp. 1 Chron. viii. 33; ix. 39). In the genealogies in Chronicles, a fourth son, *Esh-baal*, is mentioned, who was evidently the same as *Ishbosheth*. Merab and Michal are introduced with a view to their after-story. Ewald says: "With ch. xiv. Saul ceases to be the true king, in the prophetic meaning of that term. Hence the history of his reign is here closed with the usual general remarks."

both at home and abroad, and his sudden fall and rejection, to show forth that grand truth which all history is evolving : Jehovah reigneth !

Israel's oldest and hereditary enemies were the Amalekites. Descended from Esau (Gen. xxxvi., 12, 16; 1 Chron. i. 36; comp. Josephus' *Antiq.* ii., 1, 2), they occupied the territory to the south and south-west of Palestine.   They had been the first wantonly to attack Israel in the wilderness[1] (Ex. xvii. 8, etc.), and "war against Amalek from generation to generation," had been the Divine sentence upon them.   Besides that first attack we know that they had combined with the Canaanites (Num. xiv. 43–45), the Moabites (Judg. iii. 12, 13), and the Midianites (Judg. vii. 12) against Israel.   What other more direct warfare they may have carried on, is not expressly mentioned in Scripture, because, as frequently observed, it is not a record of the national history of Israel.   But from 1 Sam. xv. 33 we infer that, at the time of which we write, they were not only in open hostility against Israel, but behaved with extreme and wanton cruelty.   Against this unrelenting hereditary foe of the kingdom of God the ban had long been pronounced (Deut. xxv. 17–19). The time had now arrived for its execution, and Samuel summoned Saul in the most solemn manner to this work.   It was in itself a difficult expedition.   To be carried out in its full sweep as a "ban," it would, in Saul's then state of mind, have required peculiar self-abnegation and devotion.   Looking back upon it from another stage of moral development and religious dispensation, and in circumstances so different that such questions and duties can never arise,[2] and that they seem immeasurably far behind, as the dark valley to the traveller

---

[1] See Vol. II. of this History, pp. 101–103.

[2] This accommodation of the law to each stage of man's moral state, together with the continuous moral advancement which the law as a schoolmaster was intended to bring about, and which in turn was met by progressive revelation, renders it impossible to judge of a Divine command by trying to put it as to our own times, and as applicable to us.   If we put forward the finger-hand on the dial of time, and the clock still strikes the old hour, we must not infer that the clock is out of order, but rather that

who has climbed the sunlit height, or as perhaps events and phases in our own early history, many things connected with the "ban" may appear mysterious to us. But the history before us is so far helpful as showing that, besides its direct meaning as a judgment, it had also another and a moral aspect, implying, as in the case of Saul, self-abnegation and real devotedness to God.

Thus viewed, the command to execute the "ban" upon Amalek was the second and final test of Saul's fitness for being king over God's people. The character of this kingdom had been clearly explained by Samuel at Gilgal in his address to king and people (1 Sam. xii. 14, 20, 21, 24). There is evidently an internal connection between the first (1 Sam. xiii. 8–14) and this second and final trial of Saul. The former had brought to light his want of faith, and even of simple obedience, and it had been a *test of his moral qualification for the kingdom;* this second was *the test of his moral qualification for being king.* As the first trial, so to speak, developed into the second, so Saul's *want* of moral qualification had ripened into absolute *dis*qualification— and as the former trial determined the fate of his line, so this second decided his own as king. After the first trial his line was rejected; after the second his own standing as theocratic king ceased. As God-appointed king he was henceforth rejected ; Jehovah withdrew the sanction which He had formerly given to his reign by the aid of His power and the Presence of His Spirit. Henceforth "the Spirit of Jehovah departed from Saul "(1 Sam. xvi. 14), and he was left, in the judgment of God, to the influence of that evil spirit to whom his natural disposi-

---

we have unskilfully meddled with it. The principle for which we have here contended is clearly laid down in the teaching of our blessed Lord about divorce (Matt. xix. 8), and also implied in what St. Paul saith about the law (Gal. iii. 24). The whole of this subject is most admirably and exhaustively treated by Canon Mozley in his *Ruling Ideas in Early Ages, and their Relation to Old Testament Faith.* See especially Lecture VIII., on "The Law of Retaliation," and Lecture X., "The End the Test of a Progressive Revelation."

tion and the circumstances of his position laid him specially open (comp. Matt. xii. 43–45).

In view of the great moral trial which this expedition against Amalek would involve, Samuel had been careful to make it clear that the call to it came by Divine authority, reminding the king that he had been similarly sent to anoint him (1 Sam. xv. 1). From the circumstance that Saul seems to have marched against Amalek, not with a chosen host, but to have summoned the people as a whole[1] to execute the "ban," we infer that he had understood the character of his commission. Moving from *Telaim* ("the place of lambs"[2]), probably in the eastern part of the south country, he came to "the city of Amalek," which is not named, where he "laid an ambush in the valley." Before proceeding farther, he found means to communicate with that branch of the tribe of the Kenites who, from ancient times, had been on terms of friendship with Israel[3] (Num. x. 29; Judg. i. 16). In consequence they removed from among the Amalekites. Then a general slaughter began, which is described as "from Havilah," in the south-east, on the boundaries of Arabia, to the wilderness of Shur "over against," or eastward of Egypt. Every Amalekite who fell into their hands was destroyed,[4] with the notable exception, however, of Agag,[5] their king. And as they spared him, so also "the best of the sheep, and of the oxen, and of those of the second sort,[6] and the (wilderness-) fed lambs,

---

[1] So we understand the figures (1 Sam. xv. 4), which otherwise would be disproportionately large.

[2] Perhaps the same as *Telem* (Josh. xv. 24). Rashi has it, that Saul numbered the people by making each pick out a lamb, since it was unlawful to number the people directly.

[3] Another branch of that tribe was hostile to Israel: comp. Numb. xxiv. 21, etc.

[4] Of course, not literally *all* the Amalekites, but all who fell into their hands: comp. xxvii. 8; xxx. 1; 2 Sam. viii. 12; 1 Chron. iv. 43.

[5] Not a personal but an appellative name, like Pharaoh. Agag means "the fiery."

[6] The word must be rendered either so, or else, according to some of the Rabbis, "animals of the second birth" (*animalia secundo partu edita*), which are supposed to be better than the first-born.

and all that was good." The motives for the latter are, of course, easily understood ; not so that for sparing Agag. Did they wish to have in his person a sort of material guarantee for the future conduct of Amalek,—or did it flatter the national as well as the royal vanity to carry with them such a captive as Agag,—or did they really wish a sort of alliance and fraternity with what remained of Amalek ? All these motives may have operated. But of the character of the act as one of rebellion and disobedience there could be no doubt, in view of the direct Divine command (xv. 3).

If in the case of Saul's first failure it was difficult to withhold sympathy, however clearly his sin and unfitness for the theocratic kingdom appeared, it is not easy even to frame an excuse for his utterly causeless disregard of so solemn a command as that of "the ban." All Jewish history, from Achan downwards, rose in testimony against him ; nay, remembering his proposal to kill even Jonathan, when he had unwittingly infringed his father's rash vow, Saul stood convicted out of his own mouth ! Nor was there any tangible motive for his conduct, nor anything noble or generous either about it, or about his after-bearing towards Samuel. Rather, quite the contrary. What now follows in the sacred narrative is tragic, grand, and even awful. The first scene is laid at night in Samuel's house at Ramah. It is God Who speaketh to the aged seer. "It repenteth Me that I have made Saul king, for he has returned from after Me, and My Word he has not executed" (literally, set up). "And it kindled in Samuel" (intense feeling, wrath), "and he cried unto Jehovah the whole night." [1] It is one of the most solemn, even awful thoughts— that of the Divine repentance, which we should approach with

---

[1] The distinction generally made, that the expression in ver. 11 is used *anthropopathically* (ἀνθρωποπαθῶς),—after the feelings of man—while that in ver. 29 is θεοπρεπῶς (*theoprepos*, according to the dignity and character of God), seems but partially correct. Better is the remark of Theodoret : Divine repentance is a change of His dispensation (re-arrangement of His household)—μεταμέλεια θεοῦ ἡ τῆς οἰκονομίας μεταβολή.

worshipful reverence.   God's repentance is not like ours, for
"the Strength of Israel will not lie, nor repent ; for He is not
a man that He should repent."   Man's repentance implies a
change of mind, God's a change of circumstances and relations.
He has not changed, but is ever the same ; it is man who has
changed in his position relatively to God.   The Saul whom
God had made king was not the same Saul whom God repented
to have thus exalted ; the essential conditions of their relationship were changed.   God's repentance is the unmovedness of
Himself, while others move and change.   The Divine finger
ever points to the same spot ; but man has moved from it
to the opposite pole.   But as in all repentance there is sorrow,
so, reverently be it said, in that of God.   It is God's sorrow
of love, as, Himself unchanged and unchanging, He looks at the
sinner who has turned from Him.   But, although not wholly
unexpected, the announcement of this change on the part of
Saul, and of his consequent rejection, swept like a terrible
tempest over Samuel, shaking him in his innermost being.
The greatness of the sin, the terribleness of the judgment, its
publicity in the sight of all Israel, who knew of his Divine
call, and in whose presence Samuel, acting as Divine messenger,
had appointed him,—all these thoughts "kindled within him"
feelings which it would be difficult to analyse, but which led
to a "cry" all that long night, if perchance the Lord would
open a way of deliverance or of pardon.

With the morning light came calm resolve and the terrible
duty of going in search of Saul on this errand of God.   Nor
did the stern Nazarite now shrink from aught which this might
imply, however bitterly he might have to suffer in consequence.
Saul had returned to Gilgal, as if in his infatuation he had
intended to present himself in that place of so many sacred
memories before the God Whose express command he had
just daringly set aside.   By the way he had tarried at Carmel,[1]

---

[1] The modern Kurmul, three hours south of Hebron, the place of Nabal's
possessions (xxv. 2, 5, 7, 40).

where he "had set him up a monument" [1] of his triumph over
Agag. And now as Samuel met him, he anticipated his
questions by claiming to have executed Jehovah's behest. But
the very bleating of the sheep and lowing of the oxen betrayed
his failure, and the excuse which he offered was so glaringly
untrue,[2] that Samuel interrupted him [3] to put the matter plainly
and straightforwardly in its real bearing: "Was it not when
thou wast small in thine own eyes thou becamest head of the
tribes of Israel?"—implying this as its counterpart : Now that
thou art great in thine own eyes, thou art rejected, for it was God
Who appointed thee, and against Him thou hast rebelled. Once
more Saul sought to cloak his conduct by pretence of greater
religiousness, when Samuel, in language which shows how deeply
the spiritual meaning of ritual worship was understood even in
early Old Testament times,[4] laid open the mingled folly and
presumption of the king, and announced the judgment which
the Lord had that night pronounced in his hearing. And now
the painful interest of the scene still deepens. If there had
been folly, hypocrisy, and meanness in Saul's excuses, there was
almost incredible weakness also about his attempt to cast the
blame upon the people. Evidently Saul's main anxiety was
not about his sin, but about its consequences, or rather about
the effect which might be produced upon the people if Samuel

---

[1] Ver. 12, erroneously rendered in our Authorised Version : "he set him
up a place." The word literally means "a hand," and is again used for
"monument" in 2 Sam. xviii. 18. Phœnician monuments have been found
with *hands* on them.

[2] Besides its obvious falsehood, Saul must, of course, have known that
all that was "banned" by that very fact belonged unto God (Lev. xxvii. 29),
and could not, therefore, be again offered unto Him (Deut. xiii. 16).

[3] "Stay" (ver. 16), that is, "Stop ! cease ! "

[4] It is scarcely necessary to indicate, that the words of Samuel (vers. 22,
23) do *not* imply that sacrifices were not of primary importance. This would
have run counter not only to his own practice, but to the whole Old Testament economy. But sacrifices, irrespective of a corresponding state of mind,
and in actual rebelliousness against God,—religiousness without religion,—
were not only a mere *opus operatum*, but a gross caricature, essentially
heathen, not Jewish. Comp. Psa. l. 8-14 ; li. 17, 19 ; Isa. i. 11 ; Jer.
vi. 20 ; Hos. vi. 6 ; Micah vi. 6-8.

were openly to disown him.   He entreated him to go with him, and when Samuel refused, and turned to leave, he laid such hold on the corner of his mantle that he rent it.   Not terrified by the violence of the king, Samuel only bade him consider this as a sign of how Jehovah had that day rent the kingdom from him.

At last the painful scene ended.   Saul gave up the pretence of wishing Samuel's presence from religious motives, and pleaded for it on the ground of honouring him before the elders of his people.   And to this Samuel yielded.   Throughout it had not been a personal question, nor had Samuel received directions about Saul's successor, nor would he, under any circumstances, have fomented discord or rebellion among the people. Besides, he had other and even more terrible work to do ere that day of trial closed.   And now the brief service was past, and Samuel prepared for what personally must have been the hardest duty ever laid upon him.   By his direction Agag was brought to him.   The unhappy man, believing that the bitterness of death, its danger and pang were past, and that probably he was now to be introduced to the prophet as before he had been brought to the king, came "with gladness." [1]   So far as Agag himself was concerned, these words of Samuel must have recalled his guilt and spoken its doom: "As thy sword has made women childless, so be thy mother childless above (ordinary) women." [2]   But for Israel and its king, who had transgressed the "ban" by sparing Agag, there was yet another lesson, whatever it might cost Samuel.   Rebellious, disobedient king and people on the one side, and on the other Samuel the prophet and Nazarite alone for God—such, we take it, was the meaning of Samuel having to hew Agag in pieces before Jehovah in Gilgal.

From that day forward Samuel came no more to see Saul. God's ambassador was no longer accredited to him; for he

---

[1] This, and not "delicately," as in our Authorised Version, is the meaning of the Hebrew word (comp. Prov. xxix. 21).

[2] More than ordinary women, or rather most of women, since her son was king of his people.

was no longer king of Israel in the true sense of the term. The Spirit of Jehovah departed from him. Henceforth there was nothing about him royal even in the eyes of men—except his death. But still Samuel mourned for him and over him; mourned as for one cut off in the midst of life, dead while living, a king rejected of God. And still "Jehovah repented that He had made Saul king over Israel."

CHAPTER X.

Samuel Mourns for Saul—He is directed to the house of Jesse—Anointing of David—Preparation of David for the Royal Office—The "Evil Spirit from the Lord" upon Saul—David is sent to Court—War with the Philistines—Combat between David and Goliath—Friendship of David and Jonathan.

(1 SAM. XVI.—XVIII. 4.)

I F the tragic events just recorded, and the share which Samuel had in them, had left on the mind a lingering feeling as of harshness or imperiousness on the part of the old prophet, the narrative which follows must remove all such erroneous impressions. So far from feeling calm or satisfied under the new state of things which it had been his duty to bring about, Samuel seems almost wholly absorbed by sorrow for Saul personally, and for what had happened; not unmixed, we may suppose, with concern for the possible consequences of his rejection.[1] It needed the voice of God

---

[1] Calvin remarks: "We see here the prophet affected as other men. As Samuel beholds the vessel which God's own hand had made, more than broken and minished, he is deeply moved. In this he showed pious and holy affection. But he was not wholly free from sin in the matter —not that the feeling itself was wrong, but that it exceeded the proper measure, and that he too much indulged in personal grief."

to recall the mind of the prophet to the wider interests of the theocracy, and to calm him into complete submission by showing how the difficulties which he anticipated had been provided for. A new king had already been fixed upon, and the duty was laid on Samuel to designate him for that office. Accordingly Samuel was now sent to anoint one of the sons of Jesse to be Saul's successor. From the first, and increasingly, Samuel's public career had been difficult and trying. But never before had his faith been so severely tested as by this commission. He who had never feared the face of man, and who so lately had boldly confronted Saul at Gilgal, now spake as if afraid for his life, in case Saul, who no doubt was already under the influence of the "evil spirit," or rather the spirit of evil, should hear of what might seem an attempt to dethrone him. But, as always in such circumstances, the fears, which weakness suggested, proved groundless. As in the case of Saul, so in that of David, it was not intended that the anointing should be followed by immediate outward consequences. Hence there was no need for publicity; on the contrary, privacy served important purposes. The chief present object seems to have been a solemn call to David to prepare himself, as having been set apart for some great work. Besides, in view of the meaning of this symbol, and of its results in Saul and David (1 Sam. xvi. 13), the anointing may be regarded as an ordinance in connection with the gift of the Spirit of God, Who alone qualified for the work. In view of all this, God directed Samuel to combine the anointing of Jesse's son with a sacrificial service at Bethlehem, the home of Jesse. Only the latter, or public service, required to be made generally known. Many reasons will suggest themselves why the other part of Samuel's commission should have remained secret, probably not fully understood by Jesse, or even by David himself.[1]

---

[1] There is not a trace of attempted prevarication in the narrative. Calvin and others have given too much attention to a cavil which is best refuted by an attentive study of the history.

The narrative also affords some interesting glimpses into the history of the time. Thus we infer that Samuel had been in the habit of visiting various places in the land for the purpose of sacrifice and instruction. The former was quite lawful, so long as the ark was not in its central sanctuary.[1] On the other hand, it needs no comment to show the importance of such periodical visits of the prophet at a time when religious knowledge was necessarily so scanty, and the means of grace so scarce. It helps us to understand how religion was kept alive in the land. Again, the narrative implies that the family of Jesse must have occupied a leading place in Bethlehem, and been known as devoted to the service of the Lord. Nor do we wonder at this, remembering that they were the immediate descendants of Boaz and Ruth.

As we follow Samuel to Bethlehem, we seem to mark the same primitive simplicity and life of piety as of old. When the "elders" hear of Samuel's coming, they go to meet him, yet with fear lest the unexpected visit betoken some unknown sin resting on their quiet village. This apprehension is removed by Samuel's explanation, and they are invited to attend the "sacrifice." But the sacrificial meal which usually followed was to be confined to Jesse and his family, in whose house, as we infer, Samuel was a welcome guest. It would appear that Samuel himself was not acquainted with all that was to happen, the Lord reserving it for the proper moment to point out to His servant who was to be Israel's future king. And this, as we judge, partly because the aged prophet had himself a lesson to learn in the matter, or rather to unlearn what of the ideas of his time and people unconsciously clung to him.

All this appears from the narrative. One by one the sons of Jesse were introduced to Samuel. The manly beauty of Eliab, the eldest, and his rank in the family, suggested to the prophet that he might be "Jehovah's anointed." But

[1] See our quotation on this subject from the *Mishnah* in Vol. III. of this History, p. 78.

G

Samuel was to learn that Jehovah's judgment was "not as what man seeth" (looketh to), "for man looketh to the eyes, but Jehovah looketh to the heart."[1]   And so the others followed in turn, with a like result.   Evidently, Samuel must have expressed it to Jesse that on that day one of his family was to be chosen by Jehovah, but for what purpose seems not to have been known to them.   Nor did Jesse himself, nor even David, apparently understand what was implied in the rite of anointing.   No words of solemn designation were uttered by the prophet, such as Samuel had spoken when he anointed Saul (1 Sam. x. 1).   Besides, as Saul was the first king anointed, and as none had been present when it took place, we may reasonably suppose that alike the ceremony and its meaning were unknown to the people.   Both Jesse and David may have regarded it as somehow connected with admission to the schools of the prophets, or more probably as connected with some work for God in the future, which at the proper time would be pointed out to them.[2]   And thus was David in this respect also a type of our Lord, Whose human consciousness of His calling and work appears to have been, in a sense, progressive; being gradually manifested in the course of His history.

But to return. The seven sons of Jesse had successively passed before Samuel, yet he was not among them whom the prophet had been sent to anoint.   But for all that his mission had not failed: he had only learned to own the sovereignty of God, the failure of his own judgment, and the fact that he was simply a passive instrument to carry out, not his own views, but the will of the Lord.   For, the youngest of the family still remained.   So unlikely did it seem to his

[1] So 1 Sam. xvi. 7, rendered literally.

[2] A full knowledge of his being anointed to the kingdom is incompatible alike with his after position in his father's house, and the bearing of his brothers towards him.   In general, we infer that each of the brothers only passed before Samuel, or was introduced to him, and then left his presence when no further direction in regard to him was given to the prophet.

father that he could be called to any great work, that he had been left in the field to tend the sheep. But when, at the bidding of Samuel, he came, his very bearing and appearance seemed to speak in his favour. In the language of the text, "he was reddish,[1] and fair of eyes, and goodly to look at." And now the command to anoint him was given, and immediately and unquestioningly obeyed by Samuel.[2]

The sacrifice past, and the sacrificial meal over, Samuel returned to Ramah, and David to his humble avocation in his father's household. And here also we love to mark the print of our Lord's footsteps, and to see in the history of David the same humble submission to a lowly calling, and faithful discharge of menial toil, and the same subjectness to his parents, as we adoringly trace in the life of Him Who humbled Himself to become David's son. But there was henceforth one difference in the life of the son of Jesse. From the day of his anointing forward, "the Spirit of Jehovah seized upon David," as formerly upon Saul, to qualify him by might and by power for the work of "God's anointed." But from Saul, who was no longer the king of God's appointment, had the Spirit of Jehovah departed, not only as the source of "might and of power," but even as "the Spirit of a sound mind." At his anointing, the Spirit then given him had made him "another man" (1 Sam. x. 6, 10). But Saul had resisted and rebelled, nor had he ever turned from his pride and disobedience in repentance to the Lord. And now the Spirit of God not only departed from him, but in judgment God sent an "evil spirit," or rather "a spirit of evil," to "terrify"[3] Saul. Not that God ever sends a spirit who is evil. The angels whom God sends are all good, though their commission may be in judgment to bring evil upon

---

[1] So ver. 12, literally. The expression, "reddish," or perhaps rather "auburn," refers to the colour of the hair, which is rare in Palestine.

[2] The Authorised Version renders ver. 13: "And Samuel anointed him in the midst of his brethren." But the word may mean either "in the midst" or "among," in the sense of "from among." The latter is evidently the meaning in this instance.

[3] So literally, as in the margin of our Authorised Version.

us.[1] As one has rightly remarked, "God sends good angels to punish evil men, while to chastise good men, evil angels claim the power." The "evil spirit" sent from God was the messenger of that evil which in the Divine judgment was to come upon Saul, visions of which now affrighted the king, filled him with melancholy, and brought him to the verge of madness—but not to repentance. It is thus also that we can understand how the music of David's harp soothed the spirit of Saul, while those hymns which it accompanied—perhaps some of his earliest Psalms—brought words of heaven, thoughts of mercy, strains of another world, to the troubled soul of the king.

Had he but listened to them, and yielded himself not temporarily but really to their influence ! But he was now the old Saul, only sensibly destitute of the Divine help, presence, and Spirit, and with all the evil in him terribly intensified by the circumstances. He had all the feelings of a man cast down from his high estate through his own sin, disappointed in his hopes and ambition, and apprehensive that at any moment the sentence of rejection, pronounced against him, might be executed, and that "better" one appear to whom his kingdom was to be given. And now an angel of evil from the Lord affrighted him with thoughts and visions of what would come to pass. For man can never withdraw himself from higher influences. As one of the fathers has it, "When the Spirit of the Lord departs, an evil spirit takes His place. And this should teach us to pray with David: 'Take not Thy Holy Spirit from me.'"

Yet, in the wonder-working providence of God, this very circumstance led David onwards towards his destination. The quiet retirement of the shepherd's life was evidently of deepest importance to him immediately after his anointing. We can understand what dangers—inward and outward—would have

---

[1] Comp. Delitzsch, *Comm. ü. d. Psalter*, vol. I., p. 601 ; Hofmann, *Schriftbeweis*, vol. i., pp. 188, 189. If the expression, "evil spirit," had been intended to convey that it was a spirit in itself evil, Saul's servants would have scarcely spoken of him as in 1 Sam. xvi. 15.

beset a sudden introduction to publicity or rush into fame. On the other hand, humble avocations, retirement, thought, and lonely fellowship with God would best develop his inner life in constant dependence upon God, and even call out those energies and that self-reliance which, in conjunction with the higher spiritual qualifications, were so necessary in his after-calling.   Nor was it time lost even so far as his outward influence was concerned.   It was then that the Spirit-helped youth acquired in the neighbouring country, and far as Eastern story would carry it, the reputation of " a mighty, valiant man, and a man of war," when, all unaided and un-armed, he would slay "both the lion and the bear" that had attacked the flock which he tended.   But, above all, it is to this period of inward and spiritual preparation in soli-tary communion with God that we trace the first of those Psalms which have for ever made "the sweet singer," in a sense, the "shepherd" of all spiritual Israel.   And here also we love to connect the plains and the shepherds of Bethlehem, who heard angels hymning the birth of our dear Lord, with His great ancestor and type, and to think how in those very plains the shepherd-king may have watched his flock in the quiet of the starlit night, and poured forth in accents of praise what is the faith and hope of the Church in all times.   No doubt this talent of David also, though probably only viewed as a worldly gift, became known in the neighbourhood.   And so, when the courtiers [1] of Saul suggested music as the well-known remedy in antiquity for mental disturbances, such as those from which the king suffered through the "evil spirit," one of the servant-men in attendance, probably a native of the district around Bethlehem, could from personal knowledge recommend David as "cunning in playing, . . . knowing of speech,[2] . . . and Jehovah is with him."

[1] Our Authorised Version renders the word used in 1 Sam. xvi. 15, 16, 17, and that in ver. 18 alike by "servants." But the original marks that the former were the courtiers and officials around Saul, while in ver. 18 it is "one of the lads"—belonging to the class of man-servants.

[2] So ver. 18, literally.

The words, seemingly casually spoken, were acted upon, and David was sent for to court. He came, bringing such gifts as the primitive habits of those times suggested to Jesse as fitting for a loyal subject to offer to his monarch. And as he stood before Saul in all the freshness of youth, with conscience clear, and in the Spirit-holpen vigour of a new life —so like the ideal of what Saul might have become, like him even in stature—the king's past and better self seems to have come back to him, "the king loved David greatly," and took him into his service.[1] And God's blessing rested on it : for, when the king heard, as it were, the sound of the rushing wings of the spirit of evil, and almost felt the darkness as he spread them over him, then, as David's hands swept the harp of praise, and it poured forth its melody of faith and hope, it seemed as if heaven's light fell on those wings, and the evil spirit departed from Saul. And thus we learn once more the precious lesson, how

> " God moves in a mysterious way
> His wonders to perform."

What, if the result alone had been announced, would have seemed impossible, and hence miraculous in its accomplishment, was brought about by a chain of events, each linked to the other by natural causation. It is this naturalness, in many cases, of the supernatural which most shows that "Jehovah reigneth." What He has promised in His grace that He bringeth about in His providence. Next to inward humility and strength in dependence on the Lord, erhaps the most important lessons which David could learn for his future guidance would be those which at the court of Saul, and yet not of the court, he would derive from daily observation of all that passed in the government, standing in so near and confidential relationship to the king as to know all—the good and the evil, the danger and

---

[1] The text has it, that David was made "armour-bearer" to Saul. Probably the rank was little more than nominal. We know that in military monarchies, such as in Russia, every civil official has also a nominal military rank.

the difficulty—and yet being so wholly independent as to remain unbiassed in his estimate of persons and judgment of things.

So time passed. But in the intervals of calmness, when Saul needed not the ministry of David, the young Bethlehemite was wont to return to his father's home and to his humble avocations,—to find in quiet retirement that rest and strength which he needed (1 Sam. xvii. 15). And now once more had the dark cloud of war gathered over the land. It was again Israel's hereditary enemy the Philistines, who, probably encouraged by their knowledge of Saul's state, had advanced as far into Judah as the neighbourhood of Bethlehem. About ten miles to the south-west of that city lay Shochoh (or Sochoh), the modern Shuweikeh. Here a broad wady, or valley, marking a water-course, runs north for about an hour's distance. This is the modern Wady-es-Sumt, the valley of the acacias, the ancient valley of Elah, or of the terebinth. At the modern village of Sakarieh, the ancient Shaarim, the wady divides, turning westwards towards Gath, and northwards by the Wady Surar towards Ekron. Shochoh and Ephes-Dammim, the modern Damum, about three miles north-east of Shochoh, between which two points the Philistine camp was pitched, lay on the *southern* slope of the wady, while the host of Israel was camped on the *northern* slope, the two being separated by the deep part of the wady. But no longer did the former God-inspired courage fire Israel. The Spirit of God had departed from their leader, and his followers seemed to share in the depression which this consciousness brought. In such a warfare, especially among Easterns, all depended on decision and boldness. But unbelief makes cowards; and Saul and his army were content with a merely defensive position, without venturing to attack their enemies. Day by day the two armies gathered on the opposite slopes, only to witness what was for Israel more than humiliation, even an open defiance of their ability to resist the power of Philistia—by implication, a defiance of the covenant-people as such, and of Jehovah, the covenant-God, and a challenge to a fight between might in

the flesh and power in the Spirit.   And truly Israel, under
the leadership of a Saul, was ill prepared for such a contest.
But herein also lay the significance of the Philistine challenge, and of the manner in which it was taken up by David,
as well as of his victory.   It is not too much to assert that
this event was a turning-point in the history of the theocracy,
and marked David as the true king of Israel, ready to take up
the Philistine challenge of God and of His people, to kindle
in Israel a new spirit, and, in the might of the living God, to
bring the contest to victory.

Forty days successively, as the opposing armies had stood
marshalled in battle-array, Goliath of Gath—a descendant of
those giants that had been left at the time of Joshua (Josh.
xi. 21, 22)—had stepped out of the ranks of the Philistines to
challenge a champion of Israel to single combat, which should
decide the fate of the campaign, and the subjection of either
Israel or the Philistines.   Such challenges were common enough
in antiquity.   But it indicated a terrible state of things when it
could be thrown down and not taken up,—a fearful "reproach"
when an "uncircumcised Philistine" could so "defy the armies of the living God" (1 Sam. xvii. 8–10, 26, 36).   And
yet as Goliath left the ranks of his camp, and "came down"
(ver. 8) into the valley that separated the two hosts, and, as it
were, shook his hand in scorn of high heaven and of Israel,
not a man dared answer ; till at last the Philistine, rendered
more and more bold, began to cross the wady, and "came
up" the slopes towards where Israel stood (ver. 25), when at
sight of him they " fled," and "were sore afraid."

For, where the realising sense of God's presence was wanting, the contest would only seem one of strength against
strength.   In that case, the appearance and bearing of the
Philistine must have been sufficiently terrifying to Orientals.
Measuring about nine feet nine inches,[1] he was covered

[1] This measurement is of course approximative, as we are not quite sure
of the exact equivalent of Hebrew measures and weights.   Pliny mentions
an Arab giant who measured exactly the same as Goliath, and a man and a

front and back by a coat of mail of brass, consisting of scales overlapping each other, such as we know were used in ancient times,[1] but weighing not less than about one hundred and fifty-seven pounds.[2] That armour, no doubt, descended to his legs, which were cased in "greaves of brass," while a helmet of the same material defended his head. As weapons of offence he carried, besides the sword with which he was girded (ver. 51; xxi. 9), an enormous javelin[3] of brass, which, after the manner of the ancient soldiers, was slung on his back, and a spear, the metal head of which weighed about seventeen or eighteen pounds.

Such was the sight which David beheld, when sent by his father to the army to inquire after the welfare of his three elder brothers,[4] who had followed Saul into the war, and at the same time, in true Oriental fashion, to carry certain provisions to them, and to bring a present from the dairy produce[5] to their commanding officer. The description of what follows is so vivid that we can almost see the scene. All is truly Oriental in its cast, and truly Scriptural in its spirit.

David, who had never been permanently in Saul's service,

---

woman in the time of Augustus who were even an inch taller (*Hist. Nat.*, vii. 16). Josephus speaks of a Jew who was even taller (*Ant.*, xviii. 4, 5); and Keil refers to a giant of nearly the same proportions who visited Berlin in 1859. The LXX., however, characteristically change the measurement from six to four cubits.

[1] A corselet of this kind, belonging to Rameses III., is in the British Museum.

[2] A mediæval corselet preserved in Dresden weighs more than a third of that of Goliath, which seems proportionate to his size.

[3] This is the meaning of the word, and not "target," as in our Authorised Version.

[4] The expression, ver. 18, "take a pledge of them," need not, as by most commentators, be taken literally, but may be a figurative expression for bringing back an assurance of their welfare.

[5] "Ten cheeses," or rather, "cuts of curdled milk;" possibly resembling our so-called cream-cheese.

had, on the outbreak of the war, returned to his home.[1]
When he now arrived at the "trench" which ran round
the camp, to trace and defend it, the army of Israel was
being put in battle-array against that of the Philistines on
the opposite hill.   In true Oriental fashion, they were raising
a shout of defiance while not venturing on an attack.   David
left his baggage with the keeper of the baggage, and ran
forward to the foremost ranks, where, as he knew, the position of Judah, and therefore of his brothers, must be (Num.
ii. 3; x. 14).   While conversing with them, the scene previously described was re-enacted.   As Goliath approached
nearer and nearer, the order of battle was dissolved before
him.   It is quite characteristic that these fear-stricken Israelites should have tried to excite one another by dwelling
on the insult offered to Israel, and the rewards which Saul had
promised to the victorious champion of his people.   Quite

---

[1] There is considerable difficulty about the text as it now stands.
That the narrative is strictly historical cannot be doubted.   But, on the
other hand, vers. 12–14, and still more vers. 55–58, read as if the writer
had inserted this part of his narrative from some other source, perhaps from a
special chronicle of the event.   The LXX. solve the difficulty by simply
leaving out vers. 12–31, and again vers. 55–58; that is, they boldly
treat that part as an interpolation; and it must be confessed that the narrative reads easier without it.   And yet, on the other hand, if these verses
are interpolated, the work has been clumsily done; and it is not easy to see
how any interpolator would not have at once seen the difficulties which he
created, especially by the addition of vers. 55–58.   Besides, the account,
vers. 12–31, not only fits in very well with the rest of the narrative—bating
some of the expressions in vers. 12–14—but also bears the evident impress of truthfulness.   The drastic method in which the LXX. dealt with the
text, so early as about two centuries before Christ, at least proves that, even
at that time, there were strong doubts about the genuineness of the text.
All this leads to the suggestion, that somehow the text may have become
corrupted, and that later copyists may have tried emendations and additions,
by way of removing difficulties, which, as might be expected in such a
case, would only tend to increase them.   On the whole, therefore, we
are inclined to the opinion that, while the narrative itself is strictly authentic, the text, as we possess it, is seriously corrupted in some of the
expressions, especially in the concluding verses of the chapter.   At the
same time it should be added, that its correctness has been defended by
very able critics.

characteristic also, from what we know of him, was the bearing of David. We need not attempt to eliminate from the narrative the personal element, as we may call it, in the conduct of David. God appeals to outward motives, even in what is highest—such as the loss or gain of our souls,—and the tale of what was "to be done" to him who wrought such deliverance in Israel might well fire a spirit less ardent than that of David to realise Israel's great need. But what was so distinctive in David—who probably knew Saul too well confidently to expect the literal fulfilment of his promises—was the spiritual response to the challenge of the Philistine which sprung unbidden to his lips (ver. 26), and which, when the hour for personal action came, was felt to be a deep reality to which his faith could confidently appeal (vers. 36, 37). Truly we seem to breathe another atmosphere than that hitherto in the camp of Israel; nor could his public career be more appropriately begun, who was to pasture Israel according to the integrity of his heart, and to lead them "by the skilfulness of his hands" (Psa. lxxviii. 70–72).

And here we have another instance of the prefigurative character of the history of David. As "the brothers" and near kinsfolk of our blessed Lord misunderstood His motives, and could not enter into the spirit of His work, so Eliab, when he imputed to David a dissatisfied ambition that could not rest contented with humble avocations, and when he characterised his God-inspired courage and confidence as carnal, and a delight in war and bloodshed for its own sake (ver. 28). But it was too late to arrest David by such objections. Putting them aside, as making a man an offender for a word, but without retaliating by convicting Eliab of his own uncharitableness, worldliness, and unbelief, David turned away to repeat his inquiries. Tidings of the young champion, who had displayed quite another banner against the Philistine than that of Saul, were soon brought to the king. In the interview which followed, the king bade the shepherd think of his youth and inexperience in a contest with such a warrior as Goliath. Yet

he seems to speak like one who was half convinced by the
bearing and language of this strange champion, and easily
allowed himself to be persuaded ; not so much, we take it, by
the account of his prowess and success in the past as by the
tone of spiritual assurance and confidence in the God of Israel
with which he spake.

Once more thoughts of the past must have crowded in
upon Saul.   There was that in the language of this youth
which recalled the strength of Israel, which seemed like the
dawn of another morning, like a voice from another world.
But if he went to the combat, let it be at least in what seemed
to Saul the most fitting and promising manner—arrayed in the
king's own armour,—as if the whole meaning of David's conduct—nay, of the combat itself and of the victory—had not lain
in the very opposite direction : in the confessed inadequacy of
all merely human means for every such contest, and in the
fact that the victory over Goliath must appear as the Lord's
deliverance, achieved through the faith of a personal, realising,
conscious dependence on Him.   And so Saul's armour must
be put aside as that which had " not been proved " in such a
contest, of which the champion of the Lord had never made
trial in such encounters—and of which he never could make
trial.   A deep-reaching lesson this to the Church and to
believers individually, and one which bears manifold application,
not only spiritually, but even intellectually.   The first demand
upon us is to be spiritual ; the next to be genuine and true,
without seeking to clothe ourselves in the armour of another.

A few rapid sketches, and the narrative closes.   Goliath had
evidently retired within the ranks of the Philistines, satisfied
that, as before, his challenge had remained unanswered.   And
now tidings that a champion of Israel was ready for the fray
once more called him forth.   As he advanced, David waited
not till he had crossed the wady and ascended the slope where
Israel's camp lay, but hastened forward, and picked him five
stones from the dry river-bed in the valley.   And now the
Philistine had time to take, as he thought, the full measure

of his opponent. Only a fair-looking, stout, unarmed shepherd-youth, coming against him with his shepherd's gear, as if he were a dog! Was this, then, the champion of Israel? In true Eastern fashion, he advanced, boasting of his speedy and easy victory; in true heathen spirit the while cursing and blaspheming the God in Whose Name David was about to fight. But David also must speak. To the carnal confidence in his own strength which Goliath expressed, David opposed the Name—that is, the manifestation—of *Jehovah Zevaoth*, the God of heaven's hosts, the God also of the armies of Israel. That God, Whom Goliath had blasphemed and defied, would presently take up the challenge. He would fight, and deliver the giant into the hand of one even so unequal to such contest as an unarmed shepherd. Thus would "all the earth"—all Gentile nations—see that there was a God in Israel; thus also would "all this assembly" (the *kahal*, the called)—all Israel—learn that too long forgotten lesson which must underlie all their history, that "not by sword or spear, saith Jehovah: for Jehovah's is the war, and He gives you into our hands."

Words ceased. Slowly the Philistine giant advanced to what seemed easy victory. He had not even drawn the sword, nor apparently let down the visor of his helmet,—for was not his opponent unarmed? and a well-directed thrust of his spear would lay him bleeding at his feet. Swiftly the shepherd ran to the encounter. A well-aimed stone from his sling—and the gigantic form of the Philistine, encased in its unwieldy armour, mortally stricken, fell heavily to the ground, and lay helpless in sight of his dismayed countrymen, while the unarmed David, drawing the sword from the sheath of his fallen opponent, cut off his head, and returned to the king with the gory trophy. All this probably within less time than it has taken to write it down. And now a sudden dismay seized on the Philistines. Their champion and pride so suddenly swept down, they fled in wild disorder. It was true, then, that there was a God in Israel! It was true that the war was Jehovah's, and that He had given them into Israel's hand! Israel and Judah raised a shout, and pursued the Philistines up that ravine, through that wady, to Shaarim, and beyond it to the gates of Gath, and up that other wady to Ekron.   But while the people returned to take the spoil of the Philistine tents, David had given a modest account of himself to the jealous king and his chief general; had won the generous heart of Jonathan; and had gone to lay up the armour of the Philistine as his part of the spoil in his home.   But the head of the Philistine he nailed on the gates of Jerusalem, right over in sight of the fort which the heathen Jebusites still held in the heart of the land.

CHAPTER XI.

Saul's Jealousy, and Attempts upon David's Life—David marries Michal—Ripening of Saul's Purpose of Murder—David's Flight to Samuel—Saul among the Prophets—David finally leaves the Court of Saul.

(I SAM. XVIII. 4—XX.)

THE friendship between Jonathan and David, which dated from the victory over Goliath, and the modest, genuine bearing of the young conqueror, is the one point of light in a history which grows darker and darker as it proceeds.   We can imagine how a spirit so generous as that of Jonathan would be drawn towards that unaffected, brave youth, so free from all self-consciousness or self-seeking, who would seem the very embodiment of Israelitish valour and piety. And we can equally perceive how gratitude and admiration of such real nobleness would kindle in the heart of David an affection almost womanly in its tenderness.   Ancient history records not a few instances of such love between heroes, ratified like this by a "covenant," and betokened by such gifts as when Jonathan put on David his "mantle," his "armour-coat," [1] and even his arms,—but none more pure and elevated, or penetrated, as in this instance, by the highest and best feelings of true piety.

There can be no doubt that this friendship was among the means which helped David to preserve that loyalty to Saul which was the grand characteristic of his conduct in the very trying period which now ensued. How these trials called out his faith, and consequently his patience; how they drew him closer to God, ripened his inner life, and so prepared him for his ultimate calling, will best appear from a comparison of the Psalms which date from this time. The events, as recorded in the sacred text, are not given in strict chronological order, but rather in that of their internal connection. As we understand it, after David's victory over Goliath, he was taken into the permanent employ of Saul. This and his general success [2] in all undertakings, as well as his prudence and modesty, which, at least during the first period, disarmed even the jealousy of Saul's courtiers, are indicated in general terms in 1 Sam. xviii. 5. But matters could not long progress peacefully. On the return of the army from the pursuit of the Philistines, the conquerors had, after the custom of the times, been met in every city through which they passed by choruses of women, who, with mimic dances, sung antiphonally [3] the praise of the heroes, ascribing the victory over thousands to Saul, and over ten thousands to David. It was quite characteristic of the people, and it implied not even conscious preference for David, least of all danger to Saul's throne. But it sufficed

---

[1] The same term is used in 1 Sam. xvii. 38, 39; Judg. iii. 16; 2 Sam. xx. 8. But I cannot see how (as in *The Speaker's Commentary*, vol. ii., p. 325) it can be supposed to comprise "the sword, bow, and girdle." These three are expressly connected with it by a threefold repetition of the expression, "even to."

[2] The expression in our Authorised Version, "behaved himself wisely," includes both skilfulness and success.

[3] In ver. 6 we have it, that they went to meet Saul "with hand-drums, with joy (that is, with pæans of joy), and with triangles." The picture is vivid, and true to the custom of the times.

to kindle in Saul deep and revengeful envy. Following upon what the spirit of evil from the Lord had set before him as his own fate, sealed as it was by his solemn rejection from the kingdom and the conscious departure of the Spirit of God, the popular praise seemed to point out David as his rival. And every fresh success of David, betokening the manifest help of God, and every failure of his own attempts to rid himself of this rival, would only deepen and embitter this feeling, and lead him onwards, from step to step, until the murderous passion became all engrossing, and made the king not only forgetful of Jehovah, and of what evidently was His purpose, but also wholly regardless of the means which he used. Thus Saul's dark passions were ultimately concentrated in the one thought of murder. Yet in reality it was against Jehovah that he contended rather than against David. So true is it that all sin is ultimately against the Lord; so bitter is the root of self; and so terrible the power of evil in its constantly growing strength, till it casts out all fear of God or care for man. So true also is it that "he that hateth his brother is a murderer," in heart and principle. On the other hand, these constant unprovoked attempts upon the life of David, regardlessly of the means employed, till at last the whole forces of the kingdom were used for no other purpose than to hunt down an innocent fugitive, whose only crime was that God was with him, and that he had successfully fought the cause of Israel, must have had a very detrimental effect upon the people. They must have convinced all that he who now occupied the throne was unfit for the post, while at the same time they could not but demoralise the people in regard to their real enemies, thus bringing about the very results which Saul so much dreaded.

It deserves special notice, that Saul's attempts against the life of David are in the sacred text never attributed to the influence of the spirit of evil from the Lord, although they were no doubt made when that spirit was upon him. For God never tempts man to sin; but he sinneth when he is drawn away by his own passion, and enticed by it. If proof were needed that the spirit whom God sent was not evil in himself, it would be found in this, that while formerly David's music could soothe the king, that power was lost when Saul had given way to sin. On the first occasion of this kind, Saul, in a maniacal[1] fit, twice poised[2] against David the javelin, which, as the symbol of royalty, he had by him (like the modern sceptre); and twice "David turned (bent) aside from before him."[3] The failure of his purpose only strengthened the king's conviction that, while God had forsaken him, He was with David. The result, however, was not repentance, but a feeling of fear, under which he removed David from his own presence, either to free himself of the temptation to murder, or in the hope, which he scarcely yet confessed to himself, that, promoted to the command over a thousand men, David might fall in an engagement with the Philistines. How this also failed, or rather led to results the opposite of those which Saul had wished, is briefly marked in the text.

With truest insight into the working of such a mind, the narrative traces the further progress of this history. Perhaps to test whether he really cherished ambitious designs, but with the conscious wish to rid himself of his dreaded rival, Saul now proposed to carry out his original promise to the conqueror of Goliath, by giving David his eldest daughter Merab to wife, at the same time professing only anxiety that his future son-in-law should fight "the battles of Jehovah." The reply given might have convinced him, that David had no

[1] Our Authorised Version renders ver. 10, "and he prophesied in the midst of the house;" and the word undoubtedly means this. But in the present instance it refers not to "prophecy," but to the ecstatic state which often accompanied it, even in false prophets: comp. 1 Kings xxii. 22; Acts xvi. 16; xix. 15. Saul was in a state of maniacal ecstasy.

[2] Apparently Saul did not actually throw the javelin, as in xix. 10.

[3] So literally. Our Auth rised Version gives the impression that David had left the presence of Saul.

H

exaggerated views of his position in life.[1] It is idle to ask why Saul upon this so rapidly transferred Merab to one [2] who is not otherwise known in history. The affection of Michal, Saul's younger daughter, for David, promised to afford Saul the means of still further proving David's views, and of bringing him to certain destruction. The plan was cleverly devised. Taught by experience, David took no further notice of the king's personal suggestion of such an alliance.[3] At this the courtiers were instructed secretly to try the effect of holding out a prospect so dazzling as that of being the king's son-in-law. But the bait was too clumsily put,—or rather it failed to take, from the thorough integrity of David. Next came not the suggestion merely, but a definite proposal through the courtiers, to give the king as dowry within a certain specified time a pledge that not less than a hundred heathen had fallen in "the Lord's battles." If the former merely general admonition to fight had not led to David's destruction, a more definite demand like this might necessitate personal contests, in which, as Saul imagined, every chance would be against David's escape. But once more the king was foiled. David, who readily entered on a proposal so much in harmony with his life-work, executed within less than the appointed time double the king's requirements, and Michal became his wife.

And still the story becomes darker and darker. We have marked the progress of murderous thought in the king's mind, from the sudden attack of frenzy to the scarcely self-confessed wish for the death of his victim, to designed exposure of his life,

---

[1] The expression in ver. 18, "my life," probably means my *status* in life. The rendering proposed by some, "my people," is linguistically unsupported, and implies a needless repetition.

[2] The suggestion of Keil, that it was due to want of affection on her part, is as arbitrary as that (in *The Speaker's Commentary*) of a large dowry on the part of Adriel.

[3] Ver. 21 had probably best be rendered: "Thou shalt this day be my son-in-law in a second (another) manner;" or else, become such "a second time."

and lastly to a deliberate plan for his destruction. But now all restraints were broken through. Do what he might, David prospered, and all that Saul had attempted had only turned out to the advantage of the son of Jesse. Already he was the king's son-in-law; Michal had given her whole heart to him; constant success had attended those expeditions against the heathen which were to have been his ruin; nay, as might be expected in the circumstances, he had reached the pinnacle of popularity. One dark resolve now settled in the heart of the king, and cast it shadow over every other consideration. David must be murdered. Saul could no longer disguise his purpose from himself, nor keep it from others. He spoke of it openly—even to Jonathan, and to all around him. So alarming had it become, that Jonathan felt it necessary to warn David, who, in his conscious integrity, seemed still unsuspicious of real danger. Yet Jonathan himself would fain have believed that his father's mood was only the outcome of that dreadful disease of which he was the victim. Accordingly, almost within hearing of David, who had secreted himself near by, he appealed to his father, and that in language so telling and frank, that the king himself was for the moment won. So it had been only frenzy—the outburst of the moment, but not the king's real heart-purpose—and David returned to court!

The hope was vain. The next success against the Philistines rekindled all the evil passions of the king. Once more, as he yielded to sin, the spirit of evil was sent in judgment—this time from Jehovah. As Saul heard the rushing of his dark pinions around him, it was not sudden frenzy which seized him, but he attempted deliberate murder. What a contrast: David with the harp in his hand, and Saul with his spear; David sweeping the chords to waken Divine melody in the king's soul, and the king sending the javelin with all his might, so that, as it missed its aim, it stuck in the wall close by where David had but lately sat. Meanwhile David escaped to his own house, apparently unwilling even now to believe in the king's deliberate purpose of murder. It was Saul's own

daughter who had to urge upon her husband the terrible fact
of her father's planned crime and the need of immediate flight,
and with womanly love and wit to render it possible.   How
great the danger had been; how its meshes had been laid all
around and well nigh snared him—but chiefly what had been
David's own feelings, and what his hope in that hour of
supreme danger : all this, and much more for the teaching of
the Church of all ages, we gather from what he himself tells
us in the fifty-ninth Psalm.[1]

The peril was past; and while the cowardly menials of Saul
—though nominally of Israel, yet in heart and purpose, as in
their final requital, "heathens" (Psa. lix. 6, 8) — prowled
about the city and its walls on their terrible watch of murder,
"growling" like dogs that dare not bark to betray their
presence, and waiting till the dawn would bring their victim,
lured to safety, within reach of their teeth, Michal compassed
the escape of her husband through a window—probably on
the city-wall.   In so doing she betrayed, however, alike the
spirit of her home and that of her times.   The daughter of
Saul, like Rachel of old (Gen. xxxi. 19), seems to have had
Teraphim—the old Aramæan or Chaldean household gods,
which were probably associated with fertility.   For, despite the
explicit Divine prohibition and the zeal of Samuel against all
idolatry, this most ancient form of Jewish superstition appears
to have continued in Israelitish households (comp. Judg. xvii.
5; xviii. 14; 1 Sam. xv. 23; Hos. iii. 4; Zech. x. 2).   The
Teraphim must have borne the form of a man; and Michal
now placed this image in David's bed, arranging about the
head. "the plait of camel's hair,"[2] and covering the whole

---

[1] Our space prevents not only an analysis but even a literal translation
of this Psalm.   The reader should compare it with this history.   Those
who are able to avail themselves of it, will find much help in Pro-
fessor Delitzsch's *Commentary on the Psalms* (German Ed., vol. i., pp.
441–448); translated in Clark's *Foreign Theological Library*.

[2] The Hebrew expression is somewhat difficult, and may imply that
Michal used it to cover David's face, or that she put it about the Teraphim
to appear like hair.   I have translated the words literally.

"with the upper garment" (as coverlet), to represent David lying sick. The device succeeded in gaining time for the fugitive, and was only discovered when Saul sent his messengers a second time, with the peremptory order to bring David in the bed. Challenged by her father for her deceit, she excused her conduct by another falsehood, alleging that she had been obliged by David to do so on peril of her life.

Although we are in no wise concerned to defend Michal, and in general utterly repudiate, as derogatory to Holy Scripture, all attempts to explain away the apparent wrong-doing of Biblical personages, this instance requires a few words of plain statement. First, it is most important to observe, that Holy Scripture, with a truthfulness which is one of its best evidences, simply relates events, whoever were the actors, and whatever their moral character. We are somehow prone to imagine that Holy Scripture approves all that it records, at least in the case of its worthies—unless, indeed, the opposite be expressly stated. Nothing could be more fallacious than such an inference. Much is told in the Bible, even in connection with Old Testament saints, on which no comment is made, save that of the retribution which, in the course of God's providence, surely follows all wrong-doing. And here we challenge any instance of sin which is not followed by failure, sorrow, and punishment. It had been so in the case of Abraham, of Isaac, and of Jacob; and it was so in that of David, whose every attempt to screen himself by untruthfulness ended in failure and sorrow. Holy Scripture never conceals wrong-doing—least of all seeks to palliate it. In this respect there is the most significant contrast between the Bible and its earliest (even pre-Christian) comments. Those only who are acquainted with this literature know with what marvellous ingenuity Rabbinical commentaries uniformly try, not only to palliate wrong on the part of Biblical heroes, but by some turn or alteration in the expression, or suggestion of motives, to present it as actually right.

But we must go a step further. He who fails to recognise

the gradual development of God's teaching, and regards the
earlier periods in the history of God's kingdom as on exactly
the same level as the New Testament, not only most seriously
mistakes fundamental facts and principles, but misses the
entire meaning of the preparatory dispensation.   The Old
Testament never places truth, right, or duty on any lower basis
than the New.   But while it does not lower, it does not unfold
in all their fulness the principles which it lays down.   Rather
does it adapt the application of truths, the exposition of rights,
and the unfolding of duties, to the varying capacities of each
age and stage.   And this from the necessity of the case, in
highest wisdom, in greatest mercy, and in the interest of the
truth itself.   The principle : " When I was a child, I spake as
a child, I understood as a child, I thought as a child," applies
to the relation between the Old and the New Testament standpoint, as well as to all spiritual and even intellectual progress.
The child is ignorant of all the bearings of what he learns ;
the beginner of the full meaning and application of the
axioms and propositions which he is taught.   Had it been
otherwise in spiritual knowledge, its acquisition would have
been simply impossible.

Here also we have to distinguish between what God *sanc-
tioned* and that with which *He bore* on account of the hard-
ness of the heart of those who had not yet been spiritually
trained in that "time of ignorance," which "God overlooked."   To come to the particular question in hand.   Nothing could be more clear in the Old Testament than the
Divine insistance on truthfulness.   He Himself condescends
to be His people's example in this.   The command not to
lie one to another (Lev. xix. 11) is enforced by the consideration, " I am Jehovah," and springs as a necessary
sequence from the principle: " Be ye holy: for I Jehovah
your God am holy."   It is scarcely requisite to add, that
in no other part of Holy Scripture is this more fully or frequently enforced than in the Book of Psalms.   And yet, when
occasion arose, David himself seems not to have scrupled to

seek safety through falsehood, though with what little success appears in his history. It appears as if to his mind untruth had seemed only that which was false in the intention or in its object, not that which was simply untrue in itself, however good the intention might be, or however desirable the object thereby sought.[1] And in this connection it deserves notice, how among the few express moral precepts which the New Testament gives—for it deals in principles rather than in details; it gives life, not law,—this about lying recurs with emphatic distinctness and frequency.[2]

As might almost have been anticipated, David's destination in his flight was Ramah. To tell Samuel, who had anointed him, all that had happened; to ask his guidance, and seek refreshment in his company, would obviously suggest itself first to his mind. For greater safety, the two withdrew from the city, to "Naioth," "the dwellings," which seems to have been a block of dwellings within a compound, occupied by an order of prophets, of which Samuel was the "president,"[3] and, we may add, the founder. Not that "prophetism" (if the term may be used) commenced with Samuel. In the sense of being the bearers of God's message, the patriarchs are called "prophets" (Gen. xx. 7; Psa. cv. 15). But in its strict sense the term first applied to Moses (Num. xi. 25; Deut. xxxiv. 10; Hos. xii. 13). Miriam was a prophetess (Ex. xv. 20; comp. Num. xii. 2). In the days of the Judges there were prophets (Judg. iv. 4; vi. 8). At the time of Eli, prophetic warning came through a "man of God" (1 Sam. ii. 27); and although "the word of God" (or prophecy) "was rare" in those days (1 Sam. iii. 1), yet it came

---

[1] The Germans speak of "lies of necessity" (*Nothlüge*), which to me seems a contradiction of terms, since no one duty (or moral necessity) can ever contravene another.

[2] I am bound to add that even Talmudical writings insist on the need of absolute truthfulness, though in terms far other than the New Testament.

[3] In the Authorised Version, 1 Sam. xix. 20, "Samuel standing *as appointed over them;*" in the original, "Standing as president over them."

not upon the people as a strange and unknown manifestation (comp. also 1 Sam. ix. 9).   Here, however, we must make
distinction between the *prophetic gift* and the *prophetic office.*
The latter, so far as appears, began with Samuel.   A further
stage is marked in the days of Elijah and Elisha.   Then they
were no longer designated "prophets," as at the time of
Samuel, but "sons of the prophets," or "disciples" (1 Kings
xx. 35 ; 2 Kings iv. 38 ; vi. 1).   Lastly, whereas we read of
only one prophetic community, Naioth, in the time of Samuel,
and that close to his residence at Ramah, there were several
such in the days of Elisha, in different parts of the country—
as at Gilgal, Bethel, and Jericho.   Whether there was a continuous succession in this from Samuel to Elijah can scarcely
be determined, though the probability seems in its favour
(comp. 1 Kings xviii. 13).

It is of more importance to understand the difference be
tween "prophets" and "sons of the prophets," the circumstances under which these orders or unions originated, and
the peculiar meaning attached to this prophetic calling.   The
first point seems sufficiently clear.   The "sons of the prophets" were those who of set purpose devoted themselves
to this work, and were, on the one hand, disciples of prophets, and on the other, the messengers or ministers to carry
out their behests.   Dedication and separation to the work
(symbolised even by a common abode, and by a distinctive
appearance and dress), religious instruction, and, above all,
implicit obedience, are the historical features of those "sons
of the prophets."   Quite other was the "union," "company,"
or rather "congregation[1] of prophets" (1 Sam. xix. 20) near
Ramah.   There is no evidence of their having all permanently dedicated themselves to the office ; the contrary seems
rather implied.   No doubt from among them sprung those
who were afterwards "seers," such as Gad, Nathan, and Iddo ;
but the majority seem to have joined the union under a

---

[1] The *Lahakah*, which evidently is only an inversion of the letters of the
word *Kahalah*, which generally designates "the congregation."

temporary constraining influence of the mighty Spirit of God. And although, as we gather from many passages of Holy Scripture (as 1 Sam. xxii. 5; 1 Chron. xxix. 29, and other passages in the Books of Kings), they were occupied with the composition and the study of sacred history, and no doubt with that of the law also, as well as with the cultivation of hymnology, it would be a great mistake to regard them as a class of students of theology, or to represent them as a monastic order.

In point of fact, the time of Samuel, and that of Elijah and Elisha, were great turning-points, periods of crisis, in the history of the kingdom of God. In the first, the tabernacle, the priesthood, and the God-appointed services had fallen into decay, and, for a time, may be said to have been almost in abeyance. Then it was that God provided other means of grace, by raising up faithful, devoted men, who gathered into a living sanctuary, filled not by the Shechinah, but by the mighty Spirit of God. Under the direction of a Samuel, and the influence of a "spiritual gift,"—like those of apostolic days —their presence and activity served most important purposes. And, as in apostolic days, the spiritual influence under which they were seems at times to have communicated itself even to those who were merely brought into contact with them. This, no doubt, to prove its *reality* and *power*, since even those who were strangers to its spiritual purpose, and unaffected by it, could not resist its might, and thus involuntarily bore witness to it. And something analogous to this we also witness now in the irresistible influence which a spiritual movement sometimes exercises even on those who are and remain strangers to its real meaning.[1]

---

[1] As there is unity in all God's working, we mark a similar law prevailing in the physical and intellectual world. The general influence of physical forces and causes—even atmospheric—is sufficiently known, nor can it be necessary, in these days, to attempt proving that of "the spirit of the times," which intellectually and even morally affects us all more or less, whether consciously or unconsciously, willingly or unwillingly.

Thus far as regards "the congregation of prophets" in the days of Samuel. In the time of Elijah, Israel—as distinct from Judah—was entirely cut off from the sanctuary, and under a rule which threatened wholly to extinguish the service of God, and to replace it by the vile and demoralising rites of Baal. Already the country swarmed with its priests, when God raised up Elijah to be the breaker-up of the way, and Elisha to be the restorer of ancient paths. The very circumstances of the time, and the state of the people, pointed out the necessity of the revival of the ancient "order," but now as "sons of the prophets" rather than as prophets.

Nor did this change of designation imply a retrogression. What on superficial inquiry seems such, is, on more careful consideration, often found to mark real progress. In earliest patriarchal, and even in Mosaic times, the communications between Jehovah and His people were chiefly by *Theophanies*, or Personal apparitions of God ; in the case of the prophets, by *inspiration ;* in the New Testament Church, by the *indwelling of the Holy Ghost.* It were a grievous mistake to regard this progress in the spiritual history of the kingdom of God as a retrogression. The opposite is rather the case. And somewhat similarly we may mark, in some respects, an advance in the succession of "sons of the prophets" to the order of "pro-phetics," or "prophesiers," as we may perhaps designate them by way of distinction. "But all these things worketh one and the self-same Spirit, dividing to every man" (and to every period in the Church's history) "severally as He will," and adapting the agencies which He uses to the varying necessities and spiritual stages of His people.

What has been stated will help to explain how the three embassies which Saul sent to seize David in the Naioth were in turn themselves seized by the spiritual influence, and how even Saul, when attempting personally to carry out what his messengers had found impossible, came yet more fully and manifestly than they under its all-subduing power.[1] It proved

[1] The difference between the influence on Saul and on his messengers

incontestably that there was a Divine power engaged on behalf of David, against which the king of Israel would vainly contend, which he could not resist, and which would easily lay alike his messengers and himself prostrate and helpless at its feet. If, after this, Saul continued in his murderous designs against David, the contest would manifestly be not between two men, but between the king of Israel and the Lord of Hosts, Who had wrought signs and miracles on Saul and his servants, and that in full view of the whole people. It is this latter consideration which gives such meaning to the circumstances narrated in the sacred text, that the common report, how the spiritual influence had subdued and constrained Saul, when on his murderous errand against David, led to the renewal of the popular saying: "Is Saul also among the prophets?" For all Israel must know it, and speak of it, and wonder as it learns its significance.

Thus at the end, as at the beginning of his course, Saul is under the mighty influence of the Spirit of God—now to warn, and, if possible, to reclaim, as formerly to qualify him for his work. And some result of this kind seems to have been produced. For, although David fled from Naioth on the arrival of Saul, we find him soon again near the royal residence (xx. 1), where, indeed, he was evidently expected by the king to take part in the festive meal with which the beginning of every month seems to have been celebrated (vers. 5, 25, 27). The notice is historically interesting in connection with Num. x. 10; xxviii. 11–15, [1] as also that other one (1 Sam. xx. 6, 29), according to which it appears to have been the practice in those days

---

may be thus marked. It seized him *before* he arrived at Naioth (ver. 23); and it was more powerful and of longer duration (ver. 24). The statement that "he stripped off his clothes," and "lay down naked," refers, of course, only to his upper garments. In the excitement of the ecstacy he would put these away (comp. 2 Sam. vi. 14, 16, 20).

[1] The statement that the festive meal took place on two successive days must, of course, not be understood as implying that the religious festival lasted two days.

of religious unsettledness for families to have had a yearly "sacrifice" in their own place, especially where, as in Bethlehem, there was an altar (comp. xvi. 2, etc.).

But, whatever had passed, David felt sure in his own mind that evil was appointed against him, and that there was but a step between him and death. Yet on that moral certainty alone he did not feel warranted to act. Accordingly he applied to Jonathan, whom he could so fully trust, expressly placing his life, in word as in deed, in his hands, if he were really guilty of what the king imputed to him (ver. 8). With characteristic generosity, Jonathan, however, still refused to believe in any settled purpose of murder on the part of his father, attributing all that had passed to the outbursts of temporary madness. His father had never made a secret of his intentions and movements. Why, then, should he now be silent, if David's suspicions were well founded? The suggestion that Jonathan should excuse David's absence from the feast by his attendance on the yearly family-sacrifice at Bethlehem, for which he had asked and obtained Jonathan's leave, was well calculated to bring out the feelings and purposes of the king. If determined to evil against David, he would in his anger at the escape of his victim, and his own son's participation in it, give vent to his feelings in language that could not be mistaken, the more so, if, as might be expected, Jonathan pleaded with characteristic warmth on behalf of his absent friend. But who could be trusted to bring tidings to David as he lay in hiding, "or" tell him "what" Saul would "answer" Jonathan "roughly"—or, in other words, communicate the details of the conversation?

To discuss the matter, unendangered by prying eyes and ears, the two friends betook themselves "to the field." The account of what passed between them—one of the few narratives of this kind given in Scripture—is most pathetic. It was not merely the outflowing of personal affection between the two, or perhaps it would not have been recorded at all. Rather is it reported in order to show that, though Jonathan had never spoken of it, he was fully aware of David's future destiny ; more than that, he had sad presentiment of the fate of his own house. And yet, in full view of it all, he believingly submitted to the will of God, and still lovingly clave to his friend ! There is a tone of deep faith toward God, and of full trust in David, in what Jonathan said. Far more fully and clearly than his father does he see into the future, alike as regards David and the house of Saul. But there is not a tinge of misunderstanding of David, not a shadow of suspicion, not a trace of jealousy, not a word of murmur or complaint. More touching words, surely, were never uttered than this charge which Jonathan laid on David as *his* part of their covenant, in view of what was to come upon them both : "And not only if I am still alive—not only shalt thou do with me the mercy of Jehovah" (show towards me Divine mercy) "that I die not; but thou shalt not cut off thy mercy from my house—not even" (at the time) "when Jehovah cutteth off the enemies of David, every one from the face of the earth" (xx. 14, 15). [1]

The signal preconcerted between the friends was, that on the third day David should lie in hiding at the same spot where he had concealed himself "in the day of business"— probably that day when Jonathan had formerly pleaded with his father for his friend (xix. 2–7)—beside the stone Ezel, perhaps "the stone of demarcation," marking a boundary. Jonathan was to shoot three arrows. If he told the lad in attendance that they lay nearer than he had run to fetch them, David might deem himself safe, and come out of hiding. If, on the contrary, he directed him to go farther, then David should conclude that

---

[1] The original is very difficult in its structure. We have rendered it as literally as the sense would allow. Of the other proposed translations only these two deserve special notice. "And (wilt thou) not if I am still alive, wilt thou not show the kindness of the Lord towards me, that I die not?" Or else, "And mayest thou, if I am still alive—mayest thou show towards me the kindness of the Lord—and (if) not, if I die, not withdraw thy mercy from my house for ever." But the first rendering implies, besides other difficulties, a change from a question in ver. 14 to an assertion in ver. 15, while the second necessitates a change in the Hebrew words.

his only safety lay in flight.   The result proved that David's
fears had been too well grounded.   Saul had evidently watched
for the opportunity which the New Moon's festival would offer
to destroy his hated rival.   On the first day he noticed David's
absence, but, attributing it to some Levitical defilement, made
no remark, lest his tone might betray him.   But on the following day he inquired its reason in language which too clearly
betokened his feelings.   It was then that Jonathan repeated
the false explanation which David had suggested.   Whether or
not the king saw through the hollowness of the device, it
certainly proved utterly unavailing.   Casting aside all restraint,
the king turned on his son, and in language the most insulting
to an Oriental, bluntly told him that his infatuation for David
would cause his own and his family's ruin.   To the command
to send for him for the avowed purpose of his murder, Jonathan
with characteristic frankness and generosity replied by pleading
his cause, on which the fury of the king rose to such a pitch,
that he poised his javelin against his own son, as formerly
against David.

Jonathan had left the feast in moral indignation at the scene
which had taken place before the whole court.   But deeper far
was his grief for the wrong done to his friend.   That day of
feasting became one of fasting to Jonathan.   Next morning he
went to give the preconcerted signal of danger.   But he could
not so part from his friend.   Sending back the lad to the city
with his bow, quiver, and arrows, the two friends once more
met, but for a moment.   There was not time for lengthened
speech ; the danger was urgent.   They were not unmanly tears
which the two wept, "till David wept loudly."[1]   The parting
must be brief—only just sufficient for Jonathan to remind his
friend of their covenant of friendship in God, to Whose care
he now commended him.   Then Jonathan retraced his lonely
way to the city, while David hastened on his flight southward
to Nob.   Only once again, and that in sadly altered circumstances, did these two noblest men in Israel meet.

[1] So literally, and not as in the Authorised Version.

CHAPTER XII.

(1 S٨M. XXI.—XXIII.)

A MIDST the many doubts which must have beset the mind of
David, one outstanding fact, however painful, was at least
clear. He must henceforth consider himself an outlaw, whom
not even the friendship of a Jonathan could protect. As such
he must seek some shelter—best outside the land of Israel, and
with the enemies of Saul. But the way was far, and the journey
beset by danger. On all accounts—for refreshment of the body,
for help, above all, for inward strengthening and guidance—he
would first seek the place whither he had so often resorted
(1 Sam. xxii. 15) before starting on some perilous undertaking.

The Tabernacle of the Lord was at that time in Nob, probably
the place that at present bears a name which some have rendered
"the village of Esau" (or Edom)—reminding us of its fatal
celebrity in connection with Doeg the Edomite. The village is
on the road from the north to Jerusalem—between Anathoth
and the Holy City, and only about one hour north-west from
the latter. Here Ahimelech (or Ahiah, 1 Sam. xiv. 3), the great-
grandson of Eli, ministered as high-priest—a man probably
advanced in years, with whom his son Abiathar (afterwards
appointed high-priest by David, 1 Sam. xxx. 7) was, either
for that day or else permanently,[1] conjoined in the sacred

---

[1] It is thus that we explain the notice in Mark ii 26. This would also
account for Abiathar's flight on the first tidings of his father's death (1 Sam.
xxii. 20), whereas the other priests would deem themselves safe, and so fall
into the hands of their murderer.

service. Nob was only about an hour to the south-east of Gibeah of Saul. Yet it was not immediately on parting with Jonathan that David appeared in the holy place. We can readily understand that flight along that road could not have been risked by day—nor, indeed, anywhere throughout the boundaries of the district where Saul's residence was. We therefore conclude that David lay in hiding all that night. It was the morning of a Sabbath when he suddenly presented himself, alone, unarmed, weary, and faint with hunger before the high-priest. Never had he thus appeared before Ahimelech ; and the high-priest, who must, no doubt, have been aware of dissensions in the past between the king and his son-in-law, was afraid of what this might bode. But David had a specious answer to meet every question and disarm all suspicion. If he had come unarmed, and was faint from hunger, the king's business had been so pressing, and required such secrecy, that he had avoided taking provisions, and had not even had time to arm himself. For the same reasons he had appointed his followers to meet him at a trysting-place, rather than gone forth at the head of them.

In truth, David's wants had become most pressing.[1] He needed food to support him till he could reach a place of safety. For he dared not show himself by day, nor ask any man for help. And he needed some weapon with which, in case of absolute necessity, to defend his life. We know that it was the Sabbath, because the shewbread of the previous week, which was removed on that day, had to be eaten during its course. It affords sad evidence of the decay into which the sanctuary and the priesthood had fallen, that Ahimelech and Abiathar could offer David no other provisions for his journey than this shewbread ; which, according to the letter of the law, only the priests might eat, and that within the sanctuary (Lev.

---

[1] The whole history tends to show that David was alone, alike in Nob and afterwards in Gath, though from Mark ii. 25, 26, we infer that a few faithful friends may have kept about him to watch over his safety till he reached the border of Philistia.

xxiv. 9). But there was the higher law of charity (Lev. xix. 18), which was rightly regarded as overruling every merely levitical ordinance, however solemn (comp. Matt. xii. 5 ; Mark ii. 25). If it was as David pretended, and the royal commission was so important and so urgent, it could not be right to refuse the necessary means of sustenance to those who were engaged on it, provided that they had not contracted any such levitical defile-ment as would have barred them from access to the Divine Presence (Lev. xv. 18). For, viewed in its higher bearing, what were the priests but the representatives of Israel, who were all to be a kingdom of priests? This idea seems indeed implied in the remark of David (xxi. 5): "And though the manner" (the use to which it is put) "be not sacred, yet still it will be made" (become) "sacred by the instrument,"—either referring to himself as the Divine instrument about to be employed,[1] or to the "wallet" in which the bread was to be carried, as it were, on God's errand. By a similar pretence, David also obtained from the high-priest the sword of Goliath, which seems to have been kept in the sanctuary wrapt in a cloth, behind the ephod, as a memorial of God's victory over the might of the heathen. Most important of all, David, as we infer from xxii. 10, 15, appears to have "enquired of the Lord," through the high-priest—whatever the exact terms of that inquiry may have been. In this also there was nothing strange, since David had done so on previous occasions, probably before entering on dangerous expeditions (xxii. 15).

But already David's secret was betrayed. It so happened in the Providence of God, that on this special Sabbath, one of Saul's principal officials, the "chief over the herdsmen," was in Nob, "detained before Jehovah." The expression implies that Doeg was obliged to remain in the sanctuary in consequence of some religious ceremony—whether connected with his ad-mission as a proselyte, for he was by birth an Edomite, or with

---

[1] The passage in the Hebrew is very difficult. The word which we have rendered "instrument" is applied to *human* instrumentality in Gen. xlix. 5; Isa. xiii. 5; xxxii. 7; Jer. l. 25; comp. also Acts ix. 15.

a vow, or with some legal purification. Such a witness could not be excluded, even if David had chosen to betray his secret to the priest. Once committed to the fatal wrong of his falsehood, David had to go on to the bitter end, all the while feeling morally certain that Doeg was his enemy, and would bring report of all to Saul (xxii. 22). His feelings as connected with this are, as we believe, expressed in Ps. vii.[1]

At first sight it may seem strange that on his further flight from Nob, David should have sought shelter in Gath, the city of Goliath, whom he had killed in single combat. On the other hand, not only may this have been the place most readily accessible to him, but David may have imagined that in Gath, especially, the defection of such a champion from the hosts of Saul would be hailed as a notable triumph, and that accordingly he would find a welcome in seeking its protection. The result, however, proved otherwise. The courtiers of Achish, the king,—or, to give him his Philistine title, the Abimelech (my father king) of Gath (comp. Gen. xx. 2 ; xxvi. 8) —urged on him the high position which David held in popular estimation in Israel, and his past exploits, as presumably in-

---

[1] The Psalm evidently refers to the time of Saul's persecutions. On this point critics are almost unanimous. Most of them, however, take the word "*Cush*" as the name of a *person* (though it nowhere else occurs), and date his otherwise *unknown* "*report*" in the period between 1 Sam. xxiv. and xxvii. (comp. xxvi. 19). But I regard the term "Cush"—the Cushite, Ethiopian—as an equivalent for "Edomite," and explain the expression "the Benjamite," as referring to Doeg's identification (as a proselyte) with the Benjamites, and his probable settlement among them, as evidenced by 1 Sam. xxii. 7, 9. The Rabbis have a curious conceit on this point, which, as it has not been told by any previous critic, and is incorrectly alluded to by Delitzsch and Moll, may here find a place. It occurs in *Sifré* 27 *a*, where the expression, Numb. xii. 1, is applied to Zipporah, it being explained that she is called "a Cushite" (Ethiopian), because, as the Ethiopian differed by his skin from all other men, so Zipporah by her beauty from all women. Similarly the inscription, Ps. vii. 1, is applied to Saul, the term Cush, or Ethiopian, being explained by a reference to 1 Sam. ix. 2. On the same principle, Amos ix. 7 is accounted for, because Israel differed from all others, the Law being given to them only, while, lastly, the Ebed-melech, or servant of the king, in Jer. xxxviii. 7, is supposed to have been Baruch, because he differed by his deeds from all the other servants.

dicating what not only his real feelings but his true policy towards Philistia must be, however differently it might suit his present purpose to bear himself (comp. 1 Sam. xxix. 3–5). The danger which now threatened David must have been very great. In fact, to judge from Ps. lvi. 1, the Philistine lords must have actually "taken" him, to bring him before Achish, with a view to his imprisonment, if not his destruction. We are probably warranted in inferring that it was when thus led before the king, and waiting in the court before being admitted to the audience, that he feigned madness by scribbling[1] on the doors of the gate, and letting his spittle fall upon his beard. The device proved successful. The Philistine lords, with true Oriental reverence for madness as a kind of spiritual possession, dared not harm him any more ; while Achish himself, however otherwise previously disposed (comp. xxvii. 2, 3), would not have him in his house, under the apprehension that he might "rave against"[2] him, and in a fit of madness endanger his life. And as Ps. lvi. described the feelings of David in the hour of his great danger, so Ps. xxxiv. expresses those on his deliverance therefrom. Accordingly the two should be read in connection. Indeed the eight Psalms which date from the time of the persecutions by Saul (lix., vii., lvi., xxxiv., lvii., lii., cxlii., liv.[3]) are closely connected, the servant of the Lord gradually rising to full and triumphant anticipation of deliverance. They all express the same trustfulness in God, the same absolute committal to Him, and the same sense of undeserved persecution. But what seems of such special interest, regarding, as we do, the history of David in its typical aspect, is that in these Psalms David's view is always enlarging, so that in

[1] The LXX., by a slight alteration in the Hebrew lettering, have rendered it "beating" or "drumming."

[2] Instead of, "that ye have brought this fellow to play the madman in my presence" (xxi. 15), as in our Authorised Version, translate, "that ye have brought this one to rave against me."

[3] We have arranged these Psalms in the chronological order of the events to which they refer, although we would not, of course, be understood as implying that they were exactly composed at those very periods.

the judgment of his enemies he beholds a type of that of the heathen who oppose the kingdom of God and its King (comp. for example, Ps. lvi. 7 ; vii. 9 ; lix. 5) ; thus showing that David himself must have had some spiritual understanding of the prophetic bearing of his history.

And now David was once more a fugitive—the twofold lesson which he might have learned being, that it needed no subterfuges to ensure his safety, and that his calling for the present was within, not outside the land of Israel. A comparatively short distance—about ten miles—from Gath runs " the valley of the terebinth," the scene of David's great combat with Goliath. The low hills south of this valley are literally burrowed by caves, some of them of very large dimensions. Here lay the ancient city of Adullam (Gen. xxxviii. 1 ; Josh. xii. 15 ; xv. 35, and many other passages), which has, with much probability, been identified with the modern Aid el Mia (Adlem). In the largest of the caves close by, David sought a hiding-place. What his feelings were either at that time, or later, in similar circumstances (1 Sam. xxiv.), we learn from Ps. lvii.

It has been well observed,[1] that hitherto David had always remained within easy distance of Bethlehem. This would secure him not only the means of information as to Saul's movements, but also of easy communication with his own family, and with those who would naturally sympathise with him. Adullam was only a few hours distant from Bethlehem, and David's family, who no longer felt themselves safe in their home, soon joined him in his new refuge. But not only they. Many there must have been in the troublous times of Saul's reign who were " in distress," oppressed and persecuted ; many who under such misgovernment would fall "into debt" to unmerciful and violent exactors ; many also, who, utterly

[1] See Lieutenant Conder's very interesting paper on *The Scenery of David's Outlaw Life*, in the Quarterly Report of the Palestine Exploration Fund, for Jan. 1875, p. 42. I regret, however, that in reference to this, as to other papers of the same kind, I have to dissent from not a few of the exegetical reasonings and inferences.

dissatisfied with the present state of things, would, in the expressive language of the sacred text, "be bitter of soul." Of these the more active and ardent now gathered around David, first to the number of about four hundred, which soon increased to six hundred (xxiii. 13). They were not a band in rebellion against Saul. This would not only have been utterly contrary to David's constantly avowed allegiance and oft proved loyalty to Saul, but to the higher purpose of God. The latter, if we may venture to judge, seems to have been spiritually to fit David for his calling, by teaching him constant dependence on God, and by also outwardly training him and his followers for the battles of the Lord—not against Saul, but against Israel's great enemy, the Philistines ; in short, to take up the work which the all-absorbing murderous passion of Saul, as well as his desertion by God, prevented him from doing. Thus we see once more how, in the Providence of God, the inward and the outward training of David were the result of circumstances over which he had no control, and which seemed to threaten consequences of an entirely different character. How in those times of persecution outlaws became heroes, and of what deeds of personal bravery they were capable in the wars of the Lord, we learn from the record of their names (1 Chron. xii.), and of some of their achievements (2 Sam. xxiii. 13, etc. ; comp. 1 Chron. xi. 15, etc.).

But there were among them those nearest and dearest to David, his own aged father and mother, whose presence could only impede the movements of his followers, and whose safety he must secure. Besides, as such a band could not long escape Saul's notice, it seemed desirable to find a better retreat than the caves about Adullam. For this twofold object David and his followers now passed to the other side of Jordan. From the account of the war between Saul and Moab in 1 Sam. xiv. 47, we infer that the latter had advanced beyond their own territory across the border, and were now occupying the southern part of the trans-Jordanic country which belonged to Israel. This was within easy reach of Bethlehem. Accordingly David

now went to Mizpeh Moab, the " outlook," mountain-height or
"Tor" (as we might call it) of Moab, probably over against
Jericho in the "Arboth of Moab" (Numb. xxii. 1 ; Deut. xxxiv.
1, 8 ; Josh. xiii. 32), perhaps, as the name seems to indicate,
on the fields of the Zophim (or outlookers), on the top of Pisgah
(Numb. xxiii. 14 [1]). To the king of Moab, whose protection
he could invoke in virtue of their descent from Ruth the
Moabitess, he commended his father and mother, with the
expressive remark, till he should know "what Elohim [2] would
do" unto him. He himself and his followers meantime entrenched on that "mountain-height," [3] associated with the
prophecy there delivered by Balaam concerning Israel's future.

It was impossible that such a movement on the part of
David could long remain unknown. In two quarters it excited
deep feelings, though of a very different character. It seems
highly probable that the tidings reached the Naioth, and that
it was from thence that Gad (afterwards David's "seer"
and spiritual adviser, 2 Sam. xxiv. 11–19 ; 1 Chron. xxi. 9,
and the chronicler of his reign, 1 Chron. xxix. 29) went to
David by Divine commission.[4] But the stay in the land of
Moab was not in accordance with the purpose of God. David
must not flee from the discipline of suffering, and God had
some special work for him in the land of Israel which Saul
could no longer do. In accordance with this direction, David
left his entrenched position, recrossed the Jordan, and sought
shelter in "the forest of Hareth,"[5] within the boundaries of

[1] See Vol. II. of this History, p. 199.

[2] It is significant that David speaks to the king of Moab of *Elohim*, not
of Jehovah.

[3] This is the meaning of what is rendered in our Authorised Version "in
the hold" (xxii. 4). We infer that this entrenched mountain-height was
Mizpeh of Moab.

[4] Of course, this is only our *inference*, but it seems in accordance with
the whole narrative. It is impossible to say whether Gad was sent by
Samuel, or had received the message from God directly.

[5] Lieutenant Conder proposes to follow the LXX., and by a slight change
of the letters, to read "the city of Hareth." But such a city is not otherwise
known, nor would David's unmolested stay there agree with the after history.

Judah. But meantime Saul also had heard that "David had become known, and the men that were with him" (xxii. 6). Being aware of his position, he would secure his prey.

A royal court is held at Gibeah. The king sits, as so often before, "under the tamarisk-tree on the height," his spear as sceptre in his hand, and surrounded by all his officers of state, among them Doeg, the "chief of the herdsmen." Characteristic-ally Saul seems now to have surrounded himself exclusively by "Benjamites," either because no others would serve him, or more probably because he no longer trusted any but his own clansmen. Still more characteristic is the mode in which he appeals to their loyalty and seeks to enlist their aid. He seems to recognise no motive on the part of others but that of the most sordid selfishness. Probably some of the words that had passed between Jonathan and David, when they made their covenant of friendship (xx. 42), had been overheard, and re-peated to Saul in a garbled form by one of his many spies. That was enough. As he put it, his son had made a league with David, of which the only object could be to deprive him of his throne. This could only be accomplished by violence. Everyone was aware that David and his men then held a strong position. A conspiracy so fully organised must have been known to his courtiers. If they had no sympathy with a father betrayed by his own son, at least what profit could they as Benjamites hope to derive from such a plot? It was to defend the courtiers from guilty knowledge of such a plot that Doeg now reported what he had seen and heard at Nob. David's was a conspiracy indeed, but one hatched not by the laity but by the priesthood; and of which, as he had had personal evidence, the high-priest himself was the chief abettor.

The suggestion was one which would only too readily approve itself to a mind and conscience like Saul's. There could be nothing in common between Saul and the ministers of that God Who by His prophet had announced his rejection and appointed his successor. A priestly plot against himself, and in favour of David, had every appearance of likelihood. It is only when we thus understand the real import of Doeg's account to the king, that we perceive the extent of his crime, and the meaning of the language in which David characterised it in Ps. lii. A man of that kind was not likely to shrink from any deed. Saul summoned Ahimelech and all his father's house to his presence. In answer to the charge of conspiracy, the priest protested his innocence in language the truth of which could not have been mistaken by any impartial judge.[1] But the case had been decided against the priesthood before it was heard. Yet, callous as Saul's men-at-arms were, not one of them would execute the sentence of death against the priests of Jehovah. It was left to the Edomite to carry out what his reckless malice had instigated. That day no fewer than eighty-five of the priests in actual ministry were murdered in cold blood. Not content with this, the king had "the ban" executed upon Nob. As if the priest-city had been guilty of idolatry and rebellion against Jehovah (Deut. xiii. 15), every living being, both man and beast, was cut down by the sword. Only one escaped the horrible slaughter of that day. Abiathar, the son of Ahimelech,[2] had probably received timely warning. He now fled to David, to whom he reported what had taken place. From him he received such assurance of protection as only one could give who in his strong faith felt absolute safety in the shelter of Jehovah's wings. But here also the attentive reader will trace a typical parallel between the murder at Nob and that of the children at Bethlehem—all the more striking, that in the latter case also an Edomite was the guilty party, Herod the king having been by descent an Idumæan.

When Abiathar reached David, he was already on his way from the forest of Hareth to Keilah.[3] Tidings had come to

[1] Ver. 14 reads thus: "And who among all thy servants is approved like David, and son-in-law to the king, and having access to thy private audience, and honoured in all thy house?"

[2] He may have remained behind in Nob to attend to the Sanctuary during the absence of the other priests.

[3] As from the expression, "enquired of Jehovah" (xxiii. 2, 4), it is evident that the enquiry was made by the Urim and Thummim, we must conclude

David of a Philistine raid against Keilah, close on the border —the modern Kilah, about six miles to the south-east of Adullam. Keilah was a walled city, and therefore not itself in immediate danger. But there was plenty of plunder to be obtained outside its walls ; and henceforth no threshing-floor on the heights above the city was safe from the Philistines. Here was a call for the proper employment of a band like David's. But his followers had not yet learned the lessons of trust which he had been taught. Although the expedition for the relief of Keilah had been undertaken after "enquiry," and by direction of the Lord, his men shrank from provoking an attack by the Philistines at the same time that they were in constant apprehension of what might happen if Saul overtook them. So little did they as yet understand either the source of their safety or the object of their gathering ! What happened—as we note once more in the course of ordinary events—was best calculated to teach them all this. A second formal enquiry of the Lord by the Urim and Thummim, and a second direction to go forward, brought them to the relief of the city. The Philistines were driven back with great slaughter, and rich booty was made of their cattle.

But soon the danger which David's men had apprehended seemed really at hand. When Saul heard that David had "shut himself in by coming into a town with gates and bars," it seemed to him almost as if judicial blindness had fallen upon him, or, as the king put it : "Elohim has rejected him into my hand." So thinking, Saul rapidly gathered a force to march against Keilah. But, as we learn from the course of this narrative, each side was kept well informed of the movements and plans of the other. Accordingly David knew his danger, and

---

that Abiathar had reached David either after he had been preparing his expedition to Keilah, or more probably on his way thither. But, in general, it seems to me that the language in xxiii. 6 must not be too closely pressed. The enquiry mentioned in ver. 4 must have taken place on the road to Keilah, probably near to it, and ver. 6 is manifestly intended only to explain the mode of David's enquiry.

in his extremity once more appealed to the Lord. It was not
a needless question which he put through the Urim and
Thummim,[1] but one which was connected with God's faithfulness and the truth of His promises. With reverence be it said,
God could not have given up David into the hands of Saul.
Nor did his enquiries of God resemble those by heathen oracles.
Their main element seems to have been prayer. In most earnest
language David spread his case before the Lord, and entreated
His direction. The answer was not withheld, although, significantly, each question had specially and by itself to be brought
before the Lord (xxiii. 11, 12).

Thus informed of their danger, David and his men escaped
from Keilah, henceforth to wander from one hiding-place to
another. No other district could offer such facilities for eluding
pursuit as that large tract, stretching along the territory of
Judah, between the Dead Sea and the mountains of Judah.
It bore the general designation of "the wilderness of Judah,"
but its various parts were distinguished as "the wilderness of
Ziph," "of Maon," etc., from the names of neighbouring towns.
In general it may be said of this period of his wanderings
(ver. 14), that during its course David's head-quarters were on
"mountain heights,"[2] whence he could easily observe the approach of an enemy, while "Saul sought him every day," but
in vain, since "God gave him not into his hand."

The first station in these wanderings was the "wilderness of
Ziph," on the outskirts of the town of that name, about an
hour and three-quarters to the south-east of Hebron. South
of it a solitary mountain-top rises about one hundred feet,
commanding a full prospect of the surrounding country. On
the other hand, anything that passed there could also easily
be observed from below. It seems that this was "the mountain" (ver. 14), or, as it is afterwards (ver. 19) more particularly

---

[1] This is implied in David's direction to Abiathar: "Bring hither the
ephod" (xxiii. 9).

[2] This is the correct rendering, and not "in strongholds," as in the
Authorised Version.

described, "the hill of Hachilah, on the south of the wilderness,"[1] where David had his principal station, or rather, to be more accurate, in "the thicket," or "brushwood,"[2] which covered its sides (vers. 15, 16). It was thither that in the very height of these first persecutions, Jonathan came once more to see his friend, and, as the sacred text emphatically puts it, "strengthened his hand in God." It is difficult to form an adequate conception of the courage, the spiritual faith, and the moral grandeur of this act. Never did man more completely clear himself from all complicity in guilt, than Jonathan from that of his father. And yet not an undutiful word escaped the lips of this brave man. And how truly human is his fond hope that in days to come, when David would be king, he should stand next to his throne, his trusted adviser, as in the days of sorrow he had been the true and steadfast friend of the outlaw! As we think of what it must have cost Jonathan to speak thus, or again of the sad fate which was so soon to overtake him, there is a deep pathos about this brief interview, almost unequalled in Holy Scripture, to which the ambitious hopes of the sons of Zebedee form not a parallel but a contrast.

But yet another bitter experience had David to make. As so often in the history of the Church, and never more markedly than in the case of Him Who was the great Antitype of David, it appeared that those who should most have rallied around him were his enemies and betrayers. The "citizens"[3] of

---

[1] Not, as in the Authorised Version, "on the south of Jeshimon" (ver. 19), where the word is left untranslated.

[2] Lieutenant Conder labours to show that there never could have been "a wood" in Ziph. But the text does not call it a *yaar*, "wood" or "forest," but a *choresh*, which conveys the idea of a thicket of brushwood. Our view is fully borne out by the portraiture of a scene exactly similar to that on Hachilah in Isa. xvii. 9: "In that day shall his strong cities be like the forsakenness of the thicket (*choresh*) and of the mountain-top." In the Jer. Targum to Gen. xxii. 13 the term is applied to the thicket in which the ram was caught.

[3] There is a difference between the "inhabitants" of Keilah (xxiii. 5), and the "citizens," burghers, "lords of Keilah" (the *Baalé Keilah*), ver. 12, who were ready to sell David for their own advantage.

Keilah would have given him up from fear of Saul. But the men of Ziph went further. Like those who hypocritically pretended that they would have no other king but Cæsar, they feigned a loyalty for which it is impossible to give them credit. Of their own accord, and evidently from hatred of David, they who were his own tribesmen betrayed his hiding-place to Saul, and offered to assist in his capture. It is pitiable to hear Saul in the madness of his passion invoking on such men "the blessing of Jehovah," and characterising their deed as one of "compassion" on himself (xxiii. 21). But the danger which now threatened David was greater than any previously or afterwards. On learning it he marched still further south-east, where "the Jeshimon," or desert, shelves down into the Arabah, or low table-land.[1] Maon itself is about two hours south-east from Ziph; and amidst the mountains between Maon and the Dead Sea on the west, we must follow the track of David's further flight and adventures.

But meantime the plan which Saul had suggested was being only too faithfully carried out. Slowly and surely the men of Saul, guided by the Ziphites, were reaching David, and drawing the net around him closer and closer. Informed of his danger, David hastily "came down the rock,"[2]—perhaps the round mountain-top near Maon. It was high time, for already Saul and his men had reached and occupied one side of it, while David and his men retreated to the other. The object of the king now was to surround David, when he must have succumbed to superior numbers. We are told that "David was anxiously endeavouring to go away from before Saul; and Saul and his men were surrounding David and his men to seize them."[3] *Almost* had they succeeded—but that "almost," which as so often in the history of God's people, calls out earnest faith

---

[1] In our Authorised Version (xxiii. 24): "the plain on the south of Jeshimon."

[2] Our Authorised Version has erroneously (ver. 25), "he came down into a rock."

[3] Such is the correct rendering of the second half of ver. 26.

and prayer, only proves the real impotence of this world's might as against the Lord. How David in this danger cried unto the Lord, we learn from Ps. liv.[1] How God "delivered him out of all trouble," appears from the sacred narrative. Once more all is in the natural succession of events ; but surely it was in the wonder-working Providence of God that, just when David seemed in the power of his enemies, tidings of an incursion by the Philistines reached Saul, which obliged him hastily to turn against them. And ever afterwards, as David or others passed through that "wilderness," and looked up the face of that cliff, they would remember that God is " the Helper" of His people— for to all time it bore the name " Cliff of Escape." And so we also may in our wanderings have our " cliff of escape," to which ever afterwards we attach this precious remembrance, "Behold, God is thine Helper."

━•❦•━

CHAPTER XIII.

Saul in David's power at En-gedi—The Story of Nabal—Saul a second time in David's power.

(I SAM. XXIV.—XXVI.)

WHEN Saul once more turned upon his victim, David was no longer in the wilderness of Maon. Passing to the north-west, a march of six or seven hours would bring him to En-gedi, " the fountain of the goat," which, leaping down a considerable height in a thin cascade, converts that desert into the most lovely oasis. In this plain, or rather slope, about one mile and a half from north to south, at the foot of abrupt limestone mountains, sheltered from every

---

[1] We suppose that Psa. liv. refers to this rather than to the second betrayal by the Ziphites, recorded in I Sam. xxvi.

storm, in climate the most glorious conceivable, the city of En-gedi had stood, or, as it used to be called, Hazazon Tamar (the Cutting of the Palm-trees), perhaps the oldest place in the world (2 Chron. xx. 2). Through this town (Gen. xiv. 7) the hordes of Chedorlaomer had passed; unchanged it had witnessed the destruction of Sodom and Gomorrah, which must have been clearly visible from the heights above, where the eye can sweep the whole district far up the Jordan valley, and across the Dead Sea to the mountains of Moab. Quite close to the waters of that sea, on which the doom of judgment has ever since rested, a scene of tropical beauty and wealth stretched, such as it is scarcely possible to describe. Bounded by two perennial streams, between which the En-gedi itself makes its way, it must of old have been a little paradise; the plain covered with palm-trees, the slopes up the mountains with the choicest vineyards of Judæa, scented with camphire (Sol. Song i. 14). But all above was "wilderness," bare round limestone hills rising from two hundred to four hundred feet, burrowed by numberless caves, to which the entrance is sometimes almost inaccessible. These were "the rocks of the wild goats," and here was the cave—perhaps that of Wady Charitun, which is said to have once given shelter to no less than thirty thousand men—where David sought safety from the pursuit of the king of Israel.

Wild, weird scenery this, and it reads like a weird story, when the king of Israel enters alone one of those caverns, the very cave in the farthest recesses of which David and his men are hiding. Shall it be life or death? The goal is within easy reach! They have all seen Saul coming, and now whisper it to David with bated breath, to rid himself for ever of his persecutor. The mixture of religion and personal revenge —the presenting it as "the day of which Jehovah had spoken unto him," is entirely true to Oriental nature and to the circumstances. Who would let such an opportunity pass? But it is not by our own hands that we are to be freed from our wrongs, nor is every opportunity to attain our aims, whatever they be, God-sent. There is ever the prior question of plain duty, with which nothing else, however tempting or promising of success, can come into conflict; and such seasons may be only those when our faith and patience are put on trial, so as to bring it clearly before us, whether or not, quite irrespective of all else, we are content to leave everything in the hands of God. And David conquered, as long afterwards his great Antitype overcame the tempter, by steadfast adherence to God's known will and ordinance. Stealthily crawling along, he cut off a corner from the robe which the king had laid aside. That was all the vengeance he took.

It was with some difficulty that David had restrained his men. And now the king had left the cave to rejoin his followers. But still David's conscience smote him, as if he had taken undue liberty with the Lord's anointed. Climbing one of those rocks outside the cave, whence flight would have been easy, his voice startled the king. Looking back into the wild solitude, Saul saw behind him the man who, as his disordered passion had suggested, was seeking his life. With humblest obeisance and in most dutiful language, David told what had just happened. In sharp contrast with the calumnies of his enemies, he described the king's danger, and how he had cast from him the suggestion of his murder. Then bursting into the impassioned language of loyal affection, which had been so cruelly wronged, he held up the piece of the king's mantle which he had cut off, as evidence of the fact that he was innocent of that of which he was accused. But if so—if he had refused to avenge himself even in the hour of his own great danger, leaving judgment to God, and unwilling to put forth his own hand to wickedness, since, as the common proverb had it, "wickedness proceedeth from the wicked"—then, what was the meaning of the king's humiliating pursuit after him? Rather would he, in the conscious innocence of his heart, now appeal to Jehovah, alike for judgment between them two, and for personal deliverance, should these persecutions continue.

Words like these, of which the truth was so evident, could not but make their way even to the heart of Saul. For a moment it seemed as if the dark clouds, which had gathered around his soul and prevented the light penetrating it, were to be scattered. Saul owned his wrong; he owned the justice of David's cause; he even owned the lesson which the events of the past must have so clearly taught, which, indeed, his own persecution of David had, all unconsciously to himself, prophetically indicated, just as did the words of Caiaphas the real meaning of what was done to Jesus (John xi. 49–52). He owned the future of David, and that in his hand the kingdom of Israel would be established; and all this not in words only, but practically, by insisting on a sworn promise that in that future which he foresaw, Oriental vengeance would not be taken of his house.

And yet David himself was not secure against the temptation to personal vengeance and to self-help, although he had resisted it on this occasion. The lesson of his own weakness in that respect was all the more needed, that this was one of the most obvious moral dangers to an ordinary Oriental ruler. But David was not to be such ; and when God in His good Providence restrained him as he had almost fallen, He showed him the need of inward as well as of outward deliverance, and the sufficiency of His grace to preserve him from spiritual as from temporal dangers. This may have been one reason why the history of Nabal and Abigail is preserved in Holy Scripture. Another we may find in the circumstance that this incident illustrates not only God's dealings with David, but also the fact that even in the time of his sorest persecutions David was able to take upon himself the care and protection of his countrymen, and so, in a certain sense, proved their leader and king.

The whole story is so true to all the surroundings of place, time, and people, that we can almost portray it to ourselves. Samuel had died, mourned by all Israel. Although his work had long been finished, his name must always have been a tower of strength. He was the link which connected two very different periods, being the last representative of a past which could never come back, and seemed almost centuries behind, and also marking the commencement of a new period, intended to develop into Israel's ideal future. Samuel was, so to speak, the John the Baptist who embodied the old, and initiated the new by preaching repentance as its preparation and foundation. It was probably the death of Samuel which determined David to withdraw still farther south, to the wilderness of Paran,[1] which stretched from the mountains of Judah far to the desert of Sinai. Similarly our blessed Lord withdrew Himself after the death of John the Baptist. In the wilderness of Paran David was not only safe from pursuit, but able to be of real service to his countrymen by protecting the large flocks which pastured far and wide from the predatory raids of the wild tribes of the desert. It was thus (xxv. 7, 15, 16) that David had come into contact with one whom we only know by what was apparently his by-name, Nabal, "fool"—an ominous designation in Old Testament parlance, where "the fool" represented the headstrong, self-willed person, who followed his own course, as if there were "no God" alike in heaven and on earth. And so he is described as "hard"—stubborn, stiff,—and "evil of doings" (ver. 3). His wife Abigail was the very opposite: "good of understanding, and fair of form." Nabal, as Scripture significantly always calls him, was a descendant of Caleb. His residence was in Maon, while his "business" was in Carmel, a place about half an hour to the north-west of Maon. Here, no doubt, were his large cotes and folds, whence his immense flocks of sheep and goats pastured the land far and wide. It was the most joyous time for such a proprietor—that of sheep-shearing, when every heart would be open. A time of festivity this (ver. 36), which each would keep according to what was in him. And Nabal had cause for gladness. Thanks to the

[1] The LXX., as it seems to us needlessly, alter the text by making it the wilderness of Maon.

ever watchful care of David and his men, he had not suffered the slightest loss (vers. 15, 16); and the rich increase of his flocks crowned another year's prosperity. It was quite in the spirit of an Eastern chieftain in such circumstances, that David sent what would be a specially respectful embassy of ten of his men, with a cordial message of congratulation,[1] in the expectation that at such a time some acknowledgment would be made to those who not only deserved, but must have sorely needed the assistance of a rich Judæan proprietor. But Nabal received David's message with language the most insulting to an Oriental.

The provocation was great, and David was not proof against it. Arming about four hundred of his men, he set out for Carmel, with the determination to right himself and take signal vengeance. Assuredly this was not the lesson which God had hitherto made David learn, nor that which He wished His anointed to teach to others. It was the zeal of the sons of Boanerges, not the meekness of Him Who was David's great Antitype. And so God kept His servant from presumptuous sin.[2] Once more God's interposition came in the natural course of events. A servant who had overheard what had passed, and naturally dreaded the consequences, informed Abigail. Her own resolve was quickly taken. Sending forward a present princely in amount,[3] even in comparison with that which at a later period Barzillai brought to King David when on his flight from Absalom (2 Sam. xvii. 27–29), she hastily followed. Coming down the hollow of a hill ("the covert of a hill"), she found herself of a sudden in the presence of David and his armed men. But her courage was not shaken.

---

[1] Ver. 6, which is somewhat difficult, should, I think, be thus rendered: "And ye shall say thus: To life! Both to thee peace, to thy house peace, and to all that is thine peace!"

[2] Although guilty of a rash imprecation (ver. 22), it was at least not upon himself.

[3] The "bottles" were, of course, "skins of wine;" "the clusters" and "cakes" of fruit were large compressed cakes, such as are common in the East.

With humblest Oriental obeisance, she addressed David, first taking all the guilt on herself, as one on whom David would not stoop to wreak vengeance. Surely one like Nabal was not a fit object for controversy ; and, as for herself, she had known nothing of what had passed.

But there were far weightier arguments for David's forbearance. Was it not evidently God's Providence which had sent her for a high and holy purpose? "And now, my lord, as Jehovah liveth, and as thy soul liveth, that (it is) Jehovah who has withheld thee from coming into blood-guiltiness, and from thy hand delivering thyself." This twofold sin had been averted. Such was her first argument. But further, was it not well to leave it to God—would not Jehovah Himself avenge His servant, and make all his enemies as Nabal—showing them to be but "Nabal," "fools" in the Scriptural sense, with all the impotence and ruin which this implied? It was only after having urged all this, that Abigail ventured to ask acceptance of her gift, offering it, as if unworthy of him, to David's men rather than to himself (ver. 27). Then returning to the prayer for forgiveness, she pointed David to the bright future which, she felt assured, was reserved for him, since he was not pursuing *private* aims, nor would he afterwards charge himself with any wrong in this matter. How closely all this tallied with her former pleas will be evident. In pursuance of her reasoning she continued : "And (though) a man is risen to pursue thee, and to seek thy soul, and (yet) the soul of my lord is bound up in the bundle of life with Jehovah thy God ; and the soul of thine enemies shall He sling out from the hollow of the sling." Finally, she reminded him that when God had fulfilled all His gracious promises, this would not become a "stumbling-block" to him, nor yet be a burden on his conscience, that he had needlessly shed blood and righted himself.

Wiser speech, in the highest as well as in a worldly sense, than that of Abigail can scarcely be imagined. Surely if any one, she was fitted to become the companion and adviser of

David.   Three things in her speech chiefly impress themselves on our minds as most important for the understanding
of this history.   The fact that David was God's anointed,
on whom the kingdom would devolve, seems now to have
been the conviction of all who were godly in Israel.   They
knew it, and they expected it.   Equally strong was their
belief that David's present, as his future mission, was simply to
contend for God and for His people.   But most important of
all was the deep feeling prevalent, that David must not try
to right himself, nor work his own deliverance.   This was a
thoroughly spiritual principle, which had its foundation in absolute, almost childlike trust in Jehovah the living God, whatever
might were arrayed against David, and however the probabilities
might seem other to the outward observer.   Viewed in this
light, the whole contest between David and Saul would assume
spiritual proportions.   There was nothing personal now in the
conflict; least of all, was it to be regarded as an attempt at
rebellion against, or dethronement of Saul.   The cause was
altogether God's; only David must not right himself, but in
faith and patience await the fulfilment of God's sure and steadfast promises.   To have the matter thus set before him, was
to secure the immediate assent of David's conscience.   Recognising the great spiritual danger from which he had just been
delivered, he gave thanks to God, and then to the wise and
pious woman who had been the instrument in His hand.

Meantime Nabal had been in ignorance alike of what had
threatened him, and of what his wife had done to avert it.
On her return, she found him rioting and in drunkenness.
Not till next morning, when he was once more capable of
understanding what had passed, did she inform him of all.   A
fit of impotent fury on the part of one who was scarcely sobered,
resulted in what seems to have been a stroke of apoplexy.
If this had been brought on by himself, the second and
fatal stroke, which followed ten days later, is set before us as
sent directly by God.   It is not often that Divine vengeance
so manifestly and so quickly overtakes evil-doing.   David

fully recognised this. Nor can we wonder, that on reviewing his own deliverance from spiritual danger, and the advice which had led to it, he should have wished to have her who had given it always by his side. In connection with this the sacred text also notes the union of David with Ahinoam of Jezreel,[1] consequent probably on Saul's cruel and heartless separation between David and Michal, whom he gave to one Phalti, or Phaltiel (2 Sam. iii. 15) of Gallim in Benjamin (Isa. x. 30). Thus Saul himself had wilfully and recklessly severed the last ties which had bound David to him.

Yet another bitter experience of betrayal and persecution was in store for David. Probably trusting to his new connection with two, no doubt, powerful families in the district—those of Ahinoam and of Abigail — David seems again to have advanced northwards from the wilderness of Paran. Once more we find David in the wilderness of Ziph—the most northern and the nearest to the cities of Judah. And once more the Ziphites were negociating with Saul for his betrayal, and the king of Israel was marching against him with the three thousand men, who apparently formed the nucleus of his standing army.[2] Some years before, when betrayed by the Ziphites, David had on the approach of Saul retired to the wilderness of Maon, and been only preserved by tidings to Saul of a Philistine incursion. On yet another somewhat similar occasion, in the wilderness of En-gedi, David had had his enemy in his power, when Saul had entered alone a cave in which David and his men lay concealed. In this instance, however, the circumstances were different, alike as concerned the situation of Saul's camp, the location of David, the manner in which he came into contact with Saul, and even the communication

---

[1] This Jezreel is, of course, not the place of that name in the north (Josh. xix. 18), but a town in Judah near Carmel (Josh. xv. 56).

[2] Such a nucleus seems implied in 1 Sam. xiii. 2, where we have the same number, constituting apparently Saul's standing army. From our remarks it will be seen that we entirely repudiate the rash assertion that this is only another account of what had been related in 1 Sam. xxiii. 19–xxiv. 22.

which subsequently passed between them. The points of resemblance are just those which might have been expected: the treachery of the Ziphites, the means taken by Saul against David, the suggestion made to David to rid himself of his enemy, his firm resolve not to touch the Lord's anointed, as well as an interview between David and his persecutor, followed by temporary repentance. But the two narratives are essentially different. On learning that Saul and his army were encamped on the slope of the hill Hachilah, David and two of his bravest companions—Ahimelech, the Hittite, and Abishai, the son of Zeruiah, David's sister—resolved to ascertain the exact situation of the enemy. Creeping under cover of night through the brushwood, which as we know covered the sides of the hill (xxiii. 19), they found themselves soon where the camp of Israel lay open to them. As we imagine the scene, the three had gained the height just above the camp. Faithful as was the Hittite, and none more true or brave than he (comp. 2 Sam. xi. 3, 6; xxiii. 39), it was David's nephew Abishai, probably of the same age, who now volunteered to share with him the extremely perilous attempt of "going down" into the camp itself. But there was no murderous intent in the heart of David; rather the opposite, of proving his innocence of it. And so God blessed it. A deep sleep—evidently from the Lord—weighed them all down. In the middle, by the " waggons " of the camp, lay Saul, at his head the royal spear stuck in the ground, and a cruse of water beside him. Close by lay Abner, as chief of the host, to whom, so to speak, the custody of the king was entrusted—and all round in wide circle, the people. Once more comes the tempting suggestion to David. This time it is not his own hand, but Abishai's, that is to deal the blow. But what matters it: " For who has stretched out his hand against the anointed of Jehovah, and been unpunished? If Jehovah do not (literally, 'unless Jehovah') smite him [like Nabal], or his day be come and he die, or he go down into the war and be swept away—far be it from me, through Jehovah !—to stretch forth mine hand

against Jehovah's anointed."[1] And so David stayed the hand
of his companion.

Noiselessly the two have removed the royal spear and the
cruse from the side of Saul. They have crept back through the
camp of sleepers, and through the brushwood, crossed the
intervening valley, and gained a far-off height on the other
side. Who dares break the king's slumber in the middle of
his camp? But another ear than Abner's has heard, and
has recognised the voice of David. It has gone right to the
heart of Saul, as he learns how once more his life had been
wholly in the power of him whom he has so unrelentingly and so
wickedly persecuted. Again he seems repentant, though he
heeds not David's advice that, if these constant persecutions were
the effect produced on his mind by the spirit of evil from the
Lord, he should seek pardon and help by means of sacrifice ;
but if the outcome of calumnious reports, those who brought
them should be regarded as sure of the Divine judgment,
since, as he put it, "They drive me out this day, that I
cannot join myself to the heritage of Jehovah, saying (thereby
in effect) : Go, serve other gods" (xxvi. 19). It is useless to
follow the matter farther. Saul's proposal for David's return,
and his promise of safety, were, no doubt, honestly meant at
the time, just as are the sorrow and resolutions of many into
whose consciences the light has for a time fallen. But David
knew otherwise of Saul ; and it marks an advance in his spiritual
experience that he preferred committing himself to God rather
than trusting in man.

[1] We have translated as literally as possible. David considers that the
guilt would have been equally his, although the deed had been done by
Abishai.

CHAPTER XIV.

David's Second Flight to Gath—Residence at Ziklag—Expedition of the Philistines against Israel—Saul at Jezreel—He resorts to the Witch at Endor—Apparition and Message of Samuel—David has to leave the Army of the Philistines—Capture of Ziklag by the Amalekites— Pursuit and Victory of David.

(1 SAM. XXVII.—XXX.)

THE parting appeal of David sounds specially solemn when we remember that this was the last meeting of these two. Feeling that some day he might "fall into the hand of Saul,"[1] and that henceforth there was "no good for him,"[1] he resolved once more to seek shelter with King Achish at Gath. His reception this time was very different from that on the former occasion. For years David had been treated by Saul as his avowed enemy. He came now not as a solitary fugitive, but at the head of a well-trained band of brave men, to place himself and them, as it would seem, at the disposal of Achish. He met a most friendly welcome, and for a time was located with his men in the royal city itself. This, of course, entailed restraints such as would have proved most irksome, if not impossible, to David. The pretext that the presence of such a large band under their own chieftain was scarcely becoming in the capital of his new royal master, furnished the plea for asking and obtaining another place of residence. For this purpose Ziklag was assigned to him— a city first belonging to Judah (Josh. xv. 31), and afterwards to Simeon (Josh. xix. 5), which lay close to the southern border of the land of Israel. Of course, the inference is fair that, at the time of which we write, it had been in the possession of the

---

[1] So literally (xxvii. 1).

Philistines, and was probably deserted by its former inhabitants. No other place could have suited David so well. Whether we regard his raids against the heathen tribes, which was "his manner" during the whole year and four months that he was with the Philistines, as intended to repel their inroads into the territory of Israel, or else as incursions into heathen lands, the situation of Ziklag would afford him equal facilities. On every such occasion, as he returned laden with spoil, he took care to report himself at Gath, partly to disarm suspicion,[1] and partly, no doubt, to secure the good will of Achish by giving him a large share of the booty. His reports may have been true to the letter—giving it a forced meaning,—but they were certainly untrue in spirit. But David never brought captives with him to Gath,[2] who might have betrayed him, but always destroyed all who had witnessed his attacks.

If by means of these reported frequent successes in the land of Israel David secured the confidence of Achish, as one who had irretrievably broken with his own people, and if by the rich booty which he brought he besides obtained the favour of the Philistine, he was once more to experience that real safety was not to be gained by untruthfulness. Again there was to be war between the Philistines and Israel, this time on a larger scale than any since the first contest with Saul. It was but natural that Achish should have wished to swell his contingent to the army of the united Philistine princes by so large, well-trained, and, as he believed, trusty band as that of David. Of course, there was no alternative but to obey such a summons, although it must be admitted that the words of David, both on this occasion (xxviii. 2), and afterwards, when dismissed the camp of the Philistines (xxix. 8), are capable of

---

[1] The words of the question in xxvii. 10 are so dark in the original as to need slight alteration. The rendering of the LXX., "Against whom made ye invasion?" is evidently the correct reading of the text.

[2] The Authorised Version supplies erroneously in ver. 11 "to bring *tidings*"—the reference is clearly to captives. The last clause of ver. 11 is a substantive sentence, being part of the narrative, and not of what the captives had said.

two interpretations.   Achish, however, took them in what seemed their obvious meaning, and promised in return ("therefore"—for that) to make David the chief of his body-guard. It need scarcely be told, what terrible anxieties this unexpected turn of events must have brought to David, or how earnestly he must have prayed and trusted that, at the right moment, some "way of escape" would be made for him.

The sacred narrative now carries us successively to the camp of Israel and to that of the Philistines.   The battle-field was to be once more the Plain of Jezreel, where of old Gideon with his three hundred had defeated the hosts of Midian (Judg. vii.).   A spot this full of happy, glorious memories; but, ah, how sadly altered were the circumstances! Gideon had been the God-called hero, who was to conquer in His might; Saul was the God-forsaken king, who was hastening to judgment and ruin.   And each knew and felt it— Gideon when he was content to reduce his forces to three hundred men, and then crept down with his armour-bearer to hear the enemy foretell his own destruction ; and Saul when viewing the host of the Philistines across the plain, "he was afraid, and his heart greatly trembled" (xxviii. 5), and when all his enquiries of the Lord remained without answer.   It seems strange, and yet, as we think, it is most truthfully characteristic of Saul, that, probably after the death of Samuel, he displayed special theocratic zeal by a systematic raid upon all necromancy in the land, in accordance with Lev. xix. 31 ; xx. 27 ; Deut. xviii. 10, etc.   Such outward conformity to the law of God, not only from political motives, but from those of such religiousness as he was capable of, seems to us one of the most striking psychological confirmations of the history of Saul.

The reason why the scene of battle was laid so far north, distant alike from the cities of the Philistine princes and from the residence of Saul, was, in all probability, that the Philistines now wished to obtain such undoubted supremacy in the north of Palestine as they seem to have virtually possessed in the south.

A great victory in Jezreel would not only cut the land, so to speak, in two, but give them the key both to the south and to the north. With this view, then, the Philistines chose their ground. Where the great plain of Esdraelon shelves down to the Jordan it is broken in the east by two mountain-ranges. On the southern side of the valley, which is here about three miles wide, are the mountains of Gilboa, and at their foot, or rather spur, lies Jezreel, where the spring which gushes down is gathered into a pool of considerable size. On the northern side of the valley is Little Hermon, and at its foot the rich village of Shunem (the "twain rest"). Behind and to the north of Little Hermon runs another narrow branch of the plain. On its other side is the mountain where Endor lay amidst most desolate scenery; and in one of its many lime-stone caves was the scene of Saul's last interview with Samuel. Nor is it void of significance to us that Endor was but a few miles from Nazareth; for it is the close contiguity of these contrasting scenes which often sheds such lurid light upon events.

From his camp on the slopes of Gilboa and by the spring of Jezreel, Saul had anxiously watched the gathering hosts of Philistia on the opposite side at Shunem, and his heart had utterly failed him. Where was now the Lord God of Israel? Certainly not with Saul. And where was there now a David to meet another Goliath? Saul had successively "enquired of Jehovah" by all the well-known means, from the less to the more spiritual,[1] but without answer. That alone

---

[1] We venture to regard the "dreams," the "Urim," and the "prophets," as marking progress from the lower to the higher modes of enquiry. In accordance with the principles implied when treating of the gatherings of the "prophets," it seems to us that the more passive the instrumentality employed, the lower the stage in the mode of Divine communication. What we have ventured to call the lower or more mechanical stages of communication were adapted to the varying stages of spiritual development. But the abso-lutely highest stage of intercourse with God is the indwelling of the Holy Ghost in the New Testament Church, when man's individuality is not super-seded nor suppressed, but transformed, and thus conformed to Him in spiritual fellowship.

should have been sufficient, had Saul possessed spiritual understanding to perceive its meaning. Had his been real enquiry
of *the Lord*,[1] he would have felt his desertion, and even now
returned to Him in humble penitence ; just as Judas, if his
repentance had been genuine and true, would have gone
out to seek pardon like Peter, instead of rushing in despair
to self-destruction. As the event proved, Saul did *not* really
enquire of the Lord, in the sense of seeking direction from
Him, and of being willing to be guided by it. Rather did
he, if we may so express it, wish to use the Lord as the
means by which to obtain his object. But that was essentially the heathen view, and differed only in detail, not in
principle, from the enquiry of a familiar spirit, to which he
afterwards resorted. Accordingly the latter must be regarded
as explaining his former " enquiry," and determining its character. In this sense the notice in 1 Chron. x. 14 affords a
true and spiritual insight into the transaction.

Already the utter darkness of despair had gathered around
Saul. He was condemned : he knew it, felt it, and his conscience assented to it. What was to happen on the morrow ?
To that question he must have an answer, be it what it may.
If he could not have it from God, he must get it somewhere
else. To whom should he turn in his extremity ? Only one
person, sufficiently powerful with God and man, occurred to
his mind. It was Samuel,—the very incarnation to him of
Divine power, the undoubted messenger of God, the one man
who had ever confronted and overawed him. It seems like
fate which drives him to the very man who had so sternly,
unrelentingly, and in the hour of his triumph, told him his
downfall. But how was he to meet Samuel ? By necromancy
—that is, by devilry ! The Divine through the anti-Divine,

---

[1] If it be asked how Saul could enquire by Urim, since Abiathar, and
with him "the Ephod," were with David, we reply that Saul had evidently
appointed Zadok successor to Abiathar (1 Chron. xvi. 39, comp. vi. 8,
53), and located the tabernacle at Gibeon. This explains the mention of
two high-priests in the early years of David's reign (comp. 2 Sam. viii. 17 ;
xv. 24, 29, 35 ; 1 Chron. xv. 11 ; xviii. 16).

communication from on high by means of witchcraft: terrible contrasts these—combined, alas! in the life of Saul, and strangely connecting its beginning with its ending. But no matter; if it be at all possible, he must see Samuel, however he had parted from him in life. Samuel had announced his elevation, let him now come to tell him his fate; he had pushed him to the brow of the hill, let him show what was beneath. And yet who could say what might happen, or to what that interview might lead? For deep down in the breast of each living there is still, even in his despairing, the possibility of hope.

It is the most vivid description in Holy Scripture, next to that of the night of Judas' betrayal. Putting on the disguise of a common man, and only attended by two companions, Saul starts at dark. It was eight miles round the eastern shoulder of Hermon to Endor. None in the camp of Israel must know whither and on what errand the king has gone; and he has to creep round the back of the position of the Philistines, who lie on the front slope of Hermon. Nor must "the woman, possessor of an *Ob*"—or spirit by which the dead can be conjured up (Lev. xx. 27)—know it, that he who enquires of her is the one who "hath cut off those that have familiar spirits and the wizards out of the land."

It was night when Saul and his companions wearily reached their destination. They have roused the wretched impostor, "the woman, possessor of an *Ob*," and quieted her fears by promise that her nefarious business should not be betrayed. To her utter horror it is for once truth. God has allowed Samuel to obey Saul's summons; and, to be unmistakeable, he appears, as he was wont in life, wrapped in his prophet's *meil*, or mantle. The woman sees the apparition,[1] and from her description Saul has no difficulty in recognising Samuel,

---

[1] 1 Sam. xxviii. 13: "I saw gods" (or rather, *Elohim*) "ascending out of the earth." The expression Elohim here refers not to a Divine, but simply to a supernatural appearance, indicating its *character* as not earthly. But in that supernatural light she has also recognised her visitor as the king of Israel. Verses 13 and 14 show that Saul had *not* himself seen the apparition. The question whether the vision of the woman was objective or

and he falls in lowly reverence on his face.   During the whole
interview between them the king remains on his knees.   What
a difference between the last meeting of the two and this !
But the old prophet has nothing to abate, nothing to alter.
There is inexpressible pathos in the king's cry of despair :
" Make known to me what I shall do !"   What he shall do !
But Samuel had all his life-time made it known to him, and
Saul had resisted.   The time for doing was now past.   In
quick succession it comes, like thunderbolt on thunderbolt :
" Jehovah thine enemy " ; "Jehovah hath rent the kingdom out
of thine hand, and given it to David " ; " thy sins have overtaken
thee !   All this Saul knew long ago, although he had never
realised it as now.   And then as to his fate : *to-morrow*—
defeat, death, slaughter, to Saul, to his sons, to Israel !

One by one, each stroke heavier than the other, they had
pitilessly fallen on the kneeling king, weary, faint from want of
food, and smitten to the heart with awe and terror ; and now
he falls heavily, his gigantic length, to the ground.   The woman
and Saul's companions had stood aside, nor had any heard
what had passed between the two.   But the noise of his
fall brought them to his side.   With difficulty they persuade
him to eat ere he starts on his weary return to Jezreel.   At
last he yields ; and, rising from his prostrate position, sits
down on the divan, while they wait on him.   But he has
no longer speech, or purpose, or thought.   As one driven to
the slaughter, he goes back to meet his doom.   It must have
been early morning when once more he reached Gilboa—the
morning of the dread and decisive battle.[1]

---

subjective, is really of no importance whatever.   Suffice that it was *real*, and
came to her *ab extra*.

[1] As will be seen, we regard the apparition of Samuel not as trickery by
the woman, but as real—nor yet as caused by the devil, but as allowed and
willed of God.   A full discussion of our reasons for this view would be
evidently out of place.   Of two things only will we remind the reader : the
story must not be explained on our modern Western ideas of the ecstatic,
somnambulistic, magnetic state (Erdmann), nor be judged according to the
standpoint which the Church has *now* reached.   It was *quite* in accordance
with the stage in which the kingdom of God was in the days of Saul.

The sacred narrative now turns once more to the Philistine host. The trysting-place for the contingents of the five allied "lords" or kings of the Philistines was at Aphek, probably the same as on a previous occasion (1 Sam. iv. 1).[1] As they marched past, the division of Achish formed "the rearward." When the Philistine leaders saw David and his men amongst them, they not unnaturally objected to their presence. In vain Achish urged their faithfulness since they had "fallen away" to him. As it appeared to them, one who had in the past taken such a stand as David could never be trusted; and how better could he make his peace with his master than by turning traitor to the Philistines in the hour of their supreme need? And so, however reluctantly, Achish had to yield. David's remonstrance, couched in ambiguous language, was perhaps scarcely such (1 Sam. xxix. 8), but rather intended to make sure of the real views of Achish in regard to him. But it must have been with the intense relief of a realised God-given deliverance, that early next morning, ere the camp was astir, David and his men quitted its outskirts, where the rear-guard lay, to return to Ziklag.

It was the third day when the Hebrews reached their Philistine home. But what a sight greeted them here! Broken walls, blackened ruins, and the desolateness of utter silence all around! The Amalekites had indeed taken vengeance for David's repeated raids upon them (xxvii. 8). They had made an incursion into the *Negeb*, or south country, and specially upon Ziklag. In the absence of its defenders, the place fell an easy prey. After laying it waste, the Amalekites took with them all the women and children, as well as the cattle, and any other booty on which they could lay hands. It was a

---

[1] Most writers suppose that this Aphek was close to Shunem, though the supposition by no means tallies with the narrative. There is, however, this insuperable objection to it, that as Shunem is between eighty and ninety miles from where Ziklag must be sought, David and his men could not possibly have reached the latter "on the third day."

terrible surprise, and the first effect upon David and his men was truly Oriental (xxx. 4).   But it is both characteristic of David's followers, and indicates with what reluctance they must have followed him to Aphek, that they actually thought of killing David, as if he had been the author of that ill-fated expedition after Achish which had brought them such hopeless misery.   It was bitter enough to have lost his own family, and now David was in danger of his life from the mutiny of his men.   Had God spared him for this?   On the very morning when they had broken up from Aphek, making almost forced marches to traverse the fifty miles to Ziklag, their homes had been utterly laid waste.   Why all this? Did the Lord make him tarry, as Jesus did "beyond Jordan," till Lazarus had been three days dead?   Never more than on occasion of extreme and seemingly hopeless straits did David prove the reality of his religion by rising to the loftiest heights of faith and prayer.   The text gives a marked emphasis to the contrast : "But David strengthened himself in Jehovah his God."   His resolve was quickly taken.   The first thing was to enquire of the Lord whether he should pursue the Amalekites.   The answer was even fuller than he had asked, for it promised him also complete success.   The next thing was hasty pursuit of the enemy.   So rapid was it, that when they reached the brook Besor, which flows into the sea to the south of Gaza, two hundred of his men, who, consider-ing the state in which they had found Ziklag, must have been but ill-provisioned, had to be left behind.[1]

They soon came on the track of the Amalekites.   They had found an Egyptian slave, whom his inhuman master had, on the hasty retreat from Ziklag, left by the wayside to starve rather than hamper himself with the care of a sick man.   Food soon

---

[1] It is a curious instance of the resemblance of the popular parlance of all nations and ages, that the word in vers. 10, 21, rendered by "faint," literally means "were corpsed"—the same as in some districts of our own country.   The Hebrew word is evidently a vulgarism, for it occurs only in these two verses.

revived him ; and, on promise of safety and freedom, he offered
to be the guide of the party to the place which, as he knew,
the Amalekites had fixed upon as sufficiently far from Ziklag to
permit them to feast in safety on their booty. A short-lived
security theirs. It was the twilight—the beginning, no doubt,
of a night of orgies—when David surprised them, "lying
about on the ground," "eating and drinking, and dancing."
No watch had been set ; no weapon was in any man's hands ;
no danger was apprehended. We can picture to ourselves the
scene : how David probably surrounded the camping-place ;
and with what shouts of vengeance the infuriated Hebrews fell
on those who could neither resist nor flee. All night long, all
the next day the carnage lasted. Only four hundred servant-
lads, who had charge of the camels, escaped. Everything that
had been taken by the Amalekites was recovered, besides the
flocks and herds of the enemy, which were given to David as
his share of the spoil. Best of all, the women and children
were safe and unhurt.

It was characteristic of the wicked and worthless among
the followers of David, that when on their return march they
came again to those two hundred men who had been left
behind "faint," they proposed not to restore to them what of
theirs had been recovered from the Amalekites, except their
wives and children. Rough, wild men were many among
them, equally depressed in the day of adversity, and recklessly elated and insolent in prosperity. Nor is it merely the
discipline which David knew to maintain in such a band that
shows us "the skilfulness of his hands" in guiding them, but
the gentleness with which he dealt with them, and, above
all, the earnest piety with which he knew to tame their wild
passions prove the spiritual "integrity," or "perfectness, of
his heart" (Ps. lxxviii. 72). Many a wholesome custom, which
ever afterwards prevailed in Israel, as well as that of equally
dividing the spoil among combatants and non-combatants in
an army (1 Sam. xxx. 24, 25), must have dated not only from
the time of David, but even from the period of his wanderings.

and persecutions. Thus did he prove his fitness for the government long ere he attained to it.

Yet another kindred trait was David's attachment to friends who had stood by him in seasons of distress. As among his later servants and officials we find names connected with the history of his wanderings (1 Chron. xxvii. 27–31), so even now he sent presents from his spoil to "the elders" of the various cities of the South,[1] where his wanderings had been, and who had proved "his friends" by giving him help in the time of need. It may indeed have been that the south generally had suffered from the incursion of the Amalekites against Ziklag (xxx. 1). But such loss could scarcely have been made up by "presents" from David. His main object, next to grateful acknowledgment of past aid, must have been to prepare them for publicly owning him, at the proper time, as the chosen leader of God's people, who would make "spoil of the enemies of Jehovah." At the proper time! But while these gifts were passing, all unknown to David, that time had already come.

[1] The places enumerated in 1 Sam. xxx. 27–31 were all in the south country. The Bethel mentioned in ver. 27, was, of course, not the city of that name in the tribe of Benjamin, but Bethuel, or Bethul (1 Chron. iv. 30), in the tribe of Simeon (Josh. xix. 4).

CHAPTER XV.

The Battle on Mount Gilboa—Death of Saul—Rescue of the bodies by the men of Jabesh-gilead—David punishes the false Messenger of Saul's Death—David king at Hebron—Ish-bosheth king at Mahanaim —Battle between the forces of Abner and Joab—Abner deserts the cause of Ish-bosheth—Murder of Abner—Murder of Ish-bosheth.

(1 SAM. XXXI.—2 SAM. IV.)

BRIEF as are the accounts of the battle of Gilboa (1 Sam. xxxi. ; 1 Chron. x.), we can almost picture the scene. The attack seems to have been made by the Philistines. Slowly and stubbornly the Israelites yielded, and fell back from Jezreel upon Mount Gilboa. All day long the fight lasted ; and the darkness seems to have come on before the Philistines knew the full extent of their success, or could get to the sad work of pillaging the dead. Ill had it fared with Israel that day. Their slain covered the sides of Mount Gilboa. The three sons of Saul—foremost among them the noble Jonathan— had fallen in the combat. Saul himself had retreated on Gilboa. But the battle had gone sore against him. And now the enemy's sharpshooters had "found him"[1]—come up with him. Thus the fatal moment had arrived : "Saul was sore afraid." But if he fell, let it at least not be by the hand of the Philistines, lest Israel's hereditary enemy "make sport"[2] of the disabled, dying king. Saul will die a king. The last service he asks of his armour-bearer is to save him from falling into Philistine hands by thrusting him through. But the armour-bearer dares not lift his sword against the Lord's anointed, and Saul plants his now otherwise useless sword

---

[1] So correctly, and not, as in our Authorised Version (ver. 3), "the archers hit him, and he was sore wounded."

[2] So literally in ver. 4, rendered in the Authorised Version, "abuse me."

on the ground, and tnrows himself upon it.   The faithful
armour-bearer follows his master's example.   Soon all Saul's
personal attendants have likewise been cut down (1 Sam.
xxxi. 6; comp. 1 Chron. x. 6).

And now darkness stayed further deeds of blood.   Before
the morning light the tidings of Israel's defeat had spread
far and wide.   North of the valley of Jezreel, and even across
the Jordan,[1] which rolled close by, the people deserted the
cities and fled into the open country, leaving their strongholds to the conquerors.   Meantime the plunderers were busy
searching and stripping the dead in Jezreel and on Mount
Gilboa.   They found what they could scarcely have expected:
the dead bodies of Saul and of his three sons.   To strip
them would have been comparatively little; but to add every
insult, they cut off the heads of the king and of his sons,
leaving the naked carcases unburied.   The gory heads and the
bloody armour were sent round through Philistia, "to publish it
in the houses of their idols, and among the people."   Finally,
the armour was distributed among the temples of the Ashtaroth
(the Phœnician Venus), while the skull of Saul was fastened up
in the great temple of Dagon.

But the Philistine host had not halted.   They advanced to
occupy the towns deserted by the Hebrews.   The main body
occupied Bethshan, the great mountain-fortress of Central
Palestine, which from the top of a steep brow, inaccessible to
horsemen, seemed to command not only the Jordan valley,
but also all the country round.   As if in utter scorn and
defiance, they hung out on the walls of Bethshan the headless trunks of Saul and of his sons.   And now night with
her dark mantle once more covered these horrible trophies.
Shall the eagles and vultures complete the work which, no
doubt, they had already begun?   The tidings had been carried

---

[1] Commentators have raised, as it seems to me, needless difficulties about
an expression which always means "east of the Jordan."   There cannot
be anything incredible in the border-towns on the other side of Jordan
being deserted by their inhabitants.   If such a strong fortress as Bethshan
was given up, why not smaller places across the Jordan?

across the Jordan, and wakened echoes in one of Israel's cities. It was to Jabesh-gilead that Saul, when only named but not yet acknowledged king, had by a forced night-march brought help, delivering it from utter destruction (1 Sam. xi.). That had been the morning of Saul's life, bright and promising as none other; his first glorious victory, which had made him king by acclamation, and drawn Israel's thousands to that gathering in Gilgal, when, amidst the jubilee of an exultant people, the new kingdom was inaugurated. And now it was night; and the headless bodies of Saul and his sons, deserted by all, swung in the wind on the walls of Bethshan, amid the hoarse music of vultures and jackals.

But it must not be so; it cannot be so. There was still truth, gratitude, and courage in Israel. And the brave men of Jabesh-gilead marched all the weary night; they crossed Jordan; they climbed that steep brow, and silently detached the dead bodies from the walls. Reverently they bore them across the river, and ere the morning light were far out of reach of the Philistines. Though it had always been the custom in Israel to bury the dead, they would not do so to these mangled remains, that they they might not, as it were, perpetuate their disgrace. They burned them just sufficiently to destroy all traces of insult, and the bones they reverently laid under their great tamarisk tree, themselves fasting for seven days in token of public mourning. All honour to the brave men of Jabesh-gilead, whose deed Holy Scripture has preserved to all generations!

It was the third day after the return of David and his men to Ziklag. Every heart must have been heavy with anxiety for tidings of that great decisive struggle between the Philistines and Saul which they knew to be going on, when all at once a messenger came, whose very appearance betokened disaster and mourning (comp. 1 Sam. iv. 12). It was a stranger, the son of an Amalekite settler in Israel, who brought sad and strange tidings. By his own account, he had fled to Ziklag straight out of the camp of Israel, to tell of the defeat and slaughter of Israel, and of the death of Saul and of Jonathan.

As he related the story, he had, when the tide of battle turned against Israel, come by accident upon Saul, who stood alone on the slope of Gilboa leaning upon his spear, while the Philistine chariots and horsemen were closing in around him. On perceiving him, and learning that he was an Amalekite, the king had said, "Stand now to me and slay me, for cramp has seized upon me—for my life is yet wholly in me."[1] On this the Amalekite had "stood to" him, and killed him, "for"—as he added in explanation, probably referring to the illness which from fear and grief had seized Saul, forcing him to lean for support on his spear—"I knew that he would not live after he had fallen;[2] and I took the crown that was on his head, and the arm-band which was upon his arm, and I brought them to my lord—here !"

Improbable as the story would have appeared on calm examination, and utterly untrue as we know it to have been, David's indignant and horrified expostulation, how he had dared to destroy Jehovah's anointed (2 Sam. i. 14), proves that in the excitement of the moment he had regarded the account as substantially correct. The man had testified against himself: he held in his hand as evidence the king's crown and arm-band. If he had not murdered Saul, he had certainly stripped him when dead. And now he had come to David, evidently thinking he had done a deed grateful to him, for which he would receive reward, thus making David a partaker in his horrible crime. David's inmost soul recoiled from such a deed as murder of his sovereign and daring presumption against Jehovah, Whose anointed he was. Again and again, when defending precious life, Saul had been in his power, and he had rejected with the strongest energy of which he was capable the suggestion to ensure his own safety by the death of his persecutor. And that from which in the hour of his supreme

---

[1] This is the correct rendering of 2 Sam. i. 9.

[2] Most critics understand the expression "after he had fallen," to refer to his defeat. But there really seems no occasion for this. It is quite rational to suppose that the Amalekite meant that, in his state of body, Saul would be unable to defend himself against an attack.

danger he had recoiled, this Amalekite had now done in cold blood for hope of a reward! Every feeling would rise within him to punish the deed; and if he failed or hesitated, well might he be charged before all Israel with being an accomplice of the Amalekite. "Thy blood on thy head! for thy mouth hath testified upon thyself, saying, I have slain the anointed of Jehovah." And the sentence thus spoken was immediately executed.

It was real and sincere grief which led David and his men to mourn, and weep, and fast until even for Saul and for Jonathan, and for their fallen countrymen in their twofold capacity as belonging to the Church and the nation ("the people of Jehovah and the house of Israel," ver. 12). One of the finest odes in the Old Testament perpetuated their memory. This elegy, composed by David "to teach the children of Israel," bears the general title of *Kasheth*, as so many of the Psalms have kindred inscriptions. In our text it appears as extracted from that collection of sacred heroic poetry, called *Sepher hajjashar*, "book of the just." It consists, after a general superscription, of two unequal stanzas, each beginning with the line: "Alas, the heroes have fallen!" The second stanza refers specially to Jonathan, and at the close of the ode the head-line is repeated, with an addition, indicating Israel's great loss. The two stanzas mark, so to speak, a descent from deepest grief for those so brave, so closely connected, and so honoured, to expression of personal feelings for Jonathan, the closing lines sounding like the last sigh over a loss too great for utterance. Peculiarly touching is the absence in this elegy of even the faintest allusion to David's painful relations to Saul in the past. All that is merely personal seems blotted out, or rather, as if it had never existed in the heart of David. In this respect we ought to regard this ode as casting most valuable light on the real meaning and character of what are sometimes called the vindictive and imprecatory Psalms. Nor should we omit to notice, what a German divine has so aptly pointed out: that, with the exception of the lament of Jabesh-gilead, the

only real mourning for Saul was on the part of David, whom
the king had so bitterly persecuted to the death—reminding
us in this also of David's great Antitype, Who alone of all wept
over that Jerusalem which was preparing to betray and crucify
Him ! The elegy itself reads as follows :

"The adornment of Israel on thy heights thrust through !
           Alas,[1] the heroes have fallen !
Announce it not in Gath, publish it not as glad tidings in the streets
    of Askelon,
           Lest the daughters of the Philistines rejoice,
           Lest the daughters of the uncircumcised jubilee !
O mountains in Gilboa—no dew, nor rain upon you, nor fields of first-
    fruit offerings—
    For there defiled is the shield of the heroes,
    The shield of Saul, no more anointed with oil !
    From blood of slain, from fat of heroes
    The bow of Jonathan turned not backward,
    And the sword of Saul returned not void (lacking) !
    Saul and Jonathan, the loved and the pleasant,
    In their life and in their death were not parted—
    Than eagles were they lighter, than lions stronger !
    Daughters of Israel, over Saul weep ye,
    Who clad you in purple with loveliness,
    Who put jewels of gold upon your clothing !

    Alas, the heroes have fallen in the midst of the contest—
           Jonathan, on thy heights thrust through !
    Woe is me for thee, my brother Jonathan,—
    Pleasant wast thou to me exceedingly,
    More marvellous thy love to me than the love of women !

    Alas, the heroes have fallen—
    And perished are the weapons of war ! "[2]

But the present was not a time for mourning only. So far
as men could judge, there was no further necessity for David's
exile.   But even so he would not act without express Divine

---

[1] Our translation is an attempt at a literal rendering, which in poetry is
specially desirable. The word rendered in our Authorised Version "How,"
has been translated "Alas," not only because this gives more fully the real
meaning, but also because our word "how" might be taken interrogatively instead of exclamatively.

[2] The attentive reader will notice that throughout the body of the ode,
the thoughts move forward in sentences of three lines each, indicated in
our translation by a sign of exclamation.

guidance. In answer to his enquiry by the Urim and Thummim
he was directed to take up his residence in Hebron, where
he was soon anointed king by his own tribe of Judah. As yet,
however, and for the next seven and a half years, his rule only
extended over that tribe. It is further evidence of the entire
submission of David to the leading of Jehovah, and of his
having fully learned the lesson of not seeking to compass his
own "deliverance," that he took no steps to oppose the
enthronement of Saul's son, however contrary this was to the
Divine appointment; and that the contest which ultimately
ensued originated not with David, but with his rival. On the
contrary, David's first act as king of Judah was to send an
embassy to Jabesh-gilead to express his admiration of their
noble loyalty to Saul.[1] Nor does it detract from this mark of
his generosity that, now their master was dead, he intimated
his own elevation, to bespeak, if possible, their allegiance.
The support of such men was well worth seeking. Besides,
Jabesh-gilead was the capital of the whole of that district; and
already the standard had there been set up of a rival, whose
claims were neither founded on the appointment of God, nor
on the choice of the people.

As we infer from the sacred narrative, there had been among
the fugitives from the battle of Gilboa a son of Saul—whether
the youngest or not must remain undetermined.[2] From the lan-

[1] Keil has well noticed the frequent conjunction of the expressions "mercy
and truth" (2 Sam. ii. 6; comp. Ex. xxxiv. 6; Psa. xxv. 10). It is ever so
with God: first, "mercy"—free, gracious, and forgiving; then "truth"—
faithfulness to His promises, and experience of their reality. The expression
rendered in our Authorised Version, "And I also will requite you this
kindness," should be translated: "And I also am showing you this goodness," referring to the kind message which David sent them.

[2] Although Ish-bosheth is always mentioned fourth among the sons of
Saul, it does not necessarily follow that he was the youngest. He may
have been the son of another mother, and stand last in respect of dignity
rather than of age. The different cast of his name from that of the others,
seems rather to point in that direction. This would also account for his age
—thirty-five at least—at the time of his father's death. At the same time
we would not put too much stress on *numerals* in the Hebrew text, in which,
from the nature of the case, clerical errors would most easily arise.

guage of the text (2 Sam. ii. 8), as well as from his subsequent
history, he seems to have been a weak character—a puppet in
the hands of Abner, Saul's uncle, whom that ambitious and
unscrupulous soldier used for his own purposes.   His original
name, Esh-Baal, "fire of Baal" (1 Chron. viii. 33; ix. 39),
became in popular designation Ish-Bosheth, "man of shame,"
—Baal and Bosheth being frequently interchanged according
to the state of popular religion (Judg. vi. 32; Jer. xi. 13;
Hos. ix. 10).   Even this may be regarded as indicating the
popular estimate of the man.   Immediately after the battle of
Gilboa, Abner had taken him across the Jordan to Mahanaim,
"the twain camp," where probably the broken remnants of
Saul's army also gathered.   The place was well chosen, not
only from the historical remembrances attaching to the spot
where angels' hosts had met Jacob on his return to the land of
promise (Gen. xxxii. 2), but also as sufficiently far from the
scene of the recent war to afford safe shelter.   Here Abner
raised the standard of the Pretender to the throne of Israel;
and, probably in the course of five and a half years,[1] succeeded
in gradually clearing the country from the Philistines, and sub-
jecting it, with the exception of the territory of Judah, to the
nominal rule of the "man of shame."

The first conflict between the armies of the rival kings was
undoubtedly provoked by Abner.   With all the forces at his
disposal he marched upon Gibeon, primarily with the view of
again establishing the royal residence at "Gibeah of Saul," but
with the ulterior object of placing Ish-bosheth in the room of
his father, and gradually pushing back David.   Upon this, Joab
advanced with the seasoned troops of David, to oppose his
progress.   The town of Gibeon was built on the slope of a hill,

---

[1] This probably explains the seeming discrepancy between the two years
of his reign and the seven and a half of David's over Judah.   Erdmann has
well remarked that the preposition "over," which occurs six times in ver. 9,
is represented in the Hebrew three times by *el*, and three times by *al*—the
latter indicating the gradual subjection of territory.   The word "*Ashurites*"
should probably read *Geshurites*, their land lying on the borders of Gilead
and Bashan (Deut. iii. 14; Josh. xii. 5).

overlooking a wide and fertile valley. On the eastern side of the hill deep down in a rock is a beautiful spring, the waters of which are drained into a large rectangular pool, about seventy-two feet long and forty-two feet wide (comp. also Jer. xli. 12). South of this pool lay the army of Joab, north of it that of Abner. The two generals seem to have been previously acquainted (ver. 22); and perhaps Abner may from the first have had in his mind the contingency of having to make his peace with David. Be this as it may, the provocation to actual hostilities came once more from Abner. On his proposal, — perhaps with a view to decide the conflict by a kind of duel, instead of entering upon an internecine civil war—twelve young men from either side were to engage in a personal combat.[1] But such was the embitterment and determination of parties, that each one rushed on his antagonist, and, taking hold of him, buried his sword in his side; whence the spot obtained the name : " Plot of the sharp blades." This bloody and, in the event, useless " game " having proved indecisive, a fierce battle ensued; or rather, a rout of the Israelites, in which three hundred and sixty of them fell, as against nineteen of David's seasoned and trained warriors. The pursuit was only stopped when night had fallen, and Abner had rallied his scattered forces in a strong position on the top of a hill, and then only at Abner's special request.[2]

An incident in that day's pursuit is specially recorded for its bearing on the after-history. Of the three sons of Zeruiah, David's sister (1 Chron. ii. 16),—Abishai (1 Sam. xxvi. 6), Joab, David's general-in-chief, and Asahel—the youngest was " light of foot as one of the roes in the field." Flushed with the fight, the youth singled out Abner, and followed

---

[1] The expression, ver. 14, " Let the young men play before us," refers here to the terrible "game" of single combat.

[2] The Hebrew construction of ver. 27 is difficult. The probable meaning is as follows : " As the Elohim liveth ! For unless thou hadst spoken— then if before the morning the people had returned, each from after his brother !" In other words, the pursuit would have been continued till the morning.

him in his flight.   After a little Abner, recognising his pursuer, stood still.   Probably the youth thought this meant surrender.   But Abner, having ascertained that his pursuer was
really Asahel, and deeming that his ambition would be satisfied if he carried away the armour of some enemy, bade him
gratify his wish on one of the men-at-arms around.   When
the youth, bent on the glory of slaying Abner himself, nevertheless continued the pursuit, the captain once more stopped
to expostulate.   But neither the well-meant and kindly-spoken
warning of Abner, nor the manifest discrepancy of fighting
power between the two, could stay a lad intoxicated by perhaps a first success.   To get rid of him, and almost in necessary self-defence, Abner now struck behind him with the
butt-end of his lance, which was probably sharpened with a
point, to be capable of being stuck in the ground (1 Sam.
xxvi. 7).   Mortally wounded in " the abdomen," [1] the lad fell,
and soon "died in the same place."   The sight of one so
young and brave weltering in his blood and writhing in
agony no doubt greatly increased the bitterness of that day's
pursuit (ver. 23).

The battle of Gibeon seems to have been followed rather
by a protracted state of war [2] than by any other actual
engagement between the forces of the two kings.   The general
result is described as the house of Saul waxing weaker and
weaker, and that of David stronger and stronger.   Of both
evidence appeared.   The increasing political strength of David
was shown, as usual among Eastern monarchs, by the fresh
alliances through marriage into which he now entered.   These
would not only connect him with powerful families throughout
the country, but prove to his subjects that he felt himself safe
in his position, and could now in the Oriental fashion found
a royal house.   On the other hand, the dependence of Ish-

---

[1] This is the correct rendering, and not " under the fifth rib," as in the
Authorised Version (2 Sam. ii. 23).

[2] The expression in 2 Sam. iii. 1 : " Now there was long war," refers
not to actual war, of which there is no evidence in the record, but to a state
of chronic warfare.

bosheth upon Abner became constantly more evident and humiliating. At last the all-powerful general took a public step which in those days was regarded as implying an open claim to the succession to Saul's throne (comp. 2 Sam. xvi. 21 ; 1 Kings ii. 21). Whether or not Abner had intended this when he took Rizpah, Saul's concubine, or merely wished to gratify his passion, with utter and marked disregard of the puppet whom it had suited his purpose to keep on the throne, Ish-bosheth at any rate resented this last and crowning insult. But Abner, who had no doubt for some time seen the impossibility of maintaining the present state of affairs (comp. ver. 17), was in no mood to brook even reproof. He broke into coarse invective,[1] and vowed to Ish-bosheth's face that he would henceforth espouse the cause of David, and soon bring it to a successful issue. Nor did the wretched king even dare to reply.

If Ish-bosheth had regarded it as only the threat of an angry man, Abner at least was in full earnest. Negotiations with David were forthwith set on foot. But they met with a preliminary condition—right and proper not only in itself, but also from political considerations. It was a standing memento of David's weakness in the past, and a lasting disgrace, that his wife Michal should be parted from him, and continue the wife of another—a mere subject of the kingdom. Besides, as the husband of Saul's daughter, and as recalling how he had obtained her hand, her restoration would place him on a manifest political vantage ground. Accordingly David sent Abner this message in reply : " Well, I will make a covenant with thee ; only one thing I demand of thee, viz. : Thou shalt not see my face, unless thou before bringest Michal, the daughter of Saul, when thou comest to see my face." But it would have ill become David to address such a demand to Abner, except as all-powerful with Ish-bosheth, and therefore really responsible for his acts. The formal demand

---

[1] The words of Abner (ver. 8) should be thus rendered : " Am I a dog's head which belongeth to Judah ? This day " (at present) " I show kindness to the house of Saul thy father," etc.

was made to Ish-bosheth himself, and grounded on David's rights. The son of Saul immediately complied—of course, under the direction of Abner, who himself executed the commission to fetch her from her present husband, and restore her to David. The publicity with which this was done—the husband being allowed to accompany her with his lamentations as far as the boundary of Judah—and the influential character of the embassy, as well as the act of restoration itself, must have given to the whole nation an idea of David's acknowledged position, and contributed to their speedy submission to his rule.

When Abner brought Michal to Hebron, at the head of an embassy of twenty men—whether sent by Ish-bosheth, or coming as a sort of representative deputation from Israel—he had, with characteristic energy, already taken all his measures. First he had assured himself of the co-operation of the tribal "elders," who had long been weary of a nominal rule which left them defenceless against the Philistines and others. After that he had entered into special negotiations with the tribe of Benjamin, which might naturally be jealous of a transference of royalty from themselves to Judah. Having secured the consent of all, he was able to offer to David the undivided allegiance of Israel. The king had favourably received Abner and his suite, and entertained them at a great banquet. Already the embassy was on its way back to accomplish its mission, when Joab and his men returned to Hebron from some raid, such as in the then circumstances of David might still be necessary for the support of the troops. On learning what had passed in his absence, he made his way to the king, and violently expostulated with him for not having acted treacherously towards his guest. Abner had come bent on treachery, and he ought not to have been allowed to escape. We can scarcely suppose that this pretence of zeal imposed upon any one, any more than afterwards, when he had murdered Abner, that of having acted as avenger of blood. In both instances his motives, no doubt, were envy, personal jealousy, and fear lest his position might be endangered. As David gave him no encouragement, he acted on his own responsibility, whether or not he used the name of David in so doing. A swift messenger soon brought back Abner to Hebron. Joab, who had concerted his measures with Abishai, his brother (ver. 30), met the unsuspecting victim " in the gate ;" and taking him aside from the pathway into the interior and darker roofed part, as if for some private communication, "slew" him by a wound in "the abdomen," similar to that by which Asahel had died.[1]

As we understand it, the murderers would then turn round, and addressing the bystanders, declare that they were justified, since they had acted as "avengers of blood." But that such plea could not be urged in this instance must have been evident to all, since Abner's had been an act of self-defence, and certainly not intentional murder (comp. Deut. iv. 42, etc. ; Josh. xx.). Abner, however, represented a low type of Israelitish valour. If we were to credit his protestations (vers. 9, 10, 18) of desiring to carry out the Divine will in the elevation of David, we should, of course, have to regard him as having previously acted in conscious opposition to God, and that from the most selfish motives. But probably—put in an Oriental and Jewish fashion—it meant no more than the thousand protestations of "God wills it " and the "Te Deums" which in all ages of the world have covered human ambition with a garb of religiousness.

But none the less foul and treacherous was Joab's deed, and it behoved David not only to express his personal abhorrence of it, but to clear himself of all suspicion of complicity. In this instance it was impossible for human justice to overtake the criminals. Probably public feeling would not have supported the king ; nor could he at this crisis in his affairs afford the loss of such generals, or brave the people and the army. But David did all that was possible. Those whom human justice could not overtake he left in the hands of Divine

---

[1] The difference is marked in the original of ver. 30: Joab and Abishai *slew* or murdered Abner because *he made* Asahel *die*.

vengeance to mete out the punishment appropriate to the inordinate desire after leadership which had prompted such a crime (ver. 29).[1] A public mourning was ordered, in which the murderers themselves had to take part. The king in his official character followed the murdered man to his burying, pronounced over him an appropriate elegy, and publicly announced his intention to fast, in token of personal mourning. From the remark added in the sacred text (ver. 37), it seems that such proofs of sincerity were requisite to counterbalance the suspicions otherwise excited by such an instance of treachery and deception in high places. To his own immediate surroundings—his "servants" (vers. 38, 39)—David spoke more unreservedly, lamenting the circumstances which still made him comparatively powerless in face of such reckless chiefs as the sons of Zeruiah.

But, on the other hand, increasing public confidence rewarded David's integrity of purpose. It was needed, if highhanded crime was to be suppressed in the land. Another glaring instance of the public demoralisation consequent on Saul's long misrule soon occurred. The death of Abner had naturally the most discouraging effect, not only upon Ishbosheth, but upon all his adherents. No one was now left of sufficient prominence and influence to carry out the peaceable revolution which Abner had planned. The present weak government could not long be maintained ; and if Ish-bosheth died, the only representative of Saul's line left was a crippled child, Mephi-bosheth ("the exterminator of shame," or "of Baal"[2]), the son of Jonathan, whose deformity had been caused by the nurse letting him fall when snatching him up for hasty flight on receiving tidings of the disastrous day at Jezreel. Not even the most ardent partisan could have wished to see on the throne of Israel a child thus permanently incapacitated.

---

[1] Of course, we must in all such instances not lose out of view the religious standpoint of the times, even in the case of a David.

[2] I explain the word : "He who blows down Baal," which seems best to correspond with the parallel name Merib-Baal, in 1 Chron. viii. 34.

But few could have been prepared for the tragedy which was so soon to put an end to all difficulties.

It seems that two of Ish-bosheth's "captains of bands," prompted, no doubt, by the hope of rich reward, had in the most deliberate and treacherous manner planned the murder of Ish-bosheth. They were brothers, from Beeroth, on the western boundary of Benjamin, but included in its territory (Josh. xviii. 25). Hence they were of the same tribe with Saul, which, of course, aggravated their crime. For some unexplained reason the Beerothites had fled *en masse* to Gittaim—perhaps, as has been suggested, on the occasion of Saul's slaughter of the Gibeonites (2 Sam. xxi. 1, 2). This, however, can scarcely be regarded as the motive of their crime.[1] Probably on pretence of superintending the receipt of what was necessary for the provisioning of their men, they entered the royal residence at the time when Ish-bosheth was taking the customary Eastern midday rest, made their way into his bed-chamber, stabbed him in his sleep in the abdomen, and cut off his head, to carry it to David as gory evidence of their deed.[2] The reception which they met was such as might have been expected. To the daring appeal of those interested murderers that they had been the instruments of Jehovah's vengeance upon Saul's wrongs to David, the king gave no further reply than to point to what had hitherto been the faith and experience of his heart and the motto of his life : " Jehovah liveth, Who hath redeemed my soul out of all adversity ! " It needed not man's help, least of all the aid of crime. Never—not even in his darkest hour—had he either desponded, doubted, or sought to right himself. His strength, as his confidence, had lain in realising Jehovah as the living God and his all-sufficient

---

[1] So in *The Speaker's Commentary*, Vol. II. p. 380.

[2] There is no real difficulty about the repetition in the narrative, 2 Sam. iv. 5, 6—the latter verse taking up and continuing the interrupted narrative in ver. 5. Accordingly, there is no need for the addition made in the LXX., which must be regarded not as an emendation of, but as a gloss upon, the text.

Saviour.   No other deliverance did he either need or seek. But as for this crime—had not his conduct to the lying messenger at Ziklag sufficiently shown his abhorrence of such deeds?   How much more in regard to a murder so foul as this!   Swift, sure, and signally public punishment was the the only possible reply in such a case.

And thus at last, not by his own act, but through circumstances over which he had had no control,—allowed by Him Who gives full liberty to each man, though He overrules even the darkest deeds of the wicked for the evolving of good—David was left undisputed claimant to the throne of Israel. Faith, patience, and integrity were vindicated; the Divine promises to David had come true in the course of natural events—and all this was better far than even if Saul had voluntarily resigned his place, or Abner succeeded in his plans.

CHAPTER XVI.

David anointed King over all Israel—Taking of Fort Zion—Philistine Defeat—The Ark brought to Jerusalem—Liturgical arrangements and Institutions.

(2 SAM. V., VI.; I CHRON. XI.—XVI.)

T HE cessation of the long-pending rivalry and the prospect of a strong monarchy under David must have afforded sincere relief and satisfaction to all the well-disposed in Israel.   Even during the time when his fortunes were at the lowest, David had had constant accessions of valiant and true men from all tribes, not excluding Saul's tribe of Benjamin and the country east of the Jordan.   Yet it implied no ordinary courage to face the dangers and difficulties of the life of an outlaw; no common determination to leave home and country in such a cause.   The Book of Chronicles furnishes in this as in other instances most welcome notices supplemental to the other historical writings of the Old Testament.[1] Thus it gives us (1 Chron. xii. 1–22) the names of the leading men who joined David at different periods, with their tribal connection, and even helps us to guess what motives may have actuated at least some of their number. From these notices we learn that considerable accessions had taken place on four different occasions. When David was at Ziklag (vers. 1–7), he was joined by certain tribes-men ("brothers") of Saul (vers. 1–8), and by some men from Judah (vers. 4, 6, 7). While in the mountain-fastnesses, in the wilderness of Judah (1 Sam. xxii.–xxiv), certain of the Gadites separated themselves unto him, "men of the army for war" —soldiers trained for war (ver. 8), "chief of the host" (*not* "captains of the host," ver. 14), "one to a hundred the least, and the greatest one to a thousand," who when breaking away from the army of Saul had not only crossed Jordan in the dangerous floodtime of early spring, but cut their way through those who would have barred it (ver. 15). A third con-tingent from Benjamin and Judah came during the same period (vers. 16–18). Their names are not mentioned; but they were headed by Amasai, probably another nephew of

[1] Without here entering on a detailed analysis of the Books of Chronicles (for which see the Table at the beginning of this Volume), we may remark that their position in the canon appropriately indicates their character rela-tively to the Books of Samuel and of the Kings. These latter are *prophetic*, while the Books of Chronicles are *hagiographic*. In the one series all is viewed from the *prophetic* standpoint; in the other, from that of the "sacred writer." In the one case, it is the theocracy, with its grand world-wide principles, which dominates the view; in the other, it is rather the sanctuary which is in Judah—God-appointed in its location, ordinances, priesthood, and law, allegiance to which brings blessing, while unfaithfulness entails judgments. Accordingly, after general genealogical tables (in which the work abounds), the kingdom of David is traced to the Babylonish captivity, while the history of the kingdom of Israel is wholly omitted. Even in the history of the kingdom of David and of his successors—especially in that of David and Solomon—all the merely *personal* parts are passed over, and the narrative is, if one may use the expression, rather objective than subjective. The reader will easily find for himself what parts of history are omitted, although the plan is not always con-sistently carried out, especially in regard to the later reigns.

David—the son of Abigail, David's younger sister (1 Chron. ii.
16, 17). When challenged by David as to their intentions,
Amasai had, under the influence of the Spirit, broken forth
in language which showed the character of their motives (ver.
18). The last and perhaps most important contingent joined
David on his road back to Ziklag, when dismissed from the
armies of the Philistines. It consisted of seven chieftains of
thousands of Manasseh, who gave David most valuable aid
against the Amalekites.

If such had been David's position and influence in Israel
even during Saul's lifetime, we can readily understand the
rush of enthusiasm at his accession to the throne of a people
once more united, now that there was no longer any rival
claimant left. As they afterwards told David at Hebron,
they all felt that he was their own,—just as Israel will feel
when at last in repentant faith they will turn to their Messiah
King; that in the past, even in Saul's life-time, he alone had
been the victorious leader and chief of all; and that to him
had pointed the express Divine promise as spoken through
Samuel (1 Chron xi. 3). And while the "elders of Israel"
made a regular "covenant" with David, and anointed him
king over Israel, hundreds and thousands of the men of war
marched down to Hebron from the most remote parts of
the country (1 Chron. xii. 23–40). Such enthusiasm had
never before been witnessed. Not bidden to the war, but
voluntarily they came, some bringing with them even from
the northernmost parts of the land—from Issachar, Zebulun,
and Naphtali—contributions in kind for the three days' popular
feast which David's former subjects of Judah, and especially
those around Hebron, were preparing in honour of this great
and most joyous event. From both banks of the Jordan they
came. Of course, we do not look for a large representation
from Judah and Simeon (the latter being enclosed in the territory of Judah), since they were already David's, nor from the
Levites, many of whom may previously have been in David's
territory (1 Chron. xii. 24–26). Issachar was represented by

two hundred of its most prominent public leaders, "knowing (possessing) understanding of the times, to know what Israel should do."[1] Only the contingents from Ephraim and Benjamin were comparatively small: the former, owing either to the old tribal jealousy between Ephraim and Judah, or else from a real diminution in their number, such as had appeared even in the second census taken by Moses,[2] while in the case of Benjamin it is sufficiently accounted for by the circumstance that "even till then the greatest part of them were keeping their allegiance to the house of Saul" (ver. 29). Taking all these circumstances into account, the grand total of warriors that appeared in Hebron—339,600 men, with 1222 chiefs,[3] and so many of them from the other side Jordan,—afforded a truly marvellous exhibition of national unanimity and enthusiasm. And the king who was surrounded by such a splendid array was in the prime of his vigour, having just reached the age of thirty-seven and a half years (2 Sam. v. 5). What a prospect before the

---

[1] The expression refers, of course, to these two hundred representative men, and not to the tribe as a whole.

[2] Comp. Vol. II. of this *Bible History*, p. 146.

[3] Bearing in mind our above remarks, and that, of course, units are not given, the following are the numbers of warriors and of their leaders, given in 1 Chron. xii. 24-37:

Of Judah	6,800 men	
,, Simeon	7,100 ,,	
,, Levi	4,600 ,,	
With Jehoiada, the "prince" (not high-priest of Aaron)	3,700 ,,	
Zadok and his father's house	——	22 chiefs.
Of Benjamin	3,000 ,,	
,, Ephraim	20,800 ,,	
,, half Manasseh	18,000 ,,	
,, Issachar	——	200 leaders.
,, Zebulon	50,000 ,,	
,, Naphtali	37,000 ,,	1,000 chiefs.
,, Dan	28,600 ,,	
,, Asher	40,000 ,,	
,, the 2½ tribes east of Jordan	120,000 ,,	
Total	339,600 men	1222 chiefs, etc.

nation! Well might they joy at the national feast which David gave in Hebron! Viewing this history in its higher bearing, and remembering the grounds on which the elders of Israel in Hebron based the royal claims of David, we venture to regard it as typical of Israel at last returning to their Saviour-King. And surely it is not to strain the application, if thoughts of this feast at Hebron carry us forward to that other and better feast in the "latter days," which is destined to be so full of richest joy alike to Israel and to the world (Isa. xxv. 6–10).

Surrounded by a force of such magnitude and enthusiasm, David must have felt that this was the proper moment for the greatest undertaking in Jewish history since the conquest of the land under Joshua. The first act of David's government must appropriately be the conquest of Israel's capital.[1] The city of the Jebusites must become truly Jerusalem— "the inheritance," "the abode" "of peace:" the peace of the house of David. The town itself had indeed already been taken immediately upon Joshua's death (Judg. i. 8). But "the stronghold" on Mount Zion, which dominated the city, still continued to be held by "the Jebusites." Yet Jerusalem was almost marked out by nature to be Israel's capital, from its strength, its central position, and its situation between Benjamin and Judah. Far more than this, it was the place of which the Lord had made choice : to be, as it were, a guarded sanctuary within the holy land. So long as Zion was in possession of the Jebusites, as the original Canaanite "inhabitants of the land," the land itself could not be said to have been wholly won. Thither accordingly David now directed the united forces of his people. Yet such was the natural and artificial strength of Zion that "to say (express), David shall not come hither" (ver. 5), the Jebusites

---

[1] This might have been inferred from the circumstance that both in 2 Sam. v. and in 1 Chron. xi. the capture of Jerusalem is recorded immediately after David's coronation. But the wording of 2 Sam. v. 5 places it beyond doubt.

taunted him with what afterwards became a proverb, per-
petuating among the people the fact that no conquest is too
difficult for God and with God: "He will not come in
hither, for even the blind and the lame shall drive thee
away!"[1] It was wise and right in David to take up this
defiant taunt of the heathen, when he gave his men charge
—perhaps directing them to scale the bare rock by the
water-course,[2] which may at that time have come down the
brow of Zion: "Whoever smiteth Jebusites—let him throw
(them) down the water-course: both ' the blind and the lame '
who are hated of David's soul !"[3] At the same time no
means were neglected of encouraging the leaders in the attack. As we learn from the Book of Chronicles (1 Chron.
xi. 6), the leader who first scaled the walls was to be made
general-in-chief. This honour was won by Joab, who had
commanded David's separate army, before his elevation to the
throne had united the whole host of Israel. And so, in face
of the Jebusite boast, the impregnable fort was taken, and
called "the City of David,"—a lesson this full of encouragement to the people of God at all times. Henceforth David
made it his residence. To render it more secure, " he built,"
or rather fortified, "round about from (fort) Millo and in-
wards,"[4] or, as in 1 Chron. xi. 8 : " From the surrounding
(wall) and to the surrounding,"—that is, as we understand
it : Zion, which had hitherto been surrounded by three walls,
had now a fourth added on the north, reaching from Castle

---

[1] So the words in the original, and not as in our Authorised Version.

[2] The expression rendered in the Authorised Version "gutter," occurs only
again in the *plural* in Ps. xlii. 7, where it undoubtedly means "cataracts"
or "waterfalls." Accordingly we translate the singular of the noun by
"watercourse down a steep brow." Keil, Ewald, and Erdmann render
it "abyss." The interpretation of this difficult verse (ver. 8) in *The
Speaker's Bible* seems to us not warranted by the language of the text.

[3] This is the best rendering of this somewhat difficult verse.

[4] Mr. Lewin's theory (*Siege of Jerusalem*, pp. 256, etc.) that Millo was
the Temple-area is wholly untenable. There was, for example, another
Millo in Shechem (Judg. ix. 6), which is also designated as the migdal,
or tower of Shechem (vers. 46, 49).

Millo (either at the north-eastern or at the north-western angle)
to where the other wall ended.   Similarly, Joab repaired the
rest of the city walls (1 Chron. xi. 8).

What we have just related must, of course, not be taken as
indicating a strict chronological succession of events.   The
building of these walls no doubt occupied some time, and many
things occurred in the interval, which are related afterwards.
Apparently the intention of the sacred historian was to complete
his sketch of all connected with David's conquest of Zion and
his making it the royal residence, not to write in chronological
order.   Hence we have also here notices of the palace which
David built on Mount Zion, and of the help which Hiram,
king of Tyre, gave him both in men and materials, and even of
David's fresh alliances and of their issues, although the children
were born at a much later period than this.[1]   As we understand
it, soon after his accession, probably after the capture of Jerusalem and the final defeat of the Philistines, Hiram sent an
embassy of congratulation to David, which led to an interchange
of courtesies and to the aid which the king of Tyre gave in
David's architectural undertakings.[2]

Different feelings from those in Israel were awakened in Philistia by the tidings of David's elevation to the throne of united
Israel, and of his conquest of the Jebusite fort.   The danger to
their supremacy was too real to be overlooked.   On their approach,
David retired to the stronghold of Zion.   While the Philistines
advanced unopposed as far as the valley of Rephaim, which is
only separated by a mountain-ridge from that of Ben-Hinnom,
David "enquired of Jehovah."   So near had danger come,
and so strongly did the king feel that he must take no step

---

[1] So, notably, the four sons of Bathsheba or Bathshua (comp. 1 Chron.
iii. 5), and, of course, the others also.   In 1 Chron. iii. 6, 7, two names
(Eliphelet and Nogah) are mentioned, which do not occur in 2 Sam.   These
two must have died.

[2] The building of David's palace must have taken place in the first years
of his reign in Jerusalem.   This is evident from many allusions to this
palace.   We must, therefore, in this, as in so many other instances, consider
the *dates* given by Josephus as incorrect (*Ant.* viii. 3, 1 ; *Ag. Ap.* i. 18).

without Divine direction to avert it. For, placing ourselves on the standpoint of those times, this was the best, if not the only way of manifesting entire dependence on God's guidance —even to the incurring of what seemed near danger in so doing, and also the best if not the only way of teaching his followers much-needed lessons of allegiance to Jehovah, with all that religiously and morally followed from it.

The answer of the Lord conveyed promised assurance of help, and hence of victory. And in this light David afterwards described his triumph, exclaiming, " Broken in hath Jehovah upon mine enemies before me." To perpetuate this higher bearing of the victory, the spot was ever afterwards called " Baal-perazim " ("possessor of breaches "),—and from Isa. xxviii. 21, we know that the solemn import of the name never passed from memory. The victory and its meaning were the more notable that the Philistines had brought their gods with them to the battle, as Israel the Ark on a former occasion. Their idols were now burned by command of David, in accordance with Deut. vii. 5, 25. Yet a second time did the Philistines come up to Rephaim to retrieve their disaster. On this occasion also David was divinely directed—no doubt the more clearly to mark the Divine interposition : " Thou shalt not go up (viz., against them *in front*) ; turn thyself upon their rear, and come upon them from opposite the Bacha-trees.[1] And when thou hearest the sound of marching in the tops of the Bacha-trees, then be quick, for then shall Jehovah go forth before thee to smite in the host of the Philistines." It was as David had been told ; and the rout of the Philistines extended from Gibeon[2] to the Gazer road, which runs from Nether Bethhoron to the sea.

[1] I have left the word untranslated. The guess of the Rabbis, who render it by *mulberry-trees*, is as unsupported as that of the LXX. who translate : *pear-trees*. The word is derived from *bacha*, to flow, then to weep. Ewald and Keil suggest with much probability that it was a balsam-tree (as in the Arabic), of which the sap dropped like tears.

[2] So in 1 Chron. xiv. 16. The word *Geba*, in 2 Sam. v. 25, is evidently a clerical error, since Geba lay in quite another direction.

Thus far for the political results of David's elevation, which are placed first in the " Book of Samuel," as dealing primarily with the political aspect of his kingdom, while in the Book of Chronicles, which views events primarily in their theocratic bearing, they are recorded after another of greatest importance for the religious welfare of the new kingdom.[1]   For the same reason also, the Book of Chronicles adds details not recorded in that of Samuel, about David's consultation with his chiefs, and the participation of the priests and Levites in what related to the removal of the ark of the Lord.

About seventy years had passed since the ark of Jehovah had stood in the Tabernacle,[2] according to the express ordinance of God.   And now that Israel was once more united, not only in a political, but in the best and highest sense, and its God-appointed capital had at last been won, it was surely time to restore the ancient worship which had been so sadly disturbed.   Nor could there be any question as to the location of the Ark.   No other place fit for it but the capital of the land.   For was it not the " ark of God " over which the Lord specially manifested His Presence and His glory to His people? —or, in the language of Holy Scripture[3] (2 Sam. vi. 2): " over which is called the Name, the NAME of Jehovah Zevaoth, Who throneth upon the cherubim."   Much, indeed, had still to be left in a merely provisional state.   We cannot doubt that David from the first contemplated a time when the Lord would no longer dwell, so to speak, in tents, but when a stable form would be given to the national worship by the erection of a

---

[1] If the reader will keep in view this fundamental difference in the object of the two histories, he will readily understand not only why events are differently arranged in them, but also the reason why some events are left unrecorded, or more briefly narrated in one or the other of these works.

[2] Keil reckons about twenty years to the victory of Ebenezer, forty years in the time of Samuel and Saul, and about ten in that of David.

[3] We have translated the verse correctly, as our Authorised Version is manifestly in error.

central sanctuary. But for the present it must remain—if in Jerusalem—yet in a "tabernacle." Nay, more than that, the tent which David would prepare would not be the tabernacle which Moses had made. This was in Gibeah, and there, since the murder of the priests at Nob, Zadok officiated, while Abiathar acted as high-priest with David. Neither of these two could be deposed ; and so there must be two tabernacles, till God Himself should set right what the sin of men had made wrong. And for this, as we believe, David looked forward to the building of a house for the God of Israel.

An undertaking of such solemn national importance as the transference of the Ark to Jerusalem must be that of the whole people, and not of David alone. Accordingly representatives from the whole land assembled to the number of thirty thousand, with whom he went to bring in solemn procession the Ark from [1] Baalah of Judah, as Kirjath-Jearim ("the city of the woods") also used to be called [2] (Josh. xv. 9 ; 1 Chron. xiii. 6 ; comp. also Ps. cxxxii. 6). One thing only David had omitted, but its consequences proved fatal. The act of David and of Israel was evidently intended as a return to the Lord, and as submission to His revealed ordinances. But if so, the obedience must be complete in every particular. Viewed symbolically and typically, all these ordinances formed one complete whole, of which not the smallest detail could be altered without disturbing the symmetry of all, and destroying their meaning. Viewed legally, and, so far as Israel was concerned, even morally, the neglect of any single ordinance involved a breach of all, and indeed, in principle, that of obedience and absolute submission to Jehovah, in consequence of which the people had already so terribly suffered. Once more we must here place ourselves on the stand-point of the stage

[1] In our text (2 Sam. vi. 2) we have it : " David arose and went . . . . from Baale "—probably a clerical error instead of "to Baale" (comp. 1 Chron. xiii. 6).

[2] Baalah " of Jehudah," to distinguish it from others of that name (Josh. xix. 8, 44), or also Kirjath-Baal (Josh. xv. 60 ; xviii. 14) was the same as Kirjath-Jearim. Comp. also Delitzsch *Com.* ii. d., Ps. vol. II. p. 264.

of religious development then attained.   For only thus can we understand either the grave fault committed by David, or the severity of the punishment by which it was followed.

The arrangements which David had made for the transport of the Ark differed in one most important particular from those which God had originally prescribed.   According to God's ordinance (Numb. iv.) the Ark was only to be handled by the Levites—for symbolical reasons on which we need not now enter—nor was any other even to touch it (Numb. iv. 15). Moreover the Levites were to carry it on their shoulders, and not to place it in a waggon.   But the arrangements which David had made for the transport of the Ark were those of the heathen Philistines when they had restored it to Israel (1 Sam. vi. 7, etc.), not those of the Divine ordinance.   If such was the case on the part of the king, we can scarcely wonder at the want of reverence on the part of the people.   It was a question of the safe transport of a sacred vessel, not of the reverent handling of the very symbol of the Divine Presence.   It had been placed in a new cart, driven by the sons of Abinadab,[1] in whose house the Ark had been these many years, while David and all Israel followed with every demonstration of joy,[2] and with praise. At a certain part of the road, by the threshing-floor of "the stroke" (*Nachon*, 2 Sam. vi. 6 ; or, as in 1 Chron. xiii. 9, *Chidon*, "accident"), the oxen slipped, when Uzzah, one of Abinadab's sons, took hold of the Ark.   It scarcely needs the comment on this act, so frequently made, that Uzzah was a type of those who honestly but with unhallowed hands try to steady the ark of God when, as they think, it is in danger, to show us that some lesson was needed alike by the king and his people to remind them

---

[1] By a copyist's mistake the first two clauses of 2 Sam. vi. 3, are repeated in ver. 4.   The text of ver. 3 should continue in ver. 4 with these words : "with the ark of God : and Ahio went before the ark."

[2] A clerical error, similar to that just mentioned, occasion the wording of ver. 5, "on all manner of *instruments made of* cypress wood."   The expression should read as in 1 Chron. xiii. 8 : "with all their might and with singing."   The instruments translated in the Authorised Version (2 Sam. vi. 5) "cornets," are the *sistra*, consisting of two iron rods furnished with little bells.

that this was not merely a piece of sacred furniture, but the very emblem of God's Presence among His people. It was a sudden and terrible judgment which struck down Uzzah in his very act before all the people ; and though David was "displeased" at the unexpected check to his cherished undertaking, the more so that he must have felt that the blame lay with himself, he seems also to have learnt its lesson at least thus far, to realise, more than ever before, that holiness befitted every contact with God (2 Sam. vi. 9).

The meaning of this judgment was understood by David. When three months later the Ark was fetched from where it had been temporarily deposited in the house of Obed-Edom, a Levite of Gath-Rimmon (Josh. xxi. 24 ; xix. 45), and of that family of that Korahites (1 Chron. xxvi. 4 ; comp. Ex. vi. 21), to whom the custody of the Ark was specially entrusted (1 Chron. xv. 18, 24), David closely observed the Divine ordinance. Of this, as indeed of all the preparations made by David on this occasion, we have, as might be expected, a very full account in 1 Chron. xv. 1–25. As the procession set forward a sacrifice of an ox and a fatling[1] was offered (2 Sam. vi. 13) ; and again when the Levites had accomplished their task in safety, a thank-offering of seven bullocks and seven rams was brought (1 Chron. xv. 26). David himself, dressed as the representative of the priestly nation, in an ephod, took part in the festivities, like one of the people. It is a sad sign of the decay into which the public services of the sanctuary had fallen in the time of Saul, that Michal saw in this nothing but needless humiliation of the royal dignity. She had loved the warrior, and she could honour the king, but "the daughter of Saul"[2] could neither understand nor sympathise with such a demonstration as that in which David now took part. As she looked from her window upon the scene below, and mentally contrasted the proud grandeur of her father's court with what she regarded

---

[1] The text uses the singular, and not, as in our Authorised Version, the *plural*.

[2] Thus Michal is here significantly designated, and not as the wife of David.

as the triumph of the despicable priesthood at the cost of royalty, other thoughts than before came into her mind alike as to the past and the present, and "she despised David in her heart."

The lengthened services of that happy day were past. David had prepared for the reception of the Ark a "tabernacle," no doubt on the model of that which Moses had made. The introduction of the Ark into its "most holy place"[1] was made the feast of the dedication of the new sanctuary which had been reared for its reception, when burnt-offerings and peace-offerings were brought. But there was more than this to mark the commencement of a new religious era. For the first time the service of praise was now introduced in the public worship of Israel.[2] Shortly after it was fully organised, as also the other ritual of the sanctuary (1 Chron. xvi.). The introduction of fixed hymns of praise, with definite responses by the people (as in 1 Chron. xvi. 34–36), marks the commencement of that liturgy which, as we know, was continued in the Temple, and afterwards in the Synagogues throughout the land. The grand hymn composed for this occasion was no doubt Ps. xxiv., as its contents sufficiently indicate. But besides we have in the Book of Chronicles (xvi. 8–36), what must be considered either as a liturgical arrangement and combination of parts from other Psalms introduced at that time into the public worship, or else as a separate Psalm, parts of which were afterwards inserted into others. This question is, however, of little practical importance. In favour of the first view is the undoubted fact that the successive parts of the hymn in the Book of Chronicles occur in Ps. cv. (1–15), xcvi., cvii. (1), and cvi. (47, 48), and the circumstance that the expressions (1 Chron. xvi. 4) "to record, and to thank, and to praise," mark a liturgical division and arrangement of the Psalms. The first of the three classes indicated, the Ascharah or "memorial" Psalms, were sung

---

[1] The Hebrew expression implies the innermost part.

[2] This is expressly stated in 1 Chron. xvi. 7, omitting, of course, the words in *italics*.

when meat-offerings were brought [1] (Lev. ii. 2). Ps. xxxviii.
and lxx. in our Psalter may be mentioned as examples of this
class.   As to the second and third classes, we need only remark
that Ps. cv. is the first of the Hodim, or Thank-Psalms, and
Ps. cvi. of the " Hallelujah," or " Praise " Psalms.   Nor is it said
that the hymn in Chronicles was actually sung in the form there
indicated, the inference to that effect being derived from the
words in italics in our Authorised Version (1 Chron. xvi. 7).
These are, of course, not in the Hebrew text, which has it : " On
that day then gave " (appointed) " David first " (for the first
time) " to thank Jehovah " (*i.e.* the service of song) " by the
hand of Asaph and his brethren."   On the other hand, however,
the hymn in the Book of Chronicles is so closely and beautifully
connected in its various parts, as to give the impression of one
whole, parts of which may afterwards have been inserted in different Psalms, just as similar adaptations are found in other parts
of the Psalter (comp., for example, Ps. xl. 17, etc., with Ps. lxx.).

   But, whatever may be thought of its original form, this
" Psalm " of eight stanzas,[2] as given in the Book of Chronicles, is one of the grandest hymns in Holy Scripture.   If the
expression might be allowed, it is New Testament praise in Old
Testament language.   Only we must beware of separating the
two dispensations, as if the faith and joy of the one had differed
from that of the other except in development and form.   From
first to last the hymn breathes a missionary spirit, far beyond
any narrow and merely national aspirations.   Thus, in the fifth

   [1] At the time of our Lord the Psalms for the day were chanted when the
drink-offering was poured out.   Comp. my *Temple: its Ministry and
Services at the time of Jesus Christ*, pp. 143, 144.   But the arrangement
then prevailing may not date further back than the time of the Maccabees—at
any rate, it forms no criterion for the order of the services in the time of David.
   [2] Stanza i. (vers. 8–11) : Eulogy of God and of His wonders ; stanza ii.
(vers. 12–14) : Memorial of God's great doings ; stanza iii. (vers. 15–18) :
Memorial of the covenant and its promises ; stanza iv. (ver. 19–22) : Record
of gracious fulfilment ; stanza v. (vers. 23–27) : Missionary ; stanza vi.
(vers. 28–30) : The Universal Kingdom of God ; stanza vii. (vers. 31–33) :
The reign of God upon earth ; stanza viii. (vers. 34–36) : Eucharistic,
with doxology and liturgical close.

stanza (vs. 23–27), we have anticipation of the time when God's promise to Abraham would be made good, and all nations share in his spiritual blessing,—a hope which, in the sixth (28–30) and seventh stanzas (31–33), rises to the joyous assurance of Jehovah's reign over all men and over ransomed earth itself.

That this hymn is deeply Messianic, not only in its character but in its basis, needs no proof. In truth, we regard it and the earlier hymns of the same spirit, as that by the Red Sea (Ex. xv.) and that of Hannah (1 Sam. ii. 1–10), as forming links connecting the earlier with the later (prophetic) portions of the Old Testament, showing that, however gradually the knowledge may have come of the precise manner in which the promise would ultimately be fulfilled, the faith and hope of believers were, in substance, always the same. Nor, to pass from this to what to some may seem a comparatively secondary point, ought we to neglect noticing as an important advance, marked even by this Psalm, the establishment of a liturgical worship, apparent even in the introduction of a fixed hymnody, instead of occasional outbursts of sacred poetry, and by very distinct though brief liturgical formulas—the whole last stanza being, in fact, of that character.[1]

The solemn services of the consecration ended, David dismissed the people, giving to each individual, probably for the journey homewards, needful provisions.[2] But in that most

[1] If the reader will compare the last stanza of this hymn with corresponding parts in Ps. cvi., cvii., cxviii., and cxxxvi.—not to speak of the liturgical close of each of the five books of which the Psalter consists,—and consider such passages as 2 Chron. v. 13; vii. 3; xx. 21, or Jer. xxxiii. 11, he will understand what is meant in the text.

[2] Of the three expressions in 2 Sam. vi. 19, there can be no doubt as to the meaning of the first and the last : "a cake of bread . . . and a cake of raisins" (not "flagon of wine," as in our Authorised Version). Much doubt prevails about what the Rabbis and our Authorised Version render by "a good piece of flesh"—probably on the assumption that it had formed part of the "peace-offerings." But such a distribution of "peace-offerings" would have been quite contrary to custom—nor does the gift of "cakes of raisins" accord with it. The most probable rendering of the word in question is : "measure," viz., of wine. We venture to think that our explanation of these gifts as provisions for the journey will commend itself to the reader.

joyous hour David had once more to experience, how little sympathy he could expect, even in his own household. Although we can understand the motives which influenced Michal's "contempt" of David's bearing, we would scarcely have been prepared for the language in which she addressed him when, in the fulness of his heart, he came to bless his assembled household, nor yet for the odious representation she gave of the scene. Such public conduct on her part deserved and, in the circumstances, required the almost harsh rebuke of the king. The humiliation of the proud woman before man was ratified by her humiliation on the part of God: "Therefore Michal, the daughter of Saul, had no child unto the day of her death."

The placing of the Ark in the capital of Israel, thus making it " the city of God," was an event not only of deep national, but of such typical importance, that it is frequently referred to in the sacred songs of the sanctuary. No one will have any difficulty in recognising Ps. xxiv. as the hymn composed for this occasion. But other Psalms also refer to it, amongst which, without entering on details that may be profitably studied by each reader, we may mention Ps. xv., lxviii., lxxviii., and especially Ps. ci., as indicating, so to speak, the moral bearing of the nearness of God's ark upon the king and his kingdom.

CHAPTER XVII.

David's purpose of building the Temple, and its Postponement — The "Sure Mercies" of David in the Divine Promise—David's Thanksgiving.

(2 SAM. VII.; 1 CHRON. XVII.)

THOSE who, with devout attention, have followed the course of this history, and marked in it that of the kingdom of God in its gradual unfolding, will feel that a point had now been reached when some manifestation of the Divine purpose, fuller and clearer than ever before, might be expected. As we look back upon it, not only the whole history, but every event in it, has been deeply significant, and fraught with symbolical and typical meaning. Thus we have marked how as each event, so to speak, kindled a light, which was reflected from the polished mirror of the Psalter, it seemed to throw its brightness far beyond its own time into that future on which the day had not yet risen. But even to the men of that generation what had taken place must have carried a meaning far beyond the present. The foundation of a firm kingdom in Israel, its concentration in the house of David, and the establishment of a central worship in the capital of the land as the place which God had chosen, must have taken them back to those ancient promises which were now narrowing into special fulfilment, and have brought into greater prominence the points in these predictions which, though still towering aloft, sprung out of what was already reached, and formed part of it. A never-ending kingdom, a never-passing king; a sanctuary never to be abolished : such were the hopes still before them in the world-wide application of the promises of which they already witnessed the national and typical fulfilment. These hopes differed, not in character, but only in extent and application, from what they already enjoyed. To use our former illustration, they were not other heights than those on which they stood, but only peaks yet unclimbed. These considerations will help us properly to understand the narrative of David's purpose to build a temple, and the Divine communication consequent upon it. For clearness' sake we first sketch the facts as stated in sacred history, and then indicate their deeper meaning.

To complete the history of the religious movement of that period, the sacred writers insert in this place the account of David's purpose to build a temple. The introduction to the narrative (2 Sam. vii. 1), and the circumstance that at the time most if not all the wars mentioned in 2 Sam. viii. and x. were past, sufficiently indicate that in this, as in other instances, the history is *not* arranged according to strict chronological succession. Still it must have taken place when David's power was at its zenith, and before his sin with Bath-sheba. The king had been successful in all his undertakings. Victorious and world-famed, he inhabited his splendid palace on Mount Zion. The contrast between his own dwelling and that in which His ark abode [1] to Whom he owed all, and Who was Israel's real King, was painfully great. However frequent and unheeded a similar contrast may be in our days between the things of God and of man, David too vividly apprehended spiritual realities to remain contented under it. Without venturing to express a wish which might have seemed presumptuous, he told his feelings on this subject to his trusted friend and adviser, the prophet Nathan.[2] As might have been expected,

---

[1] The expression (2 Sam. vii. 2) is : "Abideth in the midst (within) the *Yeriah,*" or "curtain," that is the *Yeriah* (in the singular), composed of the ten *Yerioth* (in the plural), mentioned in Ex. xxvi. 1. These formed the *Mishcan,* or dwelling—thus proving that "the curtains" hung *within* the wooden framework, and constituted the "dwelling" itself.

[2] *Nathan,* "given"—a *prophet* (whereas Gad is designated as a "seer," 1 Sam. ix. 9), whose name here appears for the first time. For further notices of him see 2 Sam. xii. ; 1 Kings i. 10, 22, 34 ; 1 Chron. xxix. 29; 2 Chron. ix. 29. From the latter two passages it appears that Nathan wrote a history of David and (at least in part also) of Solomon.

Nathan responded by a full approval of the king's unspoken purpose, which seemed so accordant with the glory of God. But Nathan had spoken—as ancient writers note—from his own, though pious, impulse, and not by direction of the Lord. Ofttimes our thoughts, although springing from motives of real religion, are not God's thoughts ; and the lesson here conveyed is most important of not taking our own impressions, however earnestly and piously derived, as necessarily in accordance with the will of God, but testing them by His revealed word,—in short, of making our test in each case not subjective feeling, but objective revelation.

That night, as Nathan was busy with thoughts of the great future which the king's purpose seemed to open, God spake to him in vision, forbidding the undertaking ; or rather, while approving the motive, delaying its execution. All this time, since He had brought them up out of Egypt, God's Presence had been really among Israel ; He had walked about with them in all their wanderings and state of unsettledness. Thus far, then, the building of an house could not be essential to God's Presence, while the " walking about in tent and dwelling" had corresponded to Israel's condition. Another period had now arrived. Jehovah Zevaoth [1] had chosen David, and established his kingdom. And in connection with it as concerned Israel (ver. 10) and David (ver. 11) : " And I have appointed a place for My people Israel, and have planted it that it may abide in its place, and no more tremble ; and that the children of wickedness " (malice) " may no more oppress it as at the first, and from the day when I appointed judges over My people Israel.[2]   And I give thee rest from all thine enemies, and Jehovah intimates to thee that a house will Jehovah make to thee."

[1] The use here of the name "Jehovah of Hosts" is very significant. It marks, on the one hand, the infinite exaltation of the Lord above all earthly dwellings, and, on the other, the real source of David's success in war.

[2] It is quite evident that the sentences must be arranged and punctuated as we have done, and not as in our Authorised Version. The same remark applies to the tenses of the verbs.

Thus much for the present. As for the future, it was to be as always in the Divine arrangement. For God must build us a house before we can build one to Him. It was not that David was first to rear a house for God, but that God would rear one for David. Only afterwards, when all Israel's wanderings and unrest were past, and He had established the house of His servant, would the son of that servant, no longer a man of war (1 Chron. xx. 8; xxviii. 3), but a man of peace, "Solomon," build the house of peace. There was inward and even outward congruity in this : a kingdom which was peace ; a king the type of the Prince of peace ; and a temple the abode of peace. This, then, was the main point : a promise alike to David, to Israel, and in regard to the Temple, that God would build David a house, and make his kingdom not only lasting, but everlasting, in all the fulness of meaning set out in Ps. lxxii. What followed will be best given in the words of Holy Scripture itself : "I shall be to him a Father, and he shall be to Me a son, whom, if he transgress, I will correct with the rod of men, and with stripes of the children of men ; but My mercy shall not depart from him as I made it depart from Saul, whom I put away from before thee. And unfailing" (sure) "thy house and thy kingdom for ever before thee ; and thy throne shall be established for ever ! "

That this promise included Solomon is as plain as that it was not confined to him. No unprejudiced reader could so limit it ; certainly no sound Jewish interpreter would have done so. For on this promise the hope of a Messianic kingdom in the line of David and the title of the Messiah as the Son of David were based. It was not only the Angel, who pointed to the fulfilment of this promise in the Annunciation to the Virgin (Luke i. 32, 33), but no one, who believed in a Messiah, would have thought of questioning his application. All the predictions of the prophets may be said to rest upon it. While, therefore, it did not exclude Solomon and his successors, and while some of its terms are only applicable to them, the *fulfilment* of this promise was in Christ. In this view we are not hampered but helped by the clause which speaks of human chastisements as eventual on sins in the successors of David. For we regard the whole history from David to Christ as one, and as closely connected. And this prophecy refers neither only to Solomon nor only to Christ; nor has it a twofold application, but it is a covenant-promise which, extending along the whole line, culminates in the Son of David, and in all its fulness applies only to Him. These three things did God join in it, of which one necessarily implies the other, alike in the promise and in the fulfilment: a unique relationship, a unique kingdom, and a unique fellowship and service resulting from both. The unique relationship was that of Father and Son, which in all its fulness only came true in Christ (Heb. i. 5). The unique kingdom was that of the Christ, which would have no end (Luke i. 32, 33; John iii. 35). And the unique sequence of it was that brought about through the temple of His body (John ii. 19), which will appear in its full proportions when the New Jerusalem comes down out of heaven (Rev. xxi. 1–3).

Such was the glorious hope opening up wider and wider, till at its termination David could see "afar off" the dawn of the bright morning of eternal glory; such was the destiny and the mission which, in His infinite goodness, God assigned to His chosen servant. Much there was still in him that was weak, faltering, and even sinful; nor was he, whose was the inheritance of such promises, even to build an earthly temple. Many were his failings and sins, and those of his successors; and heavy rods and sore stripes were to fall upon them. But that promise never failed. Apprehended from the first by the faith of God's people, it formed the grand subject of their praise, not only in Ps. lxxxix., but in many others, such as Ps. ii., xlv., lxxii., cx., cxxxii., and continued the hope of the Church, as expressed in the burning language and ardent aspirations of all the prophets. Brighter and brighter this light grew, even unto the perfect day; and when all else seemed to fail, these were still "the sure mercies of David" (Isa. lv. 3), steadfast and stable, and at last fully realised in the resurrection of our Blessed Lord and Saviour Jesus Christ (Acts xiii. 32–34).

It was significant that when David received, through Nathan, this Divine communication, " he went in," no doubt, into that " tabernacle," which was to be to him what the Pisgah-view of the land had been to Moses, and " remained "[1] before Jehovah, uttering prayer, in which confession of unworthiness formed the first element, soon followed by thanksgiving and praise, and concluding with earnest entreaty.   such must all true prayer be—mingling humble confession with thanksgiving and with petition for the promised blessing.

CHAPTER XVIII.

Wars of David—Great Ammonite and Syrian Campaign against Israel— The Auxiliaries are Defeated in turn—The capital of Moab is taken —Edom subdued—Record of David's officers—His kindness to Mephibosheth.

(2 SAM. VIII., IX.; 1 CHRON. XVIII.—XX.)

BY a fitting arrangement, the record of God's promise to establish the kingdom of David is followed by an account of all his wars, though here also the order is not strictly chronological.   In fact, we have merely a summary of results, which is all that was necessary in a history of the kingdom of God— the only exception being in the case of the war with Ammon and their allies the Syrians, which is described in detail in 2 Sam. x. and xi. because it is connected with David's great sin.

As might be expected, the first war was with the Philistines, whom David subdued, taking " out of the hand of the Philis-

---

[1] Not "sat," as in our Authorised Version (2 Sam. vii. 18). *Sitting* was not the attitude of prayer, either under the old dispensation or in Apostolic times.

tines the bridle of the mother "[1]—that is, as we learn from
1 Chron. xviii. 1, the command of Gath, "the mother," or
principal city of the Philistine confederacy—which henceforth
became tributary to Israel.   The next victory was over the
Moabites, who must have, in some way, severely offended
against Israel, since the old friendship between them was not
only broken (1 Sam. xxii. 3, 4), but terrible punishment meted
out to them—the whole army being made to lie down, when
two-thirds, measured by line, were cut down, and only one
third left alive.   It was, no doubt, in this war that Benaiah,
one of David's heroes, "slew two lion-like men of Moab"
(1 Chron. xi. 22).

The next contest, mentioned in 2 Sam. viii. 3–6, evidently
formed only an incident in the course of the great war against
Ammon and its confederates, which is detailed at length in
the tenth and eleventh chapters of 2 Samuel. From the number
of auxiliaries whom the Ammonites engaged against Israel,
this was by far the greatest danger which threatened the
kingdom of David.   As such it is brought before the Lord
in Ps. xliv. and lx., while the deliverance Divinely granted,
with all that it typically implied concerning the future victory
of God's kingdom, is gratefully celebrated in Ps. lxviii.   In
fact, Ammon had succeeded in girdling the whole Eastern
frontier of the land with steel.   Up in the far north-east
rose Hadad-Ezer (*Hadad*, the sun-god, is *help*), and arrayed
against Israel his kingdom of Zobah, which probably lay to the
north-east of Damascus.   Nor was he alone.   With him were
the forces of the Syrian (probably) vassal-territory, south of
Hamath, between the Orontes and the Euphrates, of which
Rehob (Numb. xiii. 21 ; Judg. xviii. 28), or Beth-Rehob, was
the capital.   Descending still further south, along the north-
eastern frontier of Palestine, was the kingdom of Maacah
(Deut. iii. 14), which joined in the war against Israel, as well as

---

[1] The expression "taking the bridle," means taking the command or
supremacy (comp. Job xxx. 11).   The term "mother" is applied to the
principal city in a district, the other towns being designated "daughters."

the men of Tob, who inhabited the territory between Syria and Ammon, where Jephthah had erewhile found refuge (Judg. xi. 5). Next we reach the territory of Ammon, from which the war originally proceeded. In the far south Moab had been only just subdued, while the Edomites made a diversion by overrunning the valley south of the Dead Sea—and a stubborn enemy they proved. Thus, as already stated, the whole eastern, north-eastern, and south-eastern frontier was threatened by the enemy.

The occasion of this war was truly Oriental. Nahash, the king of the Ammonites, seems on some occasion, not otherwise known, to have shown kindness to David (2 Sam. x. 2). On his death, David, who never lost grateful remembrance, sent an embassy of sympathy to Hanun, the son and successor of Nahash. This the Ammonite princes chose to represent as only a device, preparatory to an attack on their capital, similar in character to that which so lately had laid Moab waste (viii. 2). There was something cowardly and deliberately provocative in the insult which Hanun put upon David's ambassadors, such as Orientals would specially feel, by shaving off the beard on one side of their face, and cutting off their long flowing dress from below up to the middle. It was an insult which, as they well knew, David could not brook; and Ammon accordingly prepared for war by raising, as we have described, all the border tribes as auxiliaries against Israel. A sum of not less than a thousand talents, or about £375,000, was spent on these auxiliaries (1 Chron. xix. 6), who amounted altogether to thirty-two thousand men—consisting of chariots, horsemen, and footmen [1]—besides the one thousand men whom the king of Maacah furnished (2 Sam. x. 6; 1 Chron. xix. 6, 7).

Against this formidable confederacy David sent Joab, at the head of "all the host—the mighty men," that is, the choicest

[1] By combining the accounts in 2 Sam. and 1 Chron., it will be seen that the army consisted, as might be expected, of these three kinds of forces, although only chariots and horsemen are mentioned in Chronicles, and footmen in Samuel. In general these two narratives supplement each other, and also not unfrequently enable us to detect and correct from the one text clerical errors that have crept into the other.

of his troops (2 Sam. x. 7).   Joab found the enemy in double battle-array.   The Ammonite army stood a short distance outside their capital, Rabbah, while the Syrian auxiliaries were posted on the wide unwooded plateau of Medeba (1 Chron. xix. 7), about fifteen miles south-west of Rabbah.   Thus Joab found himself shut in between two armies.   But his was not the heart to sink in face of such danger.   Dividing his men into two corps, he placed the best soldiers under his brother Abishai, to meet a possible attack of the Ammonites, encouraging him with brave and pious words, while he himself, with the rest of the army, fell upon the Syrians.   From the first the victory was his.   When the Ammonites saw the flight of their auxiliaries, they retired within the walls of Rabbah without striking a blow.   But the war did not close with this almost bloodless victory, although Joab returned to Jerusalem.   It rather commenced with it.   Possibly this may explain why only the second act in this bloody drama is recorded in the summary account given in 2 Sam. viii. 3, etc., and in 1 Chron. xviii. 4, etc.   Combining these narratives with the fuller details in 2 Sam. x. and 1 Chron. xix., we gather that, on his defeat, or rather after his precipitate flight, Hadad - Ezer "went to turn again his hand at the river [Euphrates]," that is, to recruit his forces there (2 Sam. viii. 3 ; in 1 Chron. xviii. 3 : "to establish his hand"[1])—a statement which is further explained in 2 Sam. x. 16 and 1 Chron. xix. 16 by the notice, that the Syrian auxiliaries thence derived were placed under the command of Shobach, the captain of the host of Hadad-Ezer.   The decisive battle was fought at Helam (2 Sam. x. 17), near Hamath (1 Chron. xviii. 3), and resulted in the total destruction of the Syrian host.   No less than 1000 chariots, 7000[2] horsemen, and 20,000 footmen, were

---

[1] This is the correct rendering, and not as in our Authorised Version.

[2] In 2 Sam. viii. 4 by a clerical error the number is given as 700.   In general, as already stated, the details of the two accounts must be compared, so as to correct copyists' omissions and mistakes in either of them. It need scarcely be pointed out how readily such might occur in numerals, and where the details were so numerous and intricate.

taken; while those who fell in the battle amounted to 700, or rather (according to 1 Chron. xix. 18) 7000 charioteers and horsemen, and 40,000 footmen (in 2 Sam., "horsemen"). Shobach himself was wounded, and died on the field of battle.[1] David next turned against the Syrians of Damascus, who had come to the succour of Hadad-Ezer, slew 22,000 of them, put garrisons throughout the country, and made it tributary. But all the spoil taken in that war—notably the "golden shields," and the brass from which afterwards " the brazen sea, and the pillars and the vessels of brass," were made for the Temple (1 Chron. xviii. 8)—was carried to Jerusalem. The immediate results of these victories was not only peace along the borders of Palestine, but that all those turbulent tribes became tributary to David. One of the kings or chieftains, Toi, the king of Hamath, had always been at war with Hadad-Ezer. On his complete defeat, Toi sent his son Hadoram[2] to David to seek his alliance. The gifts which he brought, as indeed all the spoil of the war, were dedicated to the Lord, and deposited in the treasury of the sanctuary for future use.

But still the formidable combination against Israel was not wholly broken up. On the return of David's army from their victory over the Syrians, they had to encounter the Edomites[3] (2 Sam. viii. 13, 14), who had advanced as far as the "valley of salt," south of the Dead Sea. The expedition was entrusted to Abishai, Joab's brother (1 Chron. xviii. 12, 13), and resulted in the total rout of the enemy, and the garrisoning of the prin-

[1] If the reader will attentively compare the brief notices in 2 Sam. viii. 3, 4 and 1 Chron. xviii. 3, 4 with those in 2 Sam. x. 15-18 and 1 Chron. xix. 16-18, no doubt will be left on his mind that they refer to one and the same event, viz., *not* to the beginning of the war with Hadad-Ezer, but to its second stage after his precipitate flight from the battle of Medeba. For detailed proof we must refer to the Commentaries.

[2] So in 1 Chron. xviii. 10. The writing *Joram*, in 2 Sam. viii. 10, is either a clerical error or the translation of the heathen into the Jewish form of the name—by changing "Hadad," or sun-god, into "Jehovah."

[3] In 2 Sam. viii. 13 the words " he smote Edom," have evidently fallen out after "when he returned from smiting of the Syrians."

cipal places in Edom by David's men ; though, to judge by
1 Kings xi. 15, 16, the operations took some time, and were
attended with much bloodshed. The account just given of
the wars of David appropriately closes with a notice of his
principal officers of state, among whom we mark Joab as
general-in-chief, Jehoshaphat as chancellor (*magister memoriæ*),
or recorder and adviser, Zadok as high-priest at Gibeon (1 Chron.
xvi. 39), and Jonathan as assistant of his father Abiathar
(1 Kings i. 7, 42 ; ii. 22–27) at Jerusalem, Seraiah as secretary
of state, and Benaiah as captain of the body-guard — the
Cherethi and *Pelethi*, or "executioners and runners"[1]—while
the king's sons acted as intimate advisers.[2]

The record of this period of David's reign — indeed, of
his life — would have been incomplete if the memory of his
friendship with Jonathan had passed without leaving a trace
behind.   But it was not so.   When he had reached the climax
of his power,[3] he made enquiry for any descendant of Saul to
whom he might show "the kindness of God" for Jonathan's
sake.   There is something deeply touching alike in this loving
remembrance of the past, and in the manner of it, while David
was at the zenith of his power, which shows his true character,
and proves that success had not yet injured his better nature.
There was but one legitimate scion of the royal house left—
Mephibosheth, who bore in his lamed body the memorial of
that sad day on Mount Gilboa.   It is another bright glimpse
into the moral state of the people that all this time the poor
neglected descendant of fallen royalty should have found a
home and support in the house of the wealthy chieftain Machir,

---

[1] This seems to us the most rational interpretation of the terms, though
not a few have regarded them as names of nationalities, in which case they
would represent a guard of foreign mercenaries.

[2] The term here used in the Hebrew is *cohen*, which is always translated
"priest," but is here employed in its root-meaning : one who represents and
pleads the case of a person.

[3] This is evident from the circumstance that, on the death of Saul, Mephibosheth was only five years old (2 Sam. iv. 4), while in the account before
us he is represented as having a young son (2 Sam. ix. 12), so that a
considerable period must have intervened.

the son of Ammiel, at Lodebar,[1] near Mahanaim, the scene of Ishbosheth's murder (2 Sam. iv.). Yet another evidence was afterwards given of the worth and character of Machir. He had evidently known to appreciate David's conduct toward Mephibosheth, and in consequence become one of his warmest adherents, not only in the time of prosperity, but in that of direst adversity, when he dared openly to espouse David's cause, and to supply him in his flight with much needed help (2 Sam. xvii. 27–29).

But to return. The first care of the king was to send for Ziba, well known as a servant of Saul's—perhaps formerly the steward of his household. It is curious to note how, even after David assured him of his friendly intentions, Ziba on mentioning Mephibosheth, immediately told that he was "lame on his feet," as if to avert possible evil consequences. So strongly did the Oriental idea seem rooted in his mind, that a new king would certainly compass the death of all the descendants of his predecessor. Something of the same feeling appeared also in the bearing of Mephibosheth when introduced to David. But far other thoughts were in the king's heart. Mephibosheth was henceforth to be treated as one of the royal princes. His residence was to be at Jerusalem, and his place at the king's table while, at the same time, all the land formerly belonging to Saul was restored to him for his support. Ziba, whom David regarded as a faithful adherent of his old master's family, was directed, with his sons and servants, to attend to the ancestral property of Mephibosheth.

---

[1] Much ingenious use has been made of the name "Lo Debar," as meaning "no pasture." It may help to control such fancies if we point out that the Masoretic writing "Lo-debar" in two words is manifestly incorrect, the place b ing probably the *Lidbir* of Josh. xiii. 26 (in our Authorised Version *Debir*). But even were it otherwise, Lo-Debar could only mean "no pasture," if the "Lo" were spelt with an *aleph*, which it is in 2 Sam. xvii. 27, but not in ix. 4, 5, where it is spelt with a *vav*, and hence would mean the *opposite* of "no pasture." We have called attention to this as one of many instances of certain interpretations of Holy Scripture, wholly unwarranted by a proper study of the text, from which, however, too often, dogmatic inferences are drawn.

We love to dwell upon this incident in the history of David, which forms, so to speak, an appendix to the narrative of the first period of his reign, not merely for what it tells us of the king, but as the last bright spot on which the eye rests. Other thoughts, also, seem to crowd around us, as we repeat to ourselves such words as " the kindness of God " and " for Jonathan's sake." Thus much would a man do, and so earnestly would he enquire for the sake of an earthly friend whom he had loved. Is there not a higher sense in which the " for Jonathan's sake " can bring us comfort and give us direction in the service of love?

CHAPTER XIX.

Siege of Rabbah—David's great Sin—Death of Uriah—Taking of Rabbah —David's seeming Prosperity — God's Message through Nathan— David's Repentance—The Child of Bathsheba dies—Birth of Solomon.

(2 SAM. XI., XII.)

THERE is one marked peculiarity about the history of the most prominent Biblical personages, of which the humbling lesson should sink deep into our hearts. As we follow their onward and upward progress, they seem at times almost to pass beyond our reach, as if they had not been compassed with the same infirmities as we, and their life of faith were so far removed as scarcely to serve as an example to us. Such thoughts are terribly rebuked by the history of their sudden falls, which shed a lurid light on the night side of their character— showing us also, on the one hand, through what inward struggles they must have passed, and, on the other, how Divine grace alone had supported and given them the victory in their many untold contests. But more than that, we find this specially exhibited just as these heroes of faith attain, so to speak, the spiritual climax of their life, as if the more clearly to set it forth from the eminence which they had reached. Accordingly, the climax of their history often also marks the commencement of their decline. It was so in the case of Moses and of Aaron, in that of David,[1] and of Elijah. But there is one exception to this—or rather we should say, one history to which the opposite of this remark applies: that of our Blessed Lord and Saviour. The climax in the history of His life among men was on the Mount of Transfiguration; and though what followed marks His descent into the valley of humiliation, even to the bitter end, yet the glory around Him only grew brighter and brighter to the Resurrection morning.

Once more spring-time had come, when the war against the Ammonites could be resumed. For hitherto only their auxiliaries had been crushed. The importance attached to the expedition may be judged from the circumstance that the ark of God now accompanied the army of Israel (2 Sam. xi. 11). Again success attended David. His army, having in its advance laid waste every town, appeared before Rabbah, the strong capital of Ammon. Here was the last stand which the enemy could make—or, indeed, so far as man could judge, it was the last stand of David's last enemy. Henceforth all would be prosperity and triumph! It was in the intoxication of hitherto unbroken success, on the dangerous height of absolute and unquestioned power, that the giddiness seized David which brought him to his fall. It is needless to go over the sad, sickening details of his sin—how he was literally "drawn away of his lust, and enticed;" and how when lust had conceived it brought forth sin—and then sin, when it was finished, brought forth death (James i. 14, 15). The heart sinks as we watch his rapid

---

[1] It need scarcely be pointed out, how this truthful account of the sins of Biblical heroes evinces the authenticity and credibility of the Scriptural narratives. Far different are the legendary accounts which seek to palliate the sins of Biblical personages, or even to deny their guilt. Thus the *Talmud* (Shab., 55. 6) denies the adultery of David on the ground that every warrior had, before going to the field, to give his wife a divorce, so that Bathsheba was free. We should, however, add, that this view was controverted. In the Talmudic tractate *Avodah Sarah* (4. *b*, 5. *a*) a very proper application is made of the sin of David, while that of Israel in making the golden calf is not only excused but actually given thanks for!

downward course—the sin, the attempt to conceal it by enticing Uriah, whose suspicions appear to have been aroused, and then, when all else had failed, the despatch of the murderous missive by Uriah's own hands, followed by the contest, with its foreseen if not intended consequences, in which Uriah, one of David's heroes and captains, who never turned his back to the foe (2 Sam. xxiii. 39), fell a victim to treachery and lust.

It was all past. "The wife of Uriah"—as the text significantly calls Bathsheba, as if the murdered man were still alive, since his blood cried for vengeance to the Lord—had completed her seven days' hypocritical "mourning," and David had taken her to his house. And no worse had come of it. Her husband had simply fallen in battle; while the wife's shame and the king's sin were concealed in the harem. Everything else was prosperous. As the siege of Rabbah can scarcely have lasted a whole year, we assume that also also to have been past. The undertaking had not been without serious difficulty. It had been comparatively easy to penetrate through the narrow gorge, and, following the "fish-stocked stream, with shells studding every stone and pebble," which made "Rabbah most truly 'a city of waters,'" to reach "the turfed plain," "completely shut in by low hills on every side," in which "the royal city" stood. This Joab took. But there still remained "the city itself," or rather the citadel, perched in front of Rabbah on "a round, steep, flat-topped mamelon," past which the stream flowed rapidly "through a valley contracted at once to a width of five hundred paces." As if to complete its natural defences, on its other side were valleys, gullies, and ravines, which almost isolated the citadel.[1] But these forts could not hold out after the lower city was taken. Only it was a feat of arms in those days — and Joab, unwilling to take from the king the credit of its capture, sent for David, who in due time reduced it. The spoil was immense — among it the royal crown of Ammon, weighing

[1] Our description is taken from Canon Tristram's *Land of Israel*, pp. 549, 550.

no less than a talent of gold,[1] and encrusted with precious stones, which David took to himself. The punishment meted out to those who had resisted was of the most cruel, we had almost said, un-Israelitish character, not justified even by the terrible war which the Ammonites had raised, nor by the cruelties which they seem to have practised against helpless Israelitish mothers (Amos i. 13), and savouring more of the ferocity of Joab than of the bearing of David—at least before his conscience had been hardened by his terrible sin. And so David returned triumphant to his royal city!

A year had passed since David's terrible fall. The child of his sin had been born. And all this time God was silent! Yet like a dark cloud on a summer's day hung this Divine sentence over him: "But the thing that David had done was evil in the eyes of Jehovah" (2 Sam. xi. 27). Soon it would burst in a storm of judgment. A most solemn lesson this to us concerning God's record of our deeds, and His silence all the while. Yet, blessed be God, if judgment come on earth—if we be judged here, that we may "not be condemned with the world!" (1 Cor. xi. 32). And all this time was David's conscience quiet? To take the lowest view of it, he could not be ignorant that the law of God pronounced sentence of death on the adulterer and adulteress (Lev. xx. 10). Nor could he deceive himself in regard to the treacherous, foul murder of Uriah. But there was far more than this. The man whom God had so exalted, who had had such fellowship with Him, had sunk so low; he who was to restore piety in Israel had given such occasion to the enemy to blaspheme; the man who, when his own life was in danger, would not put

[1] Keil and other commentators are disposed to regard this weight as approximative, as the crown would, in their opinion, have been too heavy to wear. But the text does not imply that it was habitually worn, nor was its weight really so excessive. Comp. Erdmann, *die Bücher Samuelis,* p. 442, col. *b.* The question is very fully discussed in the Talmud (*Av. S.* 44. *a*). Among the strange explanations offered—such as that there was a magnet to draw up the crown; that it was worn over the phylactery, etc. —the only one worth mention is, that its gems made up its value to a talent of gold.

forth his hand to rid himself of his enemy, had sent into pitiless death his own faithful soldier, to cover his guilt and to gratify his lust! Was it possible to sink from loftier height or into lower depth? His conscience could not be, and it was not silent. What untold agonies he suffered while he covered up his sin, he himself has told us in the thirty-second Psalm. In general, we have in this respect also in the Psalter a faithful record for the guidance of penitents in all ages—to preserve them from despair, to lead them to true repentance, and to bring them at last into the sunlight of forgiveness and peace. Throughout one element appears very prominently, and is itself an indication of "godly sorrow." Besides his own guilt the penitent also feels most keenly the dishonour which he has brought on God's name, and the consequent triumph of God's enemies. Placing these Psalms, so to speak, in the chronological order of David's experience, we would arrange them as follows: Psa. xxxviii., vi., li., and xxxii.[1]—when at last it is felt that all "transgression is forgiven," all "sin covered."

It was in these circumstances that Nathan the prophet by Divine commission presented himself to David. A parabolic story, simple, taken from every-day life, and which could awaken no suspicion of his ulterior meaning, served as introduction. Appealed to on the score of right and generosity, the king gave swift sentence. Alas, he had only judged himself, and that in a cause which contrasted most favourably with his own guilt. How the prophet's brief, sharp rejoinder: "Thou art the man" must have struck to his heart! There was no disguise now; no attempt at excuse or palliation. Stroke by stroke came down the hammer—each blow harder and more crushing than the other. What God had done for David; how David had acted towards Uriah and towards his wife—and how God would avenge what really was a despising of Himself: such was the burden of Nathan's brief-worded

[1] Comp. Delitzsch *Commentar ü. d. Psalter*, Vol. I. pp. 44, 45, 297. For reasons which, I hope, will approve themselves on careful comparison of these Psalms, I have somewhat altered the arrangement proposed by Delitzsch.

message. Had David slain Uriah with the sword of the Ammonites? Never, so long as he lived, would the sword depart from the house of David. Had he in secret possessed himself adulterously of Uriah's wife? Similar and far sorer evil would be brought upon him, and that not secretly but publicly. And we know how the one sentence came true from the murder of Amnon (2 Sam. xiii. 29) to the slaughter of Absalom (xviii. 14), and even the execution of Adonijah after David's death (1 Kings ii. 24, 25); and also how terribly the other prediction was fulfilled through the guilt of his own son (2 Sam. xvi. 21, 22).

The king had listened in silence, like one staggering and stunned under the blows that fell. But it was not sorrow unto death. Long before his own heart had told him all his sin. And now that the Divine messenger had broken through what had hitherto covered his feelings, the words of repentance sprang to his long-parched lips, as under the rod of Moses the water from the riven rock in the thirsty wilderness. They were not many words which he spoke — and in this also lies evidence of their depth and genuineness (comp. Luke xviii. 13)—but in them he owned two realities : sin and God. But to own them in their true meaning : sin as against God, and God as the Holy One, and yet God as merciful and gracious—was to have returned to the way of peace. Lower than this penitence could not descend; higher than this faith could not rise. And God *was* Jehovah—and David's sin *was* put away.

Brief as this account reads, we are not to imagine that all this passed, and passed away, in the short space of time it takes to tell it. Again we say: in this respect also let the record be searched of the penitential Psalms, that Old Testament comment, as it were, on the three days' and three nights' conflict, outlined in Rom. vii. 5-25, the history of which is marked out by the words "blasphemer," "persecutor," "injurious," and "exceeding abundant grace" (1 Tim. i. 13-16). For, faith is indeed an *act*, and *immediate ;* and pardon also is an *act, immediate* and *complete;* but only the soul that has passed through it knows the terrible reality of a personal sense of sin, or the wondrous surprise of the sunrise of grace.

Assuredly it was so in the case of David. But the sting of that wound could not be immediately removed. The child who was the offspring of his sin must die : for David's own sake, that he might not enjoy the fruit of sin ; because he had given occasion for men to blaspheme, and that they might no longer have such occasion ; and because Jehovah was God. And straightway the child sickened unto death. It was right that David should keenly feel the sufferings of the helpless innocent child ; right that he should fast and pray for it without ceasing ; right even that to the last he should hope against hope that this, the seemingly heaviest punishment of his guilt, might be remitted. We can understand how all the more dearly he loved his child ; how he lay on the ground night and day, and refused to rise or be comforted of man's comforts. We can also understand—however little his servants might—how, when it was all over, he rose of his own accord, changed his apparel, went to worship in the house of Jehovah, and then returned to his own household : for, if the heavy stroke had not been averted, but had fallen—his child was not gone, only gone before.

And once more there came peace to David's soul. Bathsheba was now truly and before God his wife. Another child gladdened their hearts. David named him, symbolically and prophetically, Solomon, "the peaceful:" the seal, the pledge, and the promise of peace. But God called him, and he was "Jedidiah," the Jehovah-loved. Once more, then, the sunshine of God's favour had fallen upon David's household—yet was it, now and ever afterwards, the sunlight of autumn rather than that of summer ; a sunlight, not of undimmed brightness, but amidst clouds and storm.

Milton Keynes UK
Ingram Content Group UK Ltd.
UKHW012151270324
440282UK00003B/32